APOCRYPHA

ALSO BY PETER BOYLE

Coming Home from the World
(Five Islands Press, Wollongong, 1994)

The Blue Cloud of Crying
(Hale and Iremonger, Sydney, 1997)

Acceptance of Silent Waters
(Vagabond Press, Sydney, 2000)

What the Painter Saw in Our Faces
(Five Islands Press, Wollongong, 2001)

Museum of Space
(University of Queensland Press, St Lucia, 2004)

The Trees: Selected Poems 1967–2004 by Eugenio Montejo
(Salt Publishing, Cambridge, 2004)

Reading Borges
(Picaro Press, Warners Bay, 2007)

The Transformation Boat
(River Road Press, Sydney, 2008) CD

How Does a Man Who is Dead Re-invent his Body?
The Belated love Poems of Thean Morris Caelli
(with MTC Cronin) (Shearsman, Exeter, 2008)

APOCRYPHA

TEXTS COLLECTED AND TRANSLATED

BY WILLIAM O'SHAUNESSY

EDITED AND WITH A

POSTSCRIPT BY

PETER BOYLE

☙

VAGABOND PRESS

ACKNOWLEDGEMENTS

Several of these poems and prose pieces appeared in the following: *Agenda* (UK), *ars poetica* (www.logolalia.com/arspoetica), *Australian Humanities Review, Blast, Ilumina, Imago, Island, La Traductière* (France), *Mascara, Meanjin, Over There: Poems from Singapore and Australia* (Ethos Books 2008), *PAN, Papertiger, Poetry International* (http://australia.poetryinternationalweb. org/piw_cms), *Sacred Australia: post-secular considerations* (Clouds of Magellan, 2009), *Shadowtrain* (UK) (www.shadowtrain.com), *Shearsman* (UK), *Snorkel Literary Magazine, Southerly, Stylus* (www.styluspoetryjournal.com). Poems and excerpts also appeared in the chapbook *Reading Borges* (Picaro Press, 2007).

Second edition, 2016

ISBN 978 1 922181 89 3

Vagabond Press, Sydney

Amore transfiguratus amata pro mea scribo.

— Lucianus of Mauretania

τὰ μικρά τε καὶ τὰ οὐράνια ὁμοίωσ τῶ σοφῶ
μακαρίαν καὶ φόβον φεροῦν.

—Irene Philologos

Transfigured by love, I write for my beloved.
—Lucianus of Mauretania

*To one who is wise the tiny and the immense
equally bring fear and blessings.*
—Irene Philologos

(W O'S)

BOOK I

I

—What is it your people are always swallowing secretively in tiny doses?

—It's Pluto. It's the furthest planet from the Sun. They break off small crumbs of it, grind it down and take it to ward off sunstroke and sun-madness, sunburn and sun-induced amnesia.

—But you live mostly in underground caverns.

—It always seeps through. It dazzles us. It torments our every waking dream.

—Is that why your people have a bluish tinge around the eyes and lips? Sometimes even a purple, ultra-violet glow?

—I don't know where you get that idea from. But surely you've noticed your own skin—how it breaks into a shimmer of fire, that edge of yellow seeping into your hair and fingernails? I must say it has terrified and worried us from the moment you first came into our lands.

(DIONYSIUS LAERTES, 3023, ALSO KNOWN AS "THE PAMPHLYGONIAN")

II

Among the Cistercii let no one be accused of opening their veins with undue haste. For them every action is so weighted with consideration that over many lifetimes each of them acts as if conversing and discussing with all others though he acts alone and in silence. When the first signs of final weakness manifest themselves, the Cistercii, preferring to enter the cauldron of oblivion with all their being intact, lift the razor with such reluctance and such precision that, it might be said, each movement is both infinitely slow and lasts no more and no less than an eaglet's birth-cry. In the language of the Cistercii the terms "alone", "loneliness", "in solitude" do not exist, nor words to say "by oneself" or "with others" since every breath is both a moment's idleness and the profound enactment of a community's decision to pass on their presence in the sun.

(NICOLAS OF TYRRENE, 4015)

III

It appears that breathing was invented in Sicyon although some claim that Pandraia, twelve kilometres to the north, was its true birthplace. Certainly the inventiveness of Sicyon was legendary. It is well known that Sicyon, not Corinth, first invented the practice of looking at the outside world.

(PLINIUS OF NOVA HUSTIA, 2299)

IV

The town of Aurelium was well known for the curative power of its waters. Those who drank from its springs could see far into the distances, according to numerous well-verified accounts. But more frightening were the waters of Paestum. It was said that whoever drank so much as a mouthful could be seen by his enemies even should he bury himself alive in deep caverns on the other side of the earth. Lovers, it was rumoured, sometimes drank these waters that they might be visible to their beloved even if they wandered far off in the underworld. Yet, of all the springs in the vast plains and foothills of Negroponte, the waters of Paestum inspired the most profound dread—so far does fear of being seen outweigh any longing to see.

(MARCUS ANDROGYNUS THE YOUNGER, 9834)

V

It is an everyday thing to light a fire and then swallow it. Rarer is the art of those who swallow the fires that have never been lit. Such procedures require the greatest care and precision. The magicians concerned seek as far as possible to conceal their choked splutterings, the grimaces of pain and the torments they struggle with, from all around them. Enough to say that in households where an adept has performed the required operations the owners will require fifty or a hundred attempts to light the simplest fire—all has been swallowed in advance. Darker are the true masters of this art, a skill banned by the strongest Imperial decree though all ignore it. Once a pact between three adepts sufficed to strip forever of the blessing of fire an unfortunate tribe where a child had accidentally insulted a wandering magician. Deprived of all fire for cooking, light or warmth, they stumbled blindly towards the northern wastes, shunned by all, seeking the lost fire they believed dwells only in the depths of ice.

Observe how the destroyers of possibility are more highly prized by humans than the destroyers of what is.

(PLINIUS THE YOUNGER, UNDATED)

—CODA: The art of destroying a love that exists between a man and a woman requires no magic at all. More esteemed are those who have learned the spells that destroy all possibility of love in a person's life.

(MARGARETA OF THUN, 8810)

Learn, then, of those who swallow the possibilities of others. In the doorway of time they stand completely still and in silence. They sense the first fragrant tremors of life. They roll invisible fragments between their fingers. Masters of the future, they erase our memories.

(UNKNOWN AUTHOR, LYDIAN FRAGMENT FROM THE TOMBS OF THE DRAVIDIAN ARCHERS.)

VI

The citizens of Eusebius were renowned for their addiction to every form of ownership and wealth. Not content with owning houses, lands, islands, factories and latifundiae of all kinds, metals and fruits named and unnamed, they began the practice of claiming everything from magic spells to words and phrases. A small group of the Eusebioli, forming themselves into a corporation for the purpose, asserted their right to the invention of the words "yesterday", "today" and "tomorrow". A rival consortium took out ownership of the present tense. So fierce was the vindictiveness of the Eusebian courts, whose jurisdiction extended beyond earth to galaxies visible and invisible, so absolute the force of their arms, that for decades no one could speak any more in the present without suffering confiscation of all their goods and the enslavement of their children for several generations. Likewise when a spell was developed to enable the sun to rise in the morning, it became the property of a corporation threatening the earth with darkness if they did not part with a third of their wealth. It was only in the eighteenth year of the fifth cycle of the Dravidians, about the time that the corn ripens, that a revolt of the bondsmen forced the collapse of the Eusebioli's ownership of spells and words. Suddenly it was found that language had died all around them, that the world had gone on growing and changing with no need for spells or phrases—adept beyond abjection, a new grammar had been writing its way into new emotions, new relationships and time-frames. It was in this era that scholars first remembered that a speech beyond words had always been the true birthplace of humans.

(*The Book of Origins*, AUTHORSHIP UNKNOWN, LIBRARY OF THE EXILES IN ALEXANDRIA, FRAGMENT INDEX No CD451)

First they took the words, then they took the children.
The children returned. The words did not return.
Seeking for the words, the elders understood how speech must be lost completely before it can be truly used.

(LUCIUS OF OCAMPO, 283)

Learn then from the Eusebioli how little their mania for possession had to do with wealth—how much with the overwhelming instinct constantly to narrow that portion of reality available to others. Closing evermore tightly the door that opened on language, they discovered in the silence of others confirmations of that same narrowing that fascinated and obsessed them.

(ARISTOBULUS THE AREOPAGITE, *Proposal for Certain Reforms to Investment Laws*, SICYON, 8898)

In the time of the Eusebeoli's monopoly of spells, words and knowledge structures, the practice developed of giving children entire spells and lengthy poems and grammar treatises as names in the vain hope that the right of a person to their own name would be respected. Birthday and name day ceremonies at times lasted several days while the name was recited and in this way, it was hoped, language might continue. The initial confusion this created with the court system is generally held to be the chief explanation for those fragments that connect us to the ancients.

(NICOLA OF SAMOTHRACE, DATE UNKNOWN)

VII

Those were the forgotten days when surrender
was a kindly way to say awakening:
being towed out into midstream and tilted slowly
around to face the stars.

~o~

On the erased hillside
your true eyes understood the wind that was our origin.

~o~

Your mouth blessed me:
I carry you with me here among the unspeaking.

(Tomb engravings ascribed to Evadne of Posidonia, quoted in the
Fragmentaria of the Aevolii)

VIII

—Is my name known on this side of the river? Speak to me of
my fate.

—Servant of gods and men, handmaiden of dawn and of the
lightning flash, poet and necromancer, bleak-eyed ibis of clouded
waters, you who invented lyre and plectrum, who tuned the fivefold
spheres, you have written two thousand poems, your words have
been sung by mortals in all the villages of Thessaly and Dodonia,
you have reached the still mirror of truth, now go and find a dustpan
and broom.

(Xeuxis of Anagoge, "The daughters of Clazominae",
Fragments of the lost tragedians)

IX

Among the Evadni to the north of the Chersonese can be found a small group known as the Phrangii who live entirely underground in small burrows. A flat low hill, perhaps two or three such hills during their years of triumph, stands shorn of trees and dotted by small holes. So great is their fear of appearing in any way different from others of their tribe that they build their homes under earth and rarely, if at all, invite another to visit. Once a day each family group sits above these holes to eat a plain but fairly lavish meal in the sunlight—in times of rain they simply remain underground. These meals in sunlight consist of various green items, assorted nuts and roots and slivers of what might be meat or might be tree bark cooked in an identical manner and consumed with no way for an observer to know what was meat and what was bark. Their clothing on these occasions is identical. But is this food their real food or do they eat more extravagantly or in greater poverty out of sight? Likewise with their clothing. Such questions are impossible to answer. The Phrangii themselves speak little, lacking words for equality, freedom, envy, jealousy, happy and unhappy—indeed their speech is confined to a very few pragmatic names. Grammatical structures do not seem to exist in their language. It may be that they are anarchists since it is well known that they have no central government, no council of elders, no taxes—but it may be that they are governed by a rigid internal code and adjust all their actions accordingly. Their women are not often seen—it may be that they suffer repression or simply that they fear the sun and its harsh rays. This observer spent nine days among them. At the daily meal in open sunlight waiting slowly and rigidly to consider each mouthful of food, I could feel my hands adjusting their movements to the tremors of others' hands as I ate. Each day I was losing myself. I could feel all words steadily draining from me. Soon I might truly become what I first was.

(FRAGMENT VARIOUSLY ASCRIBED TO HERODOTUS, TO BE FOUND IN THE EARLY ETRUSCAN TRANSLATION, *Herodotus—the uncut version*, BOOK XV)

The language of the Phrangii is well worthy of study. While consisting mostly of common names for everyday items, in moments
of annoyance or passion observers have detected certain verb-like
utterances creeping in. It is likely that their language was originally
highly complex but over time grammar was slowly omitted. Perhaps
it was felt by these people that, once grammar enters the world,
distinctions of correct and incorrect usage appear, giving birth to
that spirit which differentiates people and is the enemy of peace.

(EUPHRASTES, *Treatise on Grammar*, 410)

X

Probably no work of human endeavour has so profoundly affected
mankind, both by its creation and by its vanishing, as the lost music
of Parmenides. Among his contemporaries Parmenides' writings
on philosophy, his numerous letters, poems and plays were all
considered as nothing in comparison to his music. The story of his
two-hour improvisation for solo plectrum, "The journey beyond the
One", is well known. He fasted and meditated for a year before
its performance, permitting no one to hear more than a few notes
as he perfected the work. The audience remained mesmerised,
unable to return to normal life for a week. A repeat performance
a month later produced the same result. Parmenides resisted all
entreaties to perform the work a third time, fearing lest his own
being, thinned down by the arduous concentration required, should
vanish altogether. Five years later and then every five years for the
next century a pupil specially prepared by him, or a pupil of that
pupil in succession, performed the work. After that time warfare,
barbarian invasions and the loss of the ability to listen with the
necessary selfless rapture all contributed to its neglect. It was said
of this work that, should all else perish, it would be possible from
it alone to reinvent human knowledge and wisdom. Perhaps it was
this which doomed his music as later barbarians insisted on their

own phantasmagoria and held there was no book but the one book of their particular creed.

Of his other compositions also famous is his work for plectrum, zither and harp known as "The refusal". Played one time on a hill overlooking the sea the music prevented ships from reaching harbour and led to a year without marriages. Parmenides, apologizing that he had no idea his music would work so powerfully, set about composing a piece for flute and zither known as "The sacred union" which restored balance to the world.

Unlike the music of his contemporaries which relied heavily on speech, often providing settings for poems, chants and choruses, Parmenides' compositions were pure music although each listener heard in the notes, articulated as they were with great clarity, a supernatural speech talking uniquely to them.

Another famous solo piece "The silent waiting" seemed to guide the listener through endless doorways. It was possible to see a high plain in sunlight. At once it was known that one was standing inside one's own death. The most absolute aloneness gave way at each moment to the sensation of a shining blessedness, a radiant light that flowed back from oneself to all humanity. When performing another piece written to celebrate the seventh birthday of his son, Parmenides confessed that while playing it he realised it was written not to describe his son or his own feelings as a father but to bring again to the presence of daylight his great-grandfather and the love of his great-grandfather for a barbarian woman, shunned by all, who was the true spiritual mother of his own and his son's being. It is noted that once he articulated this the lights in all the houses of Samothrace went out for three days and a profound odour of lilacs and wild honey filled the city.

Numerous were the wonders of Parmenides' music. Yet Parmenides always insisted it was his listeners who with their attentiveness, with the inward breath and touch that reside wholly in the mind, created the music equally with him and with the gods. Around the time of the second barbarian invasions Polycrates of

Naso asserted that, if listeners of true inwardness ever returned to earth, Parmenides' music would reappear.

(MENANDER OF BRUNDISIUM, *A brief compendium of the ancients*, c. 500 AD)

XI

On his fiftieth birthday Demagorgas the sage was woken by his children who came to tell him messengers had just arrived with the news that Rome had been destroyed.

"Go back and ask them, has it sunk below the waves?" he replied.

The children returned to the messengers and then reported back to him that it was a barbarian invasion, that Rome had been sacked and all its buildings torched.

"Oh, is that all?" he replied and went back to sleep.

CODA: Demagorgas' query whether Rome had sunk below the waves concerns the well-known magic practice of reversing the universe. It was feared that various black magicians had mastered these skills and that, once the practice of putting cities under the sea began in earnest, all the world would be destroyed.

But others claim that this story concerns Alexandria not Rome, and that it was indeed suddenly and mysteriously plunged below the waves, that Demagorgas and his children had long been wandering there without realising it, that the great cities in truth had long returned to the seas that were their true homes, and that all of us dwell in the great silence that awaits us.

(POLYDOROS THE HERESIARCH, FOURTH CENTURY AD)

XII

The children of Ecbatana return on every third day.
On the two intervening days prepare your houses,
weep and let the salt dry on your hands,
lash yourselves with spikes and let the blood gather
    on your limbs.
The children will feed from your hands,
they will drink softly from your shoulder.
The enormous "Why?" that thunders in their eyes
will take away all questions.

~o~

The Melanchthoi maintain that everything returns,
the Evadni that nothing returns
and yet it is spring.

(Two fragments from *The Green Book of Ebtesum*, 8817)

XIII

Five days journey east of the Chersonese Bosphorus lies a sea that exists entirely above the earth. It is possible to walk underneath and look up at the fish circling in their thousands. The entire sea is about as wide as the Hellespont and similar in length to the distance from Athens to Euboea. The woman who travelled with me to this place is of simple origin and it is impossible to believe the sea was in any way conjured by her. The people who live nearby, distant cousins of the Mareotians, have built very tall towers which enable them to cast nets into the sea and fish. The fish they capture in this manner are many-coloured, glittering and of the most exquisite taste, although all of them perish within one day of leaving its waters, turning to a dry white paste which exudes a strong odour of snowfall and wild mint. No effort to preserve these fish for later consumption has proven successful. Dionysius of Erzerum maintains that the sea is the result of a powerful magician whose spell caused the sea to leave its bed and float in the air. After the magician died unexpectedly, Dionysius states, no counter-spell was found. However it seems more reasonable to believe with the majority that the sea requires no explanation, that it exists always and only of itself. About the fish and their transportation I believe a solution remains possible.

(PHILO OF DODONIA, KNOWN AS "THE MUCH TRAVELLED", 882)

XIV

Euridichos of Cos considered twilight the harshest of all punishments. Having perfected the art of seeing the world as either light or darkness, the shading of one into the other grated against him "as if one were slicing open an onion in order to teach the wind to speak". He attempted to demonstrate the impossibility of twilight through elaborate mathematical formulae. On one occasion he held a banquet on a cliff top to invoke an intricate spell that would enable the earth to move from light to dark without that orange-red-purple glow that so violated his sense of the well ordered and the beautiful. On that evening to the amazement of all there was no twilight on earth. The next day Euridichos died mysteriously either by chance or at the hands of agents of another realm, possibly even that force he called "the imbalance". His spell remains unknown.

(MENANDER OF BRUNDISIUM, *A Brief Compendium of the Ancients*)

XV

When Lycias was a rhetor on Crete, at the time of the twelfth Pythian, around noon, about the time that the corn ripens, Philos of Epizypherean Locri then living at Heracleion completed the definitive and final study of errors. He produced five copies of the book on the finest papyrus and sent them to the greater libraries of the world. All disappeared in transit. Iamblichus, an agent of the Alexandrian customs then working at Syracuse, stated in deposition that he saw the book, opened and in part read it—the first, middle and last ten pages, he asserts. More than a compendium of errors it was an examination that revealed the secret working of error and how by tracing its genesis it became possible to see the true nature of the world. On completing his reading he looked up: the sea gaped with myriad holes, the Imperial officials in the street had disappeared and instead there were only beggars in torn rags, birds were removing the eyes of all the statues and the corn was not yet ripe.

(PORPHYRY, *A Brief Compendium of the Great Lost Books*)

XVI

In the time of the great emergency Enobius, the Emperor of the Palmyran legions, was banished beyond the Ister on the charge of necromancy. Yet it is well known that, rather than contacting the dead, he was simply a man haunted by the future. "Wherever I go," he lamented, "I see only the future." The turning point happened on a day of unprecedented calm throughout the empire. On the battlements of a fortress on the Illyrian coast he heard angelic spirits reciting in a voice louder than all human voices long intolerably harsh lines of verse which he knew were being dictated to a poet who was to pace these same battlements over a thousand years in the future. Enobius heard only part of the angelic speech but knew that the poet of the future likewise heard only a small part. And there does not exist any one time, he found himself saying, when all the fragments of the angels can be heard simultaneously. This lack of simultaneity haunted and tormented him. He came to suspect that every true utterance slipped between the ghost future he sensed all around him and the physical future that would come. After this revelation in the Illyrian fortress, wherever he went he began to secrete notes in hiding places in the several languages he knew and whatever other languages he could master, foretelling what the whispered voices around him were saying. Yet despair overtook him as he fell under the conviction that all the languages of his world would vanish before the future could arrive. A tormented and wearied man, his one hope, he said, was death—in death, he said, he might at last be released into the limitless blessing of the past.

(DIOGENES CASERIUS, *The Deeds of the Neglected Emperors*)

FOOTNOTE: Much of Enobius's best work was lost as a result of his relentless habit of writing in as many languages as possible—most of these tongues now long since forgotten. Among the papyri in various libraries in Alexandria and Cairo are fragments thought to be in crypto-Dacian, early Numidean, mezzo-Akkanite and the secret language of Ur. In the last year of his life Enobius wrote the poem that begins "In which of my languages will I die?" but was then overwhelmed by the conviction that someone in the future was writing the same poem but with some teasing slight variation. In despair he wrote "Everything I write plagiarises the future."

(DR ANTOINE LEMESURIER, ASSISTANT CURATOR, THE SECRET LIBRARY TRUST OF LOWER EGYPT, 1855)

XVII

Anaximenes was the first to calculate accurately the size of the universe. Whereas Nepenthe, daughter of the mathematician Ptarchus, devised the constant for the weight of the sky. Her cousin Mystra proved the different weight of varying dreams. Mystra was the first to show conclusively that dreams of water are far heavier than dreams of fire. When all these great and learned calculations were presented to Sarsus the third, King of Kings and ruler of all Parthia, he remained unimpressed. After all he was a man who for the first twenty-five years of his life had lived in total seclusion, speaking only the language of spells and unaware that any other languages existed. To utter a word, for him, was to make that thing happen. He had difficulty understanding the idea of a language that merely reported what was—for him all words were there to bring things into being.

(ZENOBIA, *The Chronicles of Parthia and Palmyra*)

Know then of the three great languages. Beyond the Indus developed the language uniquely capable of expressing philosophical speculation and matched to the knotted and intricately curved play of reality. In Greece the true language of poetry arose with its fusion of beauty, power and the precise contours of human endurance. And in the lands of upper Egypt and greater Parthia was born the delicate and terrifying language of magic, the language that brings about whatever is desired to happen. Whilst the languages of Greece and India remain among us and have been well recorded, the language of the Magi and the Invisible Ones never travelled across borders. It was a speech that did not survive because it did not want to survive. Yet numerous are its fragments. It speaks itself in dreams and in water. It translates stars and rivers into birdsong. Once its spells raised cities, united lovers and gave youth back to the dying. But it became a confusion on the road of warriors. It feared the powerful and warlike—so it left earth.

(MACROBIUS, *Of the Eastern Kingdoms*)

Macrobius was wrong in supposing that the language of magic disappeared. Coptic as spoken in Egypt is one of its dialects that degenerated into the acceptance of everyday life. It is also a common second speech among the Scythians, Dacians and the peoples of the great desert of Fars.

(EVANDER, *On the folly of contemporary wisdom*)

XVIII

In the deep field where you lay with me
all the universe began.
From every distance
the beautiful enters my being.

~o~

You whose eyes spoke to me of your father
the stonecutter, the measurer of the gods

I have followed you here below earth.
Our embrace is warm as the sun in Agrigentum.

(Inscriptions found on funeral urns from the underground city of
Cos, central Bithynia, c. 169 ad)

XIX

On grey days open the doors to the sky,
beat your carpets from the high walls.
The innumerable are returning.

(from the Oracle Book of Gregorius of Tarsus)

XX

In those days the sky was much closer to the earth and it was
no uncommon thing, whenever one felt dispirited or anxious, to
steady one's composure by a brief walk across the sky. All that was
necessary was the right spell to project oneself that slight distance
above the treetops to where the smooth passageways of the sky
began. It was even feared, in those days, that discus throwers would

catapult their projectiles into those sacred passageways where they might speed forever across limitless space. But over generations these arts declined. The low point was signalled when in Minos' time Dedalus boasted his invention of wings and his son Icarus plummeted into the sea. Contrary to the misinformation spread by Athenian propagandists, the fate of Icarus was punishment not for any act of hubris in flying but for the ignorant boastfulness of his father Dedalus who, by slighting the numerous generations of skywalkers, had offended against the divine injunction that only the truthful should know the steady confidence of the air.

(ISTAREION THE YOUNGER, *A true history of Crete before the invasion of the Sea Peoples*, PAPYRUS FROM THE SACRED CITY OF PHAESTOS)

XXI

How quietly you scooped your way
through the endless waters of elsewhere,
how long those days
when the river flowed through the narrow room
of your dying. Each hand that had held you
traced its invisible fingers on the walls.
All words spoken
unfolded in those hours,
the thirst of the leaves
curved like a lizard's tongue:

you dying in Rome
remembering your other life in Gundeshapur.

(ELEGY WRITTEN BY MARINUS OF SAMARIA FOR HIS FRIEND EUDOXIS, SECRET DISCIPLE OF PLOTINUS WHO STUDIED WITH THE NESTORIANS OF BACTRIA AND THE INDUS.)

XXII

To answer the music
a planet, a world,
a cosmos shining with all its innumerable lights.

Wounded fish wander the skies in autumn.
In the depths of a lake
birds struggle to understand the silence.

To answer the music
we take you back into our life.

We do not have any other life.

(FRAGMENT FROM A LOST POEM *To Parmenides after the destruction of the last disciple* BY THEOPHRASTUS THE GODLESS OF NICOSIA.)

XXIII

Ten days journey south-west of Royal Memphis lies the Kingdom of Ebtesum. The Nile was in flood when I set off, along with guides and emissaries of the Nubian Order, to make my way to this famous centre of learning. Ebtesum is sometimes called the invisible kingdom—its boundaries wander over the years, its location is always subject to dispute. Ebtesum is preeminent among all kingdoms for its beauty—the beauty of its women, its poetry, its dance and song. Nothing in Ebtesum survives. Its inhabitants have little understanding of the desire to endure. Time flounders in the rich air of this kingdom. Since nothing is repeated, nothing is written down.

The people in Ebtesum have no knowledge of zither, plectrum or other stringed instrument, all their music consisting of drum and flute, apart from the extraordinary and subtle vocalisations in which they are unsurpassed. Improvised poetry is the high achievement of this kingdom. To write down a poem, they say, is like clinging to love and the man who copies down his own poems is like a man imprisoning a woman to keep love always at the moment of its first ecstasy. Everything must be let go—only in this way does the beautiful flood into our hands. On days of forced absence in Ebtesum love letters dissolve even as they are written.

Only those whom fate compels to leave attempt to write down the poems they heard in Ebtesum. Such is the origin of those famous collections whose copies have long changed hands and turned up in libraries throughout the earth and across all times: the Red Book of Ebtesum, the Black Book of Ebtesum, the Green Book of Ebtesum, and so on. For everything that is in the rainbow and everything that is not in the rainbow belong to Ebtesum.

It is now many years since I have been in Ebtesum but too much of its spirit remains in me to attempt the transcribing of the poems I heard. Many evenings, more and more evenings now the darkness approaches, I sit recalling the poetry and music of Ebtesum. I recall the day I sat in the caravanserai expecting to leave the next morning, summoned to join my brothers at the deathbed of my father. An exquisite music of wild teeming rapture came from a small cubicle nearby—the blended sounds of many drums and several voices, loud almost to the point of cacophony yet exquisite and subtle at the same time, creating out of their confusion an endless array of dialogues and choruses. I opened the door very cautiously, fearing to disturb those inside, yet the cubicle was empty apart from a small child, no more than eight years of age. All the voices came from his mastery of improvisation—the drumming was the clicks of his tongue, the patter of his hands on the stone wall. He was performing for himself in the darkness, yet all around him the moths circled, diving and humming.

(HERODOTUS, *The Complete Histories*, BOOK XXX, AS PRESERVED IN THE ETRUSCAN TRANSLATION OF THE TREVII.)

It has been stated by some authorities that this same Ebtesum was also Eusebius, the kingdom renowned for its ferocious greed and the savage destruction it dealt to others. It appears that the two kingdoms alternate according to certain formulae known only to the higher adepts of the Mathemasis. Eusebius itself is held to be a permanently recurring state of possibility—that it has already manifested itself three times—once in Ebtesum, once in Bactria and once in a location too small to be named.

Perhaps, despite their many apparent differences, Ebtesum and Eusebius are connected by their peculiar impermanence. Of all the great and terrible Empires of earth Eusebius is the shortest lived. Whereas other Empires have lasted three hundred or a thousand years, Eusebius is held to have shrunk to the dimension of fifty years—possibly even six weeks. With its monopolising of language, its ruthless possession of the present tense, it sped up the process of its own destruction.

Possibly Ebtesum and Eusebius alternate, the one dwindling and then vanishing as the other appears. Possibly both coexist, layered alternately across each other as two types of reality.

According to some scholars, during the times of its vanishing the elders of Eusebius shrink to the dimension of small finches trapped in a dusty cage at the back of a warehouse. They are, of course, immortal. Alternately, when Ebtesum disappears, its people live on as the myriad grains of sand that line a fishtank. The resonance they create penetrates the furthest stars.

It is prophesied that the fourth manifestation of Eusebius will be on one of the Atlantean islands. The Mani texts state that of the five islands of Atlantis all are large—roughly the same dimensions as Asia, Europe and Africa. One sentence in the text suggests that the fourth manifestation of Eusebius will herald the end of the earth but it is likely that this is a late interpolation.

(MACROBIUS, *A Brief Compendium of the Ancients*)

XXIV

There is a tribe among the Scythians whose women are so beautiful that men most often suicide before their eighteenth birthday, so great is their certainty that they could never be adequate lovers for these women. In vain do the women plead with them, weep, tear their hair, kneel in front of them—they all suicide. Occasionally a man lives to be thirty—occasionally, at most once or twice, but that is enough.

(DRUSUS MAKEDON OF EPIRUS, *Research into possible cures for beauty*)

XXV

In Clazomenae do not grieve too deeply
over life's passing.
By the harbour the fish are frying on their bed of coals
but still swim in the sea.
In winter the sun returns to live
with the stones that have captured its shape.

In Clazomenae clouds gather without haste.
Rain is a delicate script
recording glances and gestures of the seafront
where you sit.
Open your hands to the enormous drops
of each second.

In Clazomenae grief is not worth
the naming of daylight.

(FROM *Songs of Ionia, Caria and Cyprus*, COLLECTED BY AGATHON
OF MYTILINE, 335 BCE)

XXVI

Lysander and his friend Timon were just returning from the marketplace when I met them. They were both engaged in eager conversation and wished to share with me certain revelations made by the sophist Gorgias of whom they had just heard from Alcibiades the bald. "Gorgias", Lysander told me, "believes that humans are in essence animals possessed of language, that language is what distinguishes us as humans and that language is communication. It follows that we have only to learn to communicate well, I mean more efficiently, and we will fully realise ourselves as human beings."

—Hmm, I replied, let us pause a moment over this. For so deep a question requires care. Language, after all, might be anything.

—Yes, but surely in its essence language is communication. Through language, I think I am remembering Gorgias' words aright, we communicate to others what is at hand, what we feel and what we would like to happen. Surely nothing could be clearer.

—When you communicate you report something: would you agree?

—Of course.

—What does music report?

—Nothing.

—And when a child cries is he reporting?

—I'm not sure.

—And when a man and woman whisper, caressing each other with words in lovemaking, what do they report?

—Well, nothing. But those are all unusual examples of language.

—Is lying very rare or a quite frequent occurrence?

—Quite frequent.

—In lying, whether it be the lie of politeness, the kindly lie or the lie of political advantage, do we seek to communicate or is something more complicated happening?

—Something more complicated.

—And if we found a people in whose language there was no lying and no concept of lying, would we consider them more human or less human? I mean, imagine a tribe of perfectly adapted slaves, whose speech consisted solely of obeying orders and of reporting back states of the world on the request of their masters, if such beings had no capacity to lie, would it make them more like us or less like us?

—A great deal less like us. But surely you are not going to suggest that the essence of being human is the capacity to lie, so that humans are no more than the creatures of falsehood.

—No indeed, my intention does not travel that journey. Yet, in considering Gorgias' views, I think it important to pause over this definition of language as communication. If we think of communicating or reporting, the image comes to mind of a workman on the roof inquiring of his assistant how many tiles there are left in a certain room; the assistant looks and reports back. Or if one man asks another how many triremes are prepared for war, or a man seeking to buy a house asks the man selling his house how many rooms there are.

—That would be strange—for all houses have the same number of rooms.

—Here they do but in Babylon the Great houses may have many more rooms.

We smiled a little at this juncture when Thrasybulus, who had been listening intently to all and nodding at times as if we were circling slowly round and round a place he had always been in, took up the conversation.

—Why do people want us to believe that language is communication? If we accept a theory that equates being human with negotiating for houses and money and ordering slaves around, does it not serve the interests of those who see life as money and slavery? The other side of language—its deeper intuitive mission— is the enemy of such people. But I am outpacing myself a little for I wanted to mention here two tribes whose languages are both very different and instructive.

—By all means, Lysander began, tell us about these peoples and then, if possible, tell us more about your last observation.

—The other week I was conversing with a merchant who had recently returned from Bactria and he told me of the Monotanistoi whose language has no nouns, no naming words for everyday objects but only the one word signifying "thing" or "that over there" while instead they have innumerable adjectives of great subtlety—almost five hundred words for "sad", for example, and twenty five words for "love". Almost all their descriptor words incorporate emotional shadings since they would think it inexplicable that anyone should waste time recounting a merely physical world. Among the emotional states they encapsulate with a single word are "sad but with a likelihood of feeling better within a few hours", "confused but could be sad if the adjective was suggested to me" and "like a bird seeking the forest that has been destroyed in war". These people do not feel their language lacks anything but have a rich complex speech and find no need for the kind of reporting-language that those like Gorgias elevate so much, granting it, as it were, the highest seats in the theatre.

—Indeed these observations have broadened our way of seeing, Menander now remarked in the slow rather pompous drawl for which he is famous. (I should add that Menander was present from the first but until now had not joined in.) I have also heard of the language in which people sleep and the language in which one can say "I will see you this evening" but immediately it is understood to mean "The birds are flying to the east". There are also the countless languages in which there are no names for people, naming words replaced entirely by touch, especially the five ritual touch-gestures signifying "I tolerate you", "I admire you", "I want to make use of you generally", "I want to make use of you sexually" and "I intend to avoid you".

(THERE NOW APPEARS A GAP IN THE TEXT WHERE SEVERAL PAGES APPEAR TO BE MISSING. IT IS UNCLEAR WHO SPEAKS FIRST IN THE NEXT ENTRY.)

—When you are in a foreign country and wish to go out in the evening to a performance of music, do you bring an interpreter with you to translate the music?

—No, surely that is not needed.

—And in the underworld where people communicate wholly through music, they have no need to report anything since they dwell entirely in the present.

—Yes, for certainly those who have returned state this clearly.

—Well then, it would appear that music is an untranslatable language—the opposite, one might say, of a reporting-language since it dwells in the immediate and does not seek to relate one instant to another instant. It is a language of the continuous present.

—It sounds as if it is so. That reminds me and, I don't know why I did not mention this before, in my twenties I passed two years on Dendron, an island west of the Hyperboreans, where the people live according to a five-day cycle. They believe that at the end of each five days the world is destroyed and a new world created. They also pay great attention to the transformation of every object from one day to another of the cycle. "Mana", for example, means "table-day-one", "Tufa" "table-day-two" and so on. I am not sure how this relates to our argument yet it is a strange truth that on Dendron anyone arguing that we have ten fingers will be arrested for sorcery.

—What day are we now? I asked.

—I have forgotten. Since returning here things no longer make sense but they made sense over there.

(A LARGE HOLE APPEARS HERE IN THE PAPYRUS)

—If language is not communication, Lysander asked, what then is language?

—Perhaps, Thrasybulus interrupted, we should look at it differently. If language is a mirror of what it is to be human, it should come as no surprise if we cannot define language since we do not know who we are. At most sometimes we might have a faint sense of who we might be.

—You may well be correct in that, Thrasybulus, but first I would like to try a few more observations. Earlier I had thought to say that language is attunement although I believe it states somewhere in the sacred texts of the Mani that language is vulnerability. It is well known that the dead cannot speak yet they listen to music. In music the dead cling to a true language. The true languages consist only of *hapax legomena*, things said only once and then vanished. Poetry is language at the point that it begins to enter untranslatability—it has therefore made the first enormous step towards the condition of music. It is an anti-statue.

(IT IS CLEAR THAT THE TEXT HAS BECOME CORRUPTED AT THIS POINT. THE CONFUSION PERHAPS OF LATER SCRIBES SEEKING TO COVER FOR PAGES THEY HAD INADVERTENTLY DESTROYED. "HAPAX LEGOMENA" IS NOT A TERM THAT WOULD HAVE BEEN USED IN PLATO'S TIME. WHEN THE TEXT RESUMES IT IS CLEAR THAT SOCRATES IS TELLING A STORY, THE WELL KNOWN FABLE OF THE STATUE PEOPLE.)

On an island not far from the islands of tin, several weeks journey by boat in a northern direction from Gades and the Lusitanian mouth of the Tagus, out in the Great Ocean, live a learned and haughty people endowed with great skills in all the arts who are addicted to the statue. By selecting the right day in midwinter and standing in a carefully positioned manner in an open field, then watering their feet with various potions while reciting the correct spell, they turn themselves into statues. A great gathering of shining pillars was made in this way when a group of illustrious men chose to transform themselves to stone. In the form of a statue man can no longer speak. His perfection, his endurance and eternal fame are purchased at the price of speech and change. For even those who live by the five-day cycle we recognise as our brother but the stone we do not count as brother.

—Will you permit me Socrates, Thrasybulus now began, to sum up where we have come. We have accepted that language cannot simply be described as communication in any easy sense since we are not mere reporting machines. Likewise languages may well be untranslatable as music, at the one extreme, certainly is. There are the holes between words and the holes which surround words. Am I in accord with your ideas so far?

—Fairly much, though I must keep repeating I do not have ideas.

—Strictly speaking, language is not communication but poetry—a poetry which has its own journey to make. A journey that gathers who we are and takes us towards who we might be.

—Away from the statue towards music, perhaps, Lysander cheerfully added.

—Indeed, Socrates now concluded, I take it you will be going to the performance of "The peach-tinted sky" by Parmenides' pupil, Antigone, tomorrow night.

—Certainly, replied Lysander.

—Well then, let us all go there together, said Socrates.

(THIS APPEARS TO BE A FALSE ENDING. THE USE OF SOCRATES' NAME ALSO SUGGESTS INCONSISTENCY AND POSSIBLE INTERPOLATION. AFTER MANY PAGES OF WHICH ONLY A WORD HERE AND THERE IS DECIPHERABLE THERE APPEARS THE FOLLOWING PASSAGE WHICH WOULD SEEM TO BE THE TRUE ENDING.)

… at which point we saw the sea. And standing there, gazing or contemplating its wide expanse and the sun that, from moment to moment, caressed its cheek, stood the elderly Agador and his daughter Euphrosyne. Agador had been blind for many years and was dependent on his daughter, a young woman now of some twenty-eight years, tall and of dark beauty for her mother had come from lands beyond the Indus. However, wishing her to have her own life and since she had recently met a noble merchant Demetrios who lived at Neapolis on Cyprus, Agador had asked Euphrosyne to follow her heart and leave with the young man. Being always inventive, Agador had devised a book that could be read with the fingers alone whereby he could find his way throughout the city.

We had barely exchanged greetings and some brief talk when Lysander interrupted with a garbled and very rushed account of the conversation so far and asked:

—Agador, what is language?

—I am blessed by the most wondrous of daughters, bear with me if I weave around a little but I shall soon reach the place of which you are inquiring. She knows that I can manage well enough to negotiate the path to and from the marketplace, the path of the sea and the road to the reciters of books, the theatre and the various temples. Through habit, even blind, I know these places. Yet it would be sadness to be in those places alone. In truth my daughter wishes to stay with me and to be with her lover, her husband (for I see she blushes at the words), the good man Demetrios. This book was made by Euphrosyne—the cuts into the wax that are the feeling-letters I touch were made by her hands. I know, where we stand, the sea is there (he gestured with a wide but measured sweep of his arm) but her speech gives me the sea, its presence, its beauty, the sun that must be there today for I caught that in the slightly raised accent of her voice. So this book, though it is not the same as her voice, gives me the sea. It is also a way for her to be and not to be, to be with her husband on Cyprus and with me here in Athens. As I read the book I see her—I see my knowledge as made into a gift her tenderness offers towards me. Also present in the book are Endomorphos who cut the papyrus and prepared it, Evander the skilled binder of pages and Herodotus whose recording of such books among the Chaldees led me to suggest the idea. This book is language and, like language, more than providing us with knowledge of the useful, it adds to what exists the specific caress each thing summons from within itself. Of all the many things that language is, language is first of all tenderness.

(COMPLETE TEXT OF THE DIALOGUE "AGAINST LYSANDER" EITHER BY PLATO OR BY HIS PUPILS, AS GATHERED IN THE LOEB EDITION, *The Socratic Diaspora: previously uncollected writings by Plato*, LONDON, 1933)

XXVII

—For Memnon remains as a child—he speaks the language of truth. He has never been banished to a baby-talk of money and infidelities.

~o~

—... or, since true words lie most often
    at the bottom of oceans, it may be
    you have found yourself, sister
    in whom shining has accepted
    its divided mission.

~o~

—I was a man in a suit of darkness.
    I was financed by ghosts.

~o~

—But slowly, what news from the marketplace?
—The two sisters have returned.
—Is this by report or from your own eyes?

—I was there. The daughters of Simonides
stood apart, draped all in black,
and one still enclosed in the hood
of her hostage-taking. Three months they have lived
in the darkness under earth. The one stroked
her own cheek, touching gently the blush
of returning life, but for her sister, too timid
to risk yet the immensity of vision,
the black cloth was all her eyes. Then,
with words none present could hear
or sensing by intuition the edge
of caress in a sister's hand, she let fall the cloth
that lay ruffled all around her.
All covered their eyes. Her gaze
has given us back the blessing of daylight.

(FRAGMENTS FROM THE LOST TRAGEDY *The Invisible Ones* BY ARISTOBULUS
OF ALKMENAION, C. 485 BCE)

XXVIII

I entered an enormous chamber supported by the most delicately carved pillars all painted in gold and inlaid with turquoise, topaz and all manner of precious stones. The ceiling was some three hundred feet above me and the priests and officials informed me that the writings to be found carved into the rock face of the ceiling, here and throughout the many antechambers of this, the centre room of the immense underground city of Cos, were created some twelve hundred to nine hundred years before by adepts and masters of the old gods, seeking in the private darknesses of this space a way to illumination. Nowadays visitors are raised up by elaborate means of pulleys and supporting flat beds of wood so that, lying there, they may read a little of what the ancients wrote. In the times of the adepts and masters, so I was informed, no such knowledge of pulleys existed and the original poets relied entirely on meditation and certain spells to float up to the height required to inscribe their poems.

Following the standard practice, I first had to determine by repeated dice throws which small portion of the ceiling I should be raised up to read. Each visitor may read only three of the poems on the ceiling (there are perhaps two million poems there)—to read more would be unlucky, to read less would slight the inexplicable privilege of fate that has brought one to this place.

Having selected the spot in the prescribed manner, I lay down on a pallet and was raised some three hundred feet to the ceiling. There, lying on my back, I began to decipher the tiny script. At this point either my consciousness faded or I entered a trance. It may well be, as seems probable, that the pallet was delicately lowered from underneath me, so that I floated without realising it all the time I was reading the inscriptions. This seems to be what in fact happened for all assert that it is only possible to read the poems if one is in the same state as those who wrote them.

I came to, or next entered normal consciousness, on the floor with no recollection of my descent. In my hands I gripped the sheet of papyrus on which I had copied the words of the poems. For some half hour or more I had no clear sense of who I was, feeling I had perhaps come back in the body of a woman—a common phenomenon I am told, for temporary confusion of gender, as of time and place, is a frequent side effect of these writings. But within a few hours I felt as before.

I was one of the last to visit the underground city. Some two weeks later the entire region was devastated by earthquakes.

The words of the three poems read as follows:

Be with me, divine Alexis,
you who guard the realm of Hathor
and shine from beyond the Indus.

You have been the first breeze

in the time when men reassemble the rigging of boats.
In the dark marshes
you have been the place where
the houses lean on the sky.

The last gap remaining in the black wall of death,
you are the first woman I made love to
so many nights ago
in Locri when the sun was almost rising.

~o~

Among all that flowers and grows
who will gather the small seed of my being
to grant me my final oblivion?
Who will walk beside me
beyond the fields of Elysium
and, on parched summer days,
who will bring a thimbleful of water
brighter than all stars?
What god or fate has chosen me
to be sand in the million million
paths, these syllables
that only you
read?

~o~

Open my heart, god of the threefold path.*

(*Alternate translation: Open my heart, three-personed God.)

(NIKOS OF ALEXANDRIA, Travels in Bithynia, Cappadocia and Armenia,
c. 550 AD)

XXIX

When the wind is like that
the white trees, the thin light
trembling at our shoulders

When the wind enters our town
snow on the hills, the enemy
sailing towards the harbour,
the forest of their spears at daybreak

When the wind strips away our hands
if a scar remains or a tree
or light, the bringer of morning,

if there is a hill or a path
or a wall to capture shadows,
if we find we are still here
we must start to inquire
who we are.

(ATAXERXES OF HALICARNASSUS, A PERSIAN LIVING IN EXILE WHO WROTE
HIS POETRY IN GREEK, THE LANGUAGE OF HIS ADOPTIVE CITY. 459 BCE)

BOOK II

I

Returning early one evening to the small room he rented above the Caniculum Fountains, Marinus of Samaria, now in his sixty-first year, met a cloud-mountain that had materialized at the corner of an empty side street. Invisible to all others, it was his own personal cloud-mountain, the kind that generally descend in deserts or other remote waterless places, invariably to adepts who have starved themselves for forty days and nights and renounced all forms of everyday life in the hope of such visitations. The mountain did not speak or move but merely beckoned in a looming kind of way. Within its presence, Marinus later recalled, it was like a day shining with calm and expectation in another person's youth, someone quite young living many many years in the future. He would recall the exquisite innocence, "feeling the sea flow into you", he said, and suddenly a pair of torn bloodied boots left abandoned to the Roman winter, falling under the shadow of the cloud-mountain, blossomed with innumerable heliotropes, swaying steadily on their stems as if strengthened and defended by the ocean.

Marinus did not ask for words from his cloud-mountain or any tablets inscribed with prohibitions. Standing in its presence he no longer feared the divine Imbalance or argued with the vanishing of his life. Later, on his deathbed, he confessed, "For those five minutes I understood how love is always about to happen. I was a young girl on a beach in Atlantis."

(Dionysius Laertes, the "Pamphlygonian", from his lost manuscript, *Lives of those who see*)

II

The Chermetzoi recognise 27 different degrees of relationship between people, each creating its own separate variation of their language, with different tenses and alternate words. Among the Aretai to their north there are more than 55 distinct levels of intimacy, each generating a separate language. Often in the morning after a night of troubled dreams a couple will awake inside a new language, slowly recognising its shape and contours.

The Sarmenians, on the other hand, have over 300 words for different emotions, disdaining the perilous imprecision of such words as "love", "hate", "fear", "like" and "dislike". To them the vocabulary of languages outside their own fatally distorts even the most everyday levels of inner experience. They insist, indeed, on the tentative approximation of their own language, claiming the greatest element of human emotions remains yet to be discovered.

(EUPHRASTES, *Treatise on Grammar*, 410)

~o~

By night the blue dream walks on water. I stand in a room of bones, following in the notes as they fade the disembodied journey of ecstasy.

Here I go again, stepping out into one of the innumerable languages with its 75 terms to state the layered intensities of love. At each level having to speak in new tones and cadences with strange middle preterite tenses. And language modifies itself upwards and downwards over the years, shuffling inflections and sounds so that, all around one, new words are always beginning—

and the elderly say, "I stumble with joy. I do not know this world."

(FROM HIERONYMUS OF CHIOS, *Among the Illuminated*)

III

Among the Vandimini of central Gaul the word for "growth" and
the word for "belief" are the same. To them it is obvious that plants
are distinguished above all by their strong belief in themselves.
Learned scholars among these people have proven that sun, water,
soil with the richest chicken manure, all are of no value if a plant
lacks belief. Likewise to the Vandimini belief in oneself and belief
in the gods are identical.

(HELIOPHRASTUS, *The return to the sun of origins*)

IV

The minotaur, on reprieve, considers his difficulties

The minotaur in his bath
is joyful in madness.
Blessed for no reason,
his squat grey prison lies open today.
Strange thoughts come and go
across unguarded walls.
He counts the white days of sails
scattering their flakes of dawn
outside his window.
Any moment now
he will invent himself in a different language,
a new shape purged
of grotesqueries.

The minotaur in his madness
washes away the deep creases of pain.
The pure blue he waits for
does not grieve too deeply

over night's passing,
his legendary bellow
now the mute sigh of a tree trunk.
Undreaming the svelte grey cities
that walk the horizon, the minotaur
meditates on a new name
for his silence.
Ignored by all
he goes on unspinning
the thread that divides
peace from nothingness.

~o~

The dark judges address the minotaur

Celandron
your tiger-jacketed presence
paces the white collapse of the sea.
From the hill where the night-dotted sunflower
protects its homeland
the blue and rolling ocean circles
its inexhaustible drift.

Minotuar
by the stake of this thought-jagged pole
thrust and bound to earth,
do not grieve so much
that you will never again enter the waves,
that the blood-spattered mouth trailing its victims
was only an invention, a libel.

White ships pass
skirting the claws of the coastline.
Waves break day and night

against your tumbledown prison.
The spell of their sound alone
steadies the dark,
carries you fearless into our presence.

(Two poems from Andropoulos of Herakleion, the "minotaur" poet,
c 550 ad)

V

While travelling with his parents from Alexandria to Ephesus, the young Nicanor experienced something that would change his life. The boat which had been stumbling across the incertitude of ocean put in at an island that had appeared miraculously in previously uninhabited sea. After several days of crowded ship-board existence, rocking monotonously on deck in choppy seas and feeling the harsh poverty of the food, the three of them—Nicanor and his parents—set off to find oranges, for the island was said to have an immense supply of an exquisite blend of this fruit according to the Captain who had abandoned his boat in the port to go off in search of them.

After winding their way uphill for some half-hour, having lost sight of the dock, they realised that the island spoke to them. His parents registered this in the yellowish tinge that entered their eyes though they could not make out the words. Only Nicanor could hear the sounds of the island and follow the intricate delicacy of its speech.

Reaching the top of the hill where it seemed the best oranges were, they turned back to gaze at the sea below only to find their boat was no longer in the harbour. A long jagged wall extended across the island and had been circling them steadily as they walked. From time to time they caught sight of the people who lived on the other side of this wall, and from their stricken appearance it was soon obvious that the island was a giant floating leprosarium. Either from shock or the thirst inspired by their closeness to the oranges, Nicanor entered the deep sleep that protected him. In this sleep he spoke constantly with the island.

Later, when the time was right, he made himself into a statue so he could be taken off the island and finally brought to Ephesus. Of his parents, or the boat, or the other passengers, no record is kept.

(EVANDER OF KOS, *The pre-history of Nicanor, Prophet of the Darkness in Ephesus*, YEAR 12 OF THE FOURTH EUSEBIAN ERA)

The wondrous deeds and teachings of Nicanor gave rise to perhaps the most influential of all religions. Two rival versions of his life were recorded—one by the physician Adeodatus and one by his supposed cousin, the High Priestess Ademeter. Nicanor's teachings became the dominant creed of Atlantis during the fourth manifestation of Eusebius. His sermon on the righteousness of wealth found a special resonance with them, given their addiction to property of all kind and their cult of war. The saying "Death to the poor", ascribed to Nicanor in Adeodatus' Life, is translated differently in Ademeter's version as "Let the poor enjoy the depth of their sleep". The paradoxical nature of Eusebius owes much to this religion. How other than by consulting religion can one explain the peculiar ferocity of their addiction to ownership and the elimination of others? On Eusebius they shrank language so steadily that in the end no one could speak his own name for fear it was the property of another who had perhaps sold it elsewhere to invest in the future of sunrise. But did Eusebius become so warlike and self-destructive because of, or in spite of, the Nicanorean Ethics and the Creed of the Revived Statues of Ephesus? Scholars point out that similar practices arose during the third manifestation of Eusebius among the outer Dacians though not on the same scale, given the underdeveloped nature of the Dacian court system. Possibly, as hostile critics of the Nicanoreans assert, Nicanor's long time in deep sleep and his subsequent life as a statue blinded him to the value of such emotions as love, selfless generosity or artistic pursuits. Possibly the Eusebioli rewrote all the texts. Some suggest that his entire existence was a case of mistranslation.

(LUCIAN OF GADES, *A brief history of the rise of the Nicanoreans*, 858 THE ALTERNATIVE CALENDAR)

Fifty years after its first manifestation on the westernmost island of Atlantis, the Kingdom of Eusebius held a secret council to decide whether it should declare itself the World Government. The renowned archons Aegisthus and Menandros spoke in favour of the efficiencies to be gained should direct control be extended where the might of the Eusebian court and the Eusebian compulsory exchange committee already regulated all aspects of life. In this way, they argued, everyone could be more efficiently taxed to fund their own repression. Yet the majority, led on by the religious zeal of a certain Monochrastes, rejected the proposal, claiming such an act would undermine the purity of the Nicanorean faith. How could the principle of non-reciprocity be respected if all people became Eusebioli? Otherness must be maintained, Monochrastes urged, if the sacred duty of exploitation was to be extended to all corners of the galaxies. Likewise it was feared such a gesture might damage morale in the military—troops might be less enthusiastic about exterminating peripherals and non-successful entities if they too could be called Eusebioli.

(MACRONIUS OF ILLYRIUM, *The Chronicle of a Sad Kingdom*)

VI

The hand opens:
what it grasped it destroyed.

~o~

The sea casts its shadows upward:
birds cry entering the wash of blueness.

~o~

Everything we do collapses into us.

~o~

The wall that divides us joins us.

~o~

Better to eat light
with the trembling lips of the statues
than to sleep among the fragrance of oranges.

(FRAGMENTS OF NICANOR CITED IN EUMENIDES' TREATISE, *The idea of
beginnings among the simple singers of Pergamon*)

VII

Among the Cimmerians there is a small island, most commonly
referred to as Hyperborean Amorgos. The island is riddled with
holes, treacherous precipices and caves. Sometimes a lake or river is
found underneath, but mostly there is only silence and darkness. The
people who live here likewise bear gashes and holes all over their
bodies. Often the centre of the hand is missing or it may be possible
to look through another's cheek and see the sky. Mostly death awaits
these people as it awaits everyone only earlier and more painfully.
Yet immortals also live on this island who have learned from the
holes in their being to patch together a music that will save them. It
is rumoured that the Sirens were women of Hyperborean Amorgos
who had been stolen by sailors and left on the Wandering Islands.

The speech of those who dwell on Hyperborean Amorgos is curious. These people speak not one but two languages. In the first every word is built outwards from the simplest stems: earth [uk], air [aauuu], fire [hith], water [gliss]: along with twelve tones that register shifts in one's state of calm or anxiety. This speech they call "building speech" for in it they attempt to cement their longing to endure. The second speech called "hathor" is an alarming discontinuity of grief and rapture. Sometimes they call this "soaring speech". It is possible to explain everything at very rapid speed in this language but it is not a good language to use for cooking soup or preparing fish. Those who are in tune with each other naturally adjust their languages quite easily to achieve harmony while those who clash address each other inappropriately.

The subtle spontaneous modulations of these languages and their penetrating yet eternally flawed mirroring of existence are probably the chief explanation of the Sirens' song—that or the homesickness of women who, never abandoning the chasm through the centre of the chest called love, have gazed beyond death.

(FROM DIO CASSIUS, *A true account of the circumnavigation of Europe from Lusitanian Gades to the Chersonese Bosphorus*)

VIII

And darkly they all advanced, shooting
down the edges of the sky,
scooping the foam in troughs,
sifting the sea that raced beyond their fingers.
Soon they arrived among the Wandering Islands
and there the mist came on.
Breeze was there none
that rocks the trees in autumn and gladdens
sailors' hearts. A still blackness held them all
and no one knew the hand before his face.

Simonides was first to speak.
Holding his crew back and listening to the roar
of a thousand birds that feed on human kind,
he spoke:
"We have steered our ship into the future.
No one can state as certainty that time is round,
no one knows for sure that anything comes back.
Must we never more see Agrigentum,
never more drain the musk-sweet Syracusan wine?
Yet hope may still be: we must strip ourselves of flesh
and be as statues. Stone was our ancestor,
stone must be our watchword."
And his men all performed the sacred ritual,
their tears froze at their cheeks, and on that deck
they became a marble city, drifting safe
across the thousand death birds. And within night
and within the turning of the world
they sheltered, letting the mind walk by itself
as on some empty highway the wind
is the only traveller who has no sense of fear,
the wind takes what it chooses, with no knowledge
of endings

Dawn broke and the men felt life regain their limbs.
A great cry of joy broke from every lip.
Beyond death, beyond hope,
they spread once more the sails
and their ship soon came to Ebtesum,
the fair land of blossoming fragrances
and the smooth-skinned jet-dark women of soft voice,
there where the world began.

(FROM *The voyages of Simonides*, FRAGMENTS OF THE EPIC ATTRIBUTED TO
THEOGNIS OF MEGARA, AS PRESERVED ON PAPYRUS SCROLLS IN THE HOLY
CITY OF KITEZH)

IX

Nine days journey south of the great cities of the Numideans lies the kingdom of the Ventae, rumoured to be a sister kingdom of the legendary Ebtesum though some claim it is the more ancient seat of learning. The Ventae consider Kitezh, their sacred city, to be the geographic and temporal centre of the earth. The city and the immediate plain on which it is built are surrounded by a circular river. This river reverses the flow of its water at night. Because it is the centre of the world, its priests explain, the waters there become confused and do not know which direction to take. This vast circling of water spinning and turning marks the passage from day to night and by itself generates the most extraordinary music which is used to cure all manner of illness and likewise powers the many curious machines for which this kingdom is famous.

Those who lie down in the city at the centre of the world know the calm of the forests growing all around them, the green earth blessing them with its myriad flowers and colours visible and invisible. The city walls, made of a densely compounded mud found only in this river, mirror the stars by night and the sun by day. The moon is often found to fall asleep in this city, and spells frequently must be invoked to return it to the skies.

Several years after Scipio led his war of conquest into Numidea, fearing lest the spread of Roman command might interfere with the magic properties of their realm, the rulers of Kitezh asked their wise men to develop some suitable defence system. Around the same time envoys from the alternate Empire, Eusebius, arrived, demanding half of all their wealth or the Eusebian Council would invoke a curse to place all the land of the Ventae under the ocean. Diplomatic as always, the rulers of Kitezh prepared an immense document of so many clauses it would require several lifetimes to read, as well as many elephant-loads of precious stones for the envoys to take back with them. When the envoys were on their return journey they discovered that the document turned invisible at night and the precious stones merely acted as magnets attracting immense desert winds that obliterated all directions. On their eventual return to their own land the envoys were all executed for daring to suggest that the world might have some centre other than Eusebius, and the Council of the Eusebioli decreed that no such country as the Ventae could exist.

For defence the kingdom has always relied on two strategies— the immense desert winds which the priests control, and the gift of invisibility. Dwelling at the precise centre of the human world, they rest in the safety that mankind will never see them.

(FROM GREGORIUS OF ARMENIA, *On suitable defences for small kingdoms*)

X

Again that cry for help breaking from the lips.
Again no one comes.
Infinite the distance from gods and men.
Only the small voice in the still place,
still within oneself:
"I am here. I continue."

(FRAGMENT FROM *The Black Book of Ebtesum*)

~o~

When a people are to be executed, they may not make a speech or recite a poem or sing any songs. They may however, if they choose, tell a brief joke.

(DECREE 457 OF THE EUSEBIAN COUNCIL ON THE CORRECT PROCEDURES FOR GENOCIDE)

—What swallowed the earth but only swallowed itself?
—My excutioners and those who sent them.

~o~

I have lived here a long time
but I do not know where "here" is.

(FRAGMENT FROM *The Black Book of Ehtesum*)

XI

The Holy City of Kitezh has had two manifestations within recorded annals. The first occurred in Africa at the time of the growth of Roman power when the city and its surrounding countryside preserved African wisdom in its era of greatest flowering, an oasis of learning, one might say, on the fringes of Roman militarism. The second manifestation was in the land of the Rus during the great Mongol and Tartar invasions around 1500–1600. From this it would seem that the city appears according to a 2000-year cycle and might therefore be expected to return around the year 3600, though in which location is unclear, evidence from the future still being scarce despite the circularity of time.

At least this much is clear: the Holy City of Kitezh, providing a secure repository of wisdom both practical and spiritual, favours the edges of great Empires of devastation, relying always on invisibility for its survival.

(UNIDENTIFIED PAPYRUS WRITTEN IN ARAMAIC AND URDU, FOUND AMONG THE PAPERS OF THE ARCHAEOLOGIST PROFESSOR FRIEDRICH NEUGEBAUER, UNIVERSITY OF JENA, 1847–1870)

XII

Among the ancients of our people, the Hellenic homeland and its numerous colonies and sister cities, the poet was a figure uniquely admired and deeply feared. It is well known that poems can always be altered by a poet and that therefore the only way to ensure the canonical survival of a given poem is by killing the poet. For this reason poets were reluctant to write poems, let alone complete a poem.

When a poet did know that he had finished a poem of great value he immediately had to leave his home and city, first binding his fellow citizens on solemn oath to change nothing of his poem while he was away. It only remained for him to die in exile—in this way his people would be eternally obliged to preserve his work faithfully.

In Ebtesum an opposite tradition prevailed—that poems should not be preserved but that poets should endlessly invent new poems. Though poets were deeply honoured in the same way as musicians and singers, their specific names were rarely mentioned and, in the books later surreptitiously produced—such as the Black Book of Ebtesum or the Green Book of Ebtesum, ascriptions are not made to individuals. During my own stay in Ebtesum after an evening of extraordinarily moving poetry I made the mistake of thanking and congratulating a poet on his work. As if disturbed while searching bewilderedly among lost shades, his aged face looked far away into great distances. He spoke then in a language I had never heard before yet was able to understand immediately by instinct: "For these words to flow through me," he said, "it is necessary never to think thoughts like that. Only by eliminating all desire to own, even as much as the name on my grave, can speech bless me and the silent ones allow me into their home."

(FROM THEOPHRASTUS, *Compendium of poetic practices*, MOST LIKELY PRODUCED UNDER THEOPHRASTUS' SUPERVISION AS DIRECTOR OF THE LYCEUM AFTER

ARISTOTLE'S DEATH AND POSSIBLY WRITTEN BY ARISTOTLE'S PUPIL MENDRON
WHO HAD LIVED MANY YEARS IN EGYPT AND TRAVELLED EXTENSIVELY IN
DIVERSE REALMS)

XIII

There are birds which are invisible as night,
furnishing themselves with darkness for a body.
When your hand strokes
their watery presence in the air,
ripples of a great tenderness and a great fear
invade you.

Falling in love is like this,
Hypatia.
The invisible birds, they say, were those so wounded
they thread their passion through another realm
where all is glass. Their cries, unhearable
to humankind, life-rending to all frail-veined
creatures of earth, are the darkened water
that glides around or through all things, pure
as regret that stops one suddenly
in a doorway when the daylight leaves us.
Love has entirely eaten them away
or turned them inside out and set them spinning
ceaselessly through a world tangential to our own.

Think of the terror
when you descend a lonely hill, walking towards your beloved
and you imagine perhaps she has another, perhaps she has decided
you hold no future for her,
yet you go on walking, all your being so weakened
there is no other direction you could possibly walk.
These birds have gathered that pain,

that terror and that joy,
have augmented and augmented it
till their small hearts burst with openness
and all their being is night.

If I might be such a bird
I would nestle above the stillness of your body,
I would be the presence that haloes your silence
when, by night, your slender form bends to a flickering light
poring yet again over the Mathemasis
seeking the impossible formula of return,
the number that undoes time.

But here, among the prison-rocks
of this wandering island beyond furthest Corsica,
fettered by stern decrees, abandoned to a world
I no longer see …

(SOLE SURVIVING FRAGMENT OF POEM 23 BY ISTAREION OF ALEXANDRIA,
Love letter to Hypatia)

XIV

When he left the military after serving in the three-year expedition
to besiege and conquer Bactria, Erychthemios did not return to the
school of rhetoric and poetics as planned by his parents but instead
took ship to Alexandria. There he lived a humble and exemplary
life, writing his poems for performance in taverns and at the weekly
gatherings of slaves and homeless runaways he shared food with,
to live in the simplest manner possible being all his endeavour. At
the age of twenty-two he began composing a work of extraordinary
beauty, the collection of poems he later set to music, the famous
Knowings. Alone in Alexandria, surrounded by minor poets and
fashionable imitators of the ancients yet intuiting how the smallest
possible poem may capture the sky, Erycthemios aimed at a sparse

austerity in his work. He sought in what he called "the unity of life and silence" to explore how simple and ultimate the world might be. In those small gatherings where, as he said, only the essential is valued, he would speak his poems in a clear natural voice, eschewing all excess flourishes, accompanied only by a single lyre and occasionally a drum. On his deathbed he prophesied his return in the remote future as a musician living in a northern city by a river where the Greek language was unknown, stating that he would write his most famous piece of music at the age of twenty-two and it would be arranged for a larger group of musicians by a man who would have two wives. Of his entire work only fragments remain.

(MACROBIUS, *Lives of the great poets*)

just this hand
just this street
just this river
just this stone

~O~

having said
having said that the stone is round,
that the sky is waiting at the end of the street

it remains to greet you,
beloved who will live
so far beyond me

don't be concerned by the narrowness of your fate—
words will find you too
and the pure breath

that never needed words.

~O~

The dancer in the tavern
knows the love that she sells.
The soldier in battle
knows the death he deals and receives.
The amphora from beyond Bactria
captures the stars and lets the blind man
walk with them inside him.

What we offer most profoundly
is emptiness.
The bowl of offering is the first thing
our ancestors shape:
cracked and thrown aside
it is more complete than our bodies.

Know then:
to the one who sits, his heart opened,
the air that rests in the hollow of his palm
weighs more than the moon and sun.

~o~

If what is
floats up towards us,
unbearable at times,
the great night of rupture, the father's hand
violent on the face, or what was said
too lightly, too hurtfully, in youth,

if all that is
comes back, always to walk
along this seafront where the dunes
are crumbling,

how then do they continue,
the young women and men whose hands

silently touch, whose eyes filter
the distance of the sea and all its summers,

when the vortex of each second
drains a world into its grave?

(FRAGMENTS FROM *Knowings* BY ERYCTHEMIOS)

XV

On the island called "home of the gods" far beyond India the people were highly inventive, all their endeavour being to find ways to sell something others lacked—not an easy thing to do in a just world, since all men breathe air, eat what the earth produces and make shelters from the rain in similar fashion and, by nature, would have nothing rare to produce and no special lack needing completion. In the markets on this island originated the extraordinary trade in calendars. For these people had always lived with many calendars. Even for the lunar months they have the most distinct names, each household or clan devising its own elaborate names and competing to discover new resonances of beauty and aptness. In addition to the lunar months they have, among numerous other patterns and customary festivals, 15-day cycles, 200-day cycles and 1000-day cycles based on certain trees that bloom at certain times, the migration of birds, the rising and falling of rivers, the birth of animals and the mysterious loneliness of the human heart.

Yet, despite the rage for calendars and their successful export to places as far distant as India, Egypt, Rome and the islands of Atlantis, eventually their trade declined. The people of the island then discovered the possibility of selling spices which grew abundantly on the island and required indeed far less labour than calendars. Later the spice trade gave way to the age of wars when the rulers of the island's numerous city states, making war on each other, took to selling the women and children of conquered cities into slavery. (The women of this island were renowned for their beauty.) Later again the age of slavery was replaced by the age when they sold the earth under their feet. Finally there was a return to the age of calendars and the cycle began all over again. This was all in accord with the Calendar of the Great Movement.

(PLINY THE ELDER, *Notes towards a Universal History*)

~o~

Know then of the calendars:

the calendars of those who do not recognise the five or seven-day cycle—the calendars of fifteen days, the calendars of the nines— nine days, nine months, nine years

the calendars based on the cycle of sunspots, the twelve year cycle, the cycle of earthquakes and fire from heaven

the calendars that move backwards in time, telling you which days to eliminate from your life, the calendar that passes through one's birth to when earth first separated from sea

and the calendar for those who reject time, the calendar of chaotic dots sprawling across interminable papyri

the calendars that record the secret names for the months—the month River, Mountain, Hand Open, Sealed Lips, the month Acceptance and months or days dedicated to special gods—the god of the hour, the day, the year, and the god of the sacred moment, the god of what is hoarded, the god who travels the infinite distance of sleep

the calendar for immortals

the calendar for sleepwalkers

the calendar written by bees in their migrations across the earth

the calendar that will build you a shelter during the stellar winter

the calendar for cooking herbs to alleviate mindpain and loneliness

the calendar of lost children, the calendar that listens to their feet walking down a path over and over—the man who made this calendar resigned his life to breathe eternity into this calendar. Its sale to an inconsolable princess in Madras funded the feeding of all the children of the island for fifty years.

the calendar that tells you how to pace your breaths so they will be in harmony with the grass already growing on your grave

the calendar for those who live with the certainty that sooner or later they will fall off the edges of the known universe

the preferred calendar for synchronising the cooling of glass with the wanderings of the planet Jupiter

the calendar that teaches ants how to avoid water

the calendar that only has one day

(FROM XEUXIS OF ANAGOGE, *The Book of Lists*, CHAPTER XV, "ON CALENDARS")

XVI

In the settlements along the Chersonese straits they have a scarcity of all medicinal herbs, the soil being poor as much of its power is drained by enormous trees. Instead they rely on jumblewords (wordjumble) to cure all manner of illness. Far from being an idle superstition the practice is both highly efficacious and based on the soundest principles. When language continues along its smooth well-worn path we remain in the same state, whether for good or ill, the body accumulating those destructive habits and contaminated airs that soon manifest themselves as stomach cramps, painful bones, the blight that eats into the eye or other forms of illness. By breaking up that well-worn path, by putting kinks and twists to spoken words, the mouth learning babble frees the spirit within a person. For words, the ancients say, are the backbone of the mind. Cracking words open, reassembling them in new combinations, the mind gains rest and so cures itself and the body. The practice strongly resembles what happens spontaneously on the edges and furthest shores of sleep. Hippocrates himself discusses the efficacious nature of such wordsplicing and wordfusion within half-dreaming states in the third volume of his dissertation on the alternatives to surgery. He records the example of one Menandron of Corinth who, suffering from a painful swelling of the forehead, had requested the removal of his brain to alleviate the torment. From inquiries among neighbours Hippocrates learned the illness had set in shortly after the death of his son, killed through the violence of a playmate. Suspecting the means to cure the illness lay within the power of language, could it only be induced to shatter itself, to remake itself at the precise point when waking gives way to sleep and the soul slides most easily between its several lives, Hippocrates placed Menandron in a dream-like state. There words broke effortlessly from his lips in a babble of drowning sounds. Menandron found himself swimming among reeds, drawn onwards by a yellow flower of the brightest radiance. Reaching inside the flower a word came to him: *"allodendronhamratia-spreuge"*. With difficulty he seized the word, bearing it with him back into his conscious life. On waking he pronounced the word once, then left the doctor's residence as one intent on a mission, firmly believing he must complete his task before the death which he assumed was imminent. He began organising a petition to ban all gladiatorial games throughout his city—for the common practice of bringing small children to watch the games had led to the corruption of the other boy's mind and so to the death of his own son. (Frequently parents so lusted to watch the blood sports they considered leaving their children elsewhere too troublesome to arrange.) In his enthusiasm to ban the vile Roman, or as they assert Etruscan, practice, Menandron forgot his own condition and within a month the swelling had disappeared. Although the popular clamour for the game proved undefeatable, Menandron did succeed in having the ban on the presence of young children enforced.

CODA:

According to a tradition preserved among the Carian women, the name "poetry" (poesis, poemata) derives from this practise of deliberately making curative words. The rhythmic nature of these fractured or recombined words gave rise to the notion of the poetic line. A person who made such wordjumbles became known as a "poeta" as opposed to a "rhetor" or "aidos", both of which words highlight the sung nature of extended lyrics. In poetry the curative power was held to lie in the word itself, rather than the melody to which the words might or might not be sung. The respect given to poets, then, was in its origins an extension of the respect given to doctors and healers.

(FROM THEOPHRASTUS, *Compendium of poetic practices*)

XVII

In those days the sun was always sliding off the edge of the visible, vanishing then reappearing in the least likely places—a locked cupboard, a woman's sandal, a darkened mirror or the shallow mound of earth where a gardener might be planting a rosebush. Sometimes at noon it would turn itself inside out so that its black core glared terrifyingly towards the homes of men.

Then the great Continuator took measure and numbers were assigned to the heavens and the geometric forms were invented—

the circle, the rhombus, the triangle and the apeiron eidolon—the figure where an infinity of lines redraw themselves according to the secret numbers of the universe.

From all these numbers and formulae the goddess that presides over music ordered the realm of the audible, creating the five-tone scale, the nine notes and the 360 variations of resonance.

Likewise these numbers spilt into the visible and the tangible, creating architecture and the knowledge of the proportions, and the yearning for the intuitive numbers that men recognise as beauty.

Yet in the human heart the sun still vanishes at random and all formulae fail. The black core of the universe cannot be caught in the web that measures, does not answer to the laws of the Mathemasis. Heedless it burns through eye and hand. As space it is the vortex that consumes, in the world of men it is the unlimited war that destroys. [ἄπειροσ πολεμὸσ, τὸ πανορφανούμενο]

(PHOTIUS OF AEGISPOTAMI, *Against Pythagoras*)

XVIII

The Floriendi are very skilled at visualising and holding onto
the inward maps for things.
By night they climb down enormous ladders into the space of their
    dreams.
What life intends for them next
is always in the third room on the left.
What they most long for
is in the first room on the right.

When it rains in their land, they float above the downpours
to map the concourse of the rivers.
Like the fingers weary gamblers stretch across a table late at night,
the bones of the rivers of the world cannot see how they all connect.

When the dry season comes the Floriendi unroll their maps.
To a clicked litany of dry grass,
they finger the waterholes.

Beauty and coolness break in the mouths of their dreams.

(FROM *The Black Book of Ebtesum*)

XIX

On his second voyage to attempt the circumnavigation of Africa
Eudoxas had passed the Cape of the West and progressed for many
days along the shore that now lay to his north when they passed the
mouth of a wide, swift-flowing river. Here his small fleet of three
boats put in at the dock of a great and wondrous city. Their arrival
was clearly anticipated as a deputation from the Prince of the city
along with emissaries from the Kingdom of Ebtesum greeted them
on arrival, inviting them to refresh themselves in the nearby palace.

By this time Eudoxas had exhausted his supplies of food. The grains
he had brought for cultivation had been destroyed by storms and
by the intensity of the sun in those regions, while his men feared
that to sail any further would cost them their lives. Their journey
from Gades had now been more than six months and they were
warned by many villages that the time of the great rain would soon
be on them. Accordingly Eudoxas was eager to find shelter for the
coming months before resuming his journey.

Now the power of Ebtesum had secretly been following his progress
since he first sailed south beyond Mauretania. The rulers of Ebtesum
were aware of his intentions and they feared that the creation of
new trade routes to lower Africa and India would damage their
security. Seeing into the future they feared Roman intrusion and
the imminent devastation of the trade and commerce of their sister
Kingdoms. They argued with Eudoxas that his plan to round the

southern cape of Africa was doomed to failure. The map on which he relied, the great map of Eratosthenes, was mistaken in two main ways: it omitted the islands of Atlantis that lay far to the West and it seriously underestimated the enormous distances north-south. Eudoxas himself had become aware of this flaw during his journey which had so far lasted not three months, as predicted by Eratosthenes, but seven months. And soon, the emissaries informed him, the coastline would plunge not eastward but southward again, many more months than those he had already travelled. Death and disaster alone awaited him if he should continue in that direction. Apart from numerous pirates and the violence of many villages, there were the treacherous winds of the southern cape to be considered. And, most of all, they informed him, the Great Council of the African Kingdoms had solemnly resolved that any European attempting to round the cape would be put to death, as the time for such a discovery had not yet arrived.

The emissaries of Ebtesum, not wishing the blood of any man to be on their hands, offered him several alternatives. They informed him of the possibility of a safe return to Egypt or Gades via overland routes of great antiquity—the one through Ebtesum, the other through their sister Kingdom of Kitezh and the lands of the Ventae. Alternatively, if he wished, they could transport him, again via secret inland routes, to the fabulous city of Zam which lay on the Eastern coast of Africa. Zam was the sovereign trade centre between the Cinnamon Coast, southern Africa and India. His boats would be sailed there by expert mariners from the Southern Kingdom who had authority to round the Cape and knew the winds in those parts—they would deliver the boats personally to him in Zam in six months time where he might resume his life as a trader.

Considering his situation and understanding the deep veracity of all who spoke for Ebtesum, Eudoxas accepted the offer to establish himself as a merchant in Zam for he had heard of that kingdom when reaching the Cinnamon coast many years before. Now Lysander, his co-pilot and second in command, longed to return to his family on the island of Cos, and so asked that he might be escorted overland to Egypt from where he could return safely to his homeland. The emissaries agreed to all these things and arrangements were made for their departure before the season of the rains set in.

At the same time the emissaries from Ebtesum also revealed something of the deeper reasons why Eudoxas and his crew were not permitted to proceed. According to the sacred calendar held by the rulers of the stone fortresses of the south, no one born in Europe or north of the line that joins Memphis to Mauretania was due to sail around the Southern Cape till another cycle of one thousand six hundred and four years had passed, as reckoned by the solar calendar of the West. Once that happened, according to the prophecies, ruin would swiftly follow for the peoples of Africa and many other peoples throughout the earth. The rulers of Ebtesum, though they wished no harm to Eudoxas and his crew, must in conscience do all possible to delay that fate till its appointed hour.

Now the evening before their departure a great feast was held in the palace wherein those from Ebtesum, the Prince and Eudoxas, conversed freely on diverse matters concerning the nature of the Western world, of which they took Greece to be the finest exponent. Of this discussion Lysander later made notes after returning to his homeland on Cos, and these notes, I, Iamblichus his grandson, have recorded here, correcting only slightly where words appear missing or errors of grammar may have intruded.

The conversation in the Palace of Prince Nefaroponte, ruler of the great south river, wherein the emissaries from Ebtesum, the Prince and Eudoxas, discussed several matters concerning the future:

—Speak to me further of Greece, for I am puzzled. Your people have lifted marble into the shining air and breathed life into it.

Of the tragic predicament of man and the divided dignity of his going under, your renowned dramatists have written words that will last forever. And in other forms of poetry, the lyric and the epic, how wondrous your achievement. In the city of Athens you have developed the beginnings of a form of democracy in which all citizens might share in good governance and work together in liberty. Yet your people have burned themselves out with war, always distrustful of each other, always hungrily eyeing the just moment to destroy a neighbour. For among your people war has seemed to be less an instrument of policy, a last resort for survival in dark necessity, than a heady addiction. And those wars and that petty chaos of bloodshed ended only with Alexander—a small war, as they say, giving way to a large war. And, beyond Alexander, Rome now rises in your west and all the militarism that will be Rome. In our lands we have had emissaries and dark contacts from Eusebius, the kingdom that recognises no god but war and profit. In the Greek and Roman lands Eusebius has had no need to meddle since your rulers have done its work for it.

The second emissary, Astaromorph, now joined in

—Indeed, this subject of war and the double-edged nature of your people confounds us. For us, observing for many centuries from the edges, it seems the mere smallest leap could save you. For beauty in the hands of butchers bewilders us. You are a trader and a man of moderation and sound judgement, as known from your discourse of the other night. How do you explain this lust for war, this perverse reverence for war, that so obsesses your people?

Now though Eudoxas, as a trader, was no great friend of the political leaders of Hellas or the new Alexandrian kingdoms, he felt it incumbent on him as a Greek to speak as best he might in explanation of his countrymen.

—War is many things. It is natural to protect one's own interests and to favour the advantages of one's own people over others.

After the Persian War Athens felt exposed to danger on all sides and knew its survival had come to depend on its control of key ports that protected its grain flow from the north. It existed too in a climate where men perceived war to be the constant and unspoken state of relations between each people and each city. Sparta had long shown its hostile intentions towards Athens so fear was ripe among the multitude. A democracy above all is prone to government by fear and the manipulators of fear are always keen to sense this advantage. To win an election or gain high office nothing is easier than to point to one's prowess in war and whoever counsels prudence or moderation in dealings with other nations will be branded soft. So Athens' leaders, sensing any display of weakness, anything the mob might be led to decry as softness, would be the end of their careers, frantically outdid each other in the punishments they pledged to inflict on supposed enemies of the polis. For, except in an ideal world where all men have reached a calm moderation in judgement, democracy is the form of government that most favours war.

Prince Nefaroponte, who had been listening intently, now came in with well-considered words:

—Yet beyond this quest for immediate fame and gratification of private ambitions of which you speak, lies the inherent contradiction of cruelty as a means of diplomacy. The merest schoolboy knows that those who misuse power to oppress others and seize all they can for themselves, heedless of tomorrow, soon unite all against them and speed their own destruction.

To which Eudoxas replied:

—In a world of wise rulers I agree, but in my own world, despite the few great geniuses of whom Allorophon first spoke, the many with their immediate fears and insatiable greed and gullibility have always predominated. Remember that in a democracy young men compete for power and fame. No fame or honour goes to the educator or the medic or the wise trader who improves the livelihood of many people—and the way of the true statesman is hard to achieve, his success uncertain even after many years of negotiations. On the other hand the preachers of war have immediate access to men's minds.

Now pausing a while to consider their reactions and finding himself, as often happens in Ebtesum and in the poetic world that Kingdom shapes around its visitors, strangely puzzled by what once seemed merely a given of life, a thing that drifted by and never needed to be held or turned about in the dazzling rays of an altered sunlight, Eudoxas found other words flowing to him as out of a darkness he suddenly recognised he had dragged with him all his life:

—Among our own people I have heard some say that war is driven by trade and the quest for advantages in commerce. I cannot altogether see that. For war most of all brings ruin—except for the shipbuilder and the makers of helmets, breastplates and spikes. Others argue that war is the product of this or that person, or this or that dispute over who should own a peninsula or a chain of small worthless islands. And there have been wars over who should or should not pay tribute, over colonies that feel their founding city demands too high taxes for its produce, and wars over sporting contests, as in who was the rightful winner of a running race, or the famous war of the volleyball game. Always I believed that war was a specific local matter, the product of some individual's greed or ambition. So through war, or more exactly to avoid it, my family had to abandon Cos for Cyrene, then later Cyrene for Alexandria, and later, foolishly trusting the promise of the Egyptian king of that time, I travelled to the Cinnamon Coast and learnt how to use the months of the great winds to sail to India, always believing there would be a glorious elsewhere that was free of war. But I fear I speak rashly—for you of Ebtesum are renowned in all realms as the great poets, and what interest can a poet have in war?

Allorophon, sensing the glint of challenge in the last remark and wishing to dispel certain false images people all too frequently have of poetry, took up the discourse:

—On the contrary what is most pressing is always where poetry must be. When a man or woman is young and in love, it is fitting the heart sing of this. But in dark times, when a great menace absorbs our being and in the back of every waking hour is the question, why is there this terror, why does violence triumph and everywhere the peacemaker is put to shame and banished by his people, why do men trade other men for slaves or banish the poor and the sick from their kingdoms to let them die in no-man's-land, at such times poets must reach down inside the untapped waters at the core of being, not to find mere phrases or clever images, like charlatans in a bazaar do with bright beads of varied light, but simply to seek truth. You are a mariner. You sense what it is to feel the wind moving, and to know the speed of distances shining from a now fair, now black and terrifying sea. A poet is an inward mariner. And let no one underestimate the great poets of your lands, the singers of the epics, those who wrote of Jocasta and Oedipus, of Antigone and Agamemnon, and of the great mariner Odysseus himself—for poetry everywhere is indivisible, feeding itself, nourishing itself. But to speak briefly of Greek poetry, I believe it is because your people were the great mariners, open more than any to the winds of this floating sphere of earth, that poetry entered your language so completely and spread its wonders that men may savour them forever.

Prince Nefaroponte now briefly joined in

—If you will forgive my interruption, I think the short answer to your question, good Eudoxas, is that poets care deeply about war since war is the gathering terror that shapes us, and, as each poet ages, he thinks, like any man, less of himself, than of his children, or his children's children, if they should be, and fears greatly if there will be any world for them in fifty years. For the world we do not like to name, Eusebius, grows that rapidly. And poets, for I have learnt this much in my many years dealing with young or older poets of Ebtesum in residence in my city, whether here as emissaries or on summer lecture tours, care less, as they reach a certain level, about beauties of form or refining their phrases than finding the essential, naming it in a way that lets it reveal its true menace, then probing below it, deciphering the words the sand itself draws beneath the shadow of a fear, and always letting the wind that guides them free them up that they may move a little closer into the presence of truth. Forgive me, worthy emissaries, that I prattle so.

Allorophon and Astaromorph gestured to signify how much they appreciated Nefaroponte's contribution and seemed about to enlarge upon these topics. Yet before the others could speak Eudoxas, who was curious of all matters and wishing to extend the talk beyond his homeland, asked a question that had burned its way into his mind:

—Now I have heard rumours but nothing very plain about Eusebius. Briefly then, tell me of this land and why it so strikes terror?

Allorophon then replied:

—No one wishes to speak too clearly of that place. Its agents have been known to steal among us. It is of the present but mostly it looms far in the future when mankind will be hanging by a thread. It began with profits, with a strange mix of traditions—half free, half slave—and the rich plundered there in ways they had never plundered before. It is said that in Eusebius men start a war where elsewhere they would build a bridge or carve a monument, to pass time, to strike a name. And the people of Eusebius, whose skin is mostly fair, have a mania for skin colour, judging and esteeming all the peoples of the earth according to their pigmentation. Through some sickness we do not understand they despise, above all, the black races and those whose skins are like the glittering morning sun, and against these people they especially enjoy making war. For if a people are seen as not quite human war is that much easier. Like Athens, Eusebius prides itself on being a democracy, though its rulers have always been rich and contriving to suit most of all the needs of the rich, sacrificing all that inequality might reach its maximum levels for, so their religion asserts, it is the sacred duty of the state to give to those who have much and take from those who have nothing. Now throughout their history whenever a leader appeared who sought to curb the abuses of those wealthy cliques they call corporations the powerful had them murdered. In Eusebius money is all and, the country being wealthy beyond measure, the poor die there a most miserable death. For beggars, they say in Eusebius, make good soldiers.

But the pain of speaking of Eusebius is unbearable—not only for the wars they will inflict, but for the ruination of so many homelands. To speak of them is to walk in a land of future ghosts. Let us talk, then, of some other place.

Now the Prince and Astaromorph, shaking their heads in distress and clearly much moved by Allorophon's words, were about to speak when Eudoxas, like a poet sensing that the presence of war had something more it required him to say of it, and the winds of a strange sea drawing him on, resumed his discourse as the Muses prompted.

Now feeling in his heart the gathering sadness,
his face scowled over, and the words breaking
as they had never broken, pain pounding it out,
the raw-veined inner shoreline, he spoke in driven sounds,
the words so measured, the phrases almost scanning,
and just as he spoke them I have set them out in lines
for in those brief minutes
fed by passion,
touched by the sacred horror of humankind,

Eudoxas, trader and sailor out of Cos,
unskilled in harp or lyre, unskilled
in the epithets and breakwords that ease the poet's task,
was as of old the rhetor, was the aidos:

—Yet, beyond all its excuses, beyond any explanation we may give,
   war is men united as brothers in a shared endeavour,
   to violate those branded by the crime of helplessness.
   For deeds no one dares commit alone
   are honoured in a war
   and wars play first with names—
   now it is liberation, now police action,
   showing who we are, or measures required
   to safeguard national borders,
   help offered to a friendly neighbour
   or operations to clear the land of bandits.
   Under the cloak of war ports are renamed
   and houses stolen, families destroyed
   that gods may shine on walls.
   And behind the glittering carpets that hang on festive days
   war and the blood of war is what
   awaits us.

I recall, and I had never thought to speak of this again,
two days south of the Cinnamon Coast, a landfall,
a dusty village that could be anywhere, a great fire burning,
and in each doorway the bodies of men and women slaughtered,
the thick blood, the death-stench. Searching the ruins
we found in the corner of an outhouse, hidden by a fallen tree
that blocked the doorway, a frightened group
of eight small girls, the only living beings
in all that village. Fearing the murderers would return,
for what were five of us against war's madness,
we took the children with us, dividing them among our boats.

The eldest of the children explained that a neighbouring tribe
    had done this,
wanting the waterholes for their cattle, not wanting to share
and despising the girl's tribe all for the different manner of
    shaving
the edges of their hair. We had no words.
We took them with us, heading far beyond the bend of the
    horizon
to where the offshore winds would scoop us wide and drive us
hard along the edges of the sky to India. There I found
safe haven for the girls, with a goodly Prince,
who welcomed them as his eight new daughters, sent by the gods,
those the heaven-sweeping winds of the Yavanas
had brought to shelter at his hearth.

(FROM IAMBLICHUS, *The Life of Eudoxas*)

XX

At the front of our house is dawn
and the mist of the sea that enters our valley.

On tree-branches
the cold dawn-smoke rests:

notes from invisible birds
give the dead back their sleep.

~o~

Stumbling out to watch the dawn
I forget I am lonely.
Two million suns
have still
left room for me.

~O~

The most remote land
is present on my balcony
at dawn.

(FROM *The Green Book of Ehtesum*)

XXI

In the democratic republic of Hau, on the central Atlantean island not far from Eusebius, they perfected the surgical operation required to cure people of the sensation that all is not right with the world. A simple removal of a quarter of the nose, tongue and midmost brain suffices to restore equilibrium. More radical are the adaptive technologies of Naupolis, the underwater city located in the vast caves off the southernmost tip of South Atlantis. Here a buried sky-weapon radiates the water and the people breathe a green gas emitted by certain corals. Air they decry here as a fiction and any unfortunate visitor has their lungs removed as experimental adaptive surgery.

Yet consider the talking mermaid fish of north India. A native to the Ganges, one was hauled in one day in a fisherman's net in the waters off Ultima Thule. In the perpetual grey of that northernmost outpost sadly the fisherman eyed its radiant and every second changing beauty of translucent colour. Divine as no other being is divine, infused with the dazzling exposure of Himalayan snows and enfolded in the warmth of tropic waters, the fish trembled under the gaze of the fisherman. Unable to stop the endless pulsing of colour, it uttered over and over the one syllable: in the Vedic tongue *prāo*: *I burn*.

(PAUSANIAS, *Days and Nights on Atlantis*)

XXII

They danced like a severed hand torn open
then knitted back together:

not beautiful but eternal.

~o~

If the heart dreams, the rain speaks.

~o~

Arrival:
the lover we at last understand is our lover.

~o~

If the young girl who has not yet known love
and the grey-haired woman, frail as winter sun,
dance transfigured, partnered by the air,
swaying to the one music

If a man or a woman should see this
and let the music fully enter their heart
know
their wandering alone into the first night of death
will hold no fear—
death will not be loneliness.

~o~

Five cards on the table:
a single player.

~o~

Understanding is the slow walk uphill to the citadel,
always about to arrive.

Knowing is *this* and *this* and *this*.

Understanding is the dry crust
on the fortieth day of the siege.

The harbour full: the wind-crested ships of the Yavanas coming home
with mangoes, papaya, the blood-bright juice of the guava:
all this is knowing.

~o~

In the taverna
when all else is folded and put away,
when the city shuts like a leaden box—
the jewels all measured and assigned,
each with its name and date

dance
dance slowly
dance with a woman whose name you cannot say

in all her sadness and tiredness
she is stronger than death

hold her with infinite care—
in the soft of her back
rest your hand
steadier than the furthest star

let her arms guide you—
night is vanishing,
the gods are already entering the earth.

(from Erycthemios, *Knowings*, First Part)

XXIII

On arrival at Abukar, a rugged and tranquil island about a half-day's sail south of Eusebius, we were welcomed by a small deputation and escorted to meet the Department of Mystification, the organising body and sponsor of our visit. Now Abukar is a curious case. A fanatic opponent of Eusebius, yet a distorted mirror image of the very regime it decries, renowned for its repressive severity, the entire republic is a police state ruled by a single man, the eccentric Commendatore. Through the use of longevity drugs he has ruled the Republic, some assert, for ninety-nine years—by others' reckoning it is three hundred. Stability and control are achieved by using the rule of thirds—at any given time, rotating on a random basis, a third of the island's inhabitants are to be found in prison, a third fled into exile and a third accept the requirements of collaboration, being generously rewarded with permits to breathe, drink water and urinate in specially dug holes. Describing Abukar as the Paradise for the Common Man, the ideology tourism department has long showcased this island where poverty has been renamed tranquility and the total decay of roads, buildings, transport of all kinds, has all been blamed on the hostility of Eusebius. Which, as with so much in this world, is both true and not true. In fairness, compared to the terror regimes Eusebius created in many places throughout the globe and especially in parts of Atlantis where it chose to rule indirectly, Abukar is almost a benign state. As with so much in my travels it is difficult to form a just appraisal.

To our surprise the Department of Mystification, on whose impressive multi-coloured papyrus our invitation was inscribed, consists of one man. Now this man, the island's leading poet and composer of songs, was deeply disillusioned when the youthful Commendatore began the arrests and executions of his followers who might act as rivals. The poet accordingly renounced his name and took a vow of silence. At first various of the Commendatore's chief assistants planned his murder but the Commendatore, terrified at losing face, instead turned magnanimous. He renamed the poet as a Government Department that would exist in perpetuity and gave him as office space the entire peak of the island's tallest mountain, the one place in the island from which it was possible to see every village, every farm and beach, and every place on the island. Now following his vow the poet could no longer speak though he continued writing poems. The Commendatore also arranged that, though everything was in shortage on the island, the Department of Mystification would never lack for the finest papyrus and every year sent him also the finest food on the day of the long flying crane, the island's national bird and guardian deity. In the strange spirit of fraternity that typifies the island the Commendatore came to see in the poet not a rival but the embodiment of his younger self, an alternate version of who he might have been.

After making the arduous ascent of the Mountain in the company of our guides, the beautiful Tetuani and her companion Lino, we found the poet resting in the small grass and bamboo shack the locals had built for him as a shelter from the fierce tropical sun. I presented him with a cask of the sweet-scented Syracusan wine we had brought with us as well as a rare edition of the complete works of Homer for I understood that, like most of the more educated people on Abukar, he spoke Greek fluently. The poet gestured to us that we share with him a glass of the local speciality, a strong resinous wine made from crushed cane palm seeds. He gestured at the island and we understood its beauty. His hand traced the fineness of the sky and the longing of all men for freedom. With the briefest gesture of anxiety or hard labour, the four fingers patting lightly the sweat on his brow, he indicated the hard life of his countrymen, their immense value, their need for respect. And time, he pleaded, would heal the island. Later he sought among the numerous bundles of papyri that littered the corners of his shack for a specific copy of Thucydides and, opening it at a certain page, gestured that I read. It was the famous passage where the Eusebiolan ambassadors arrive, offering Athens survival if it pledged allegiance, promising that they would deliver them the secret of plunging cities and nations under the sea, enabling them to devastate the rest of the world, leaving Attica alone floating above a drowned and vanished people. To its credit Athens refused. "In the end", writes Thucydides, "the view prevailed in the assembly that humanity was a valid concept, and that it was better to live or perish faithful to human decency than to submit oneself to the unlimited greed and power-lust of Eusebius. In life, they said, the greatest thing is to choose the lesser evil, for with patience even harsh tyrants can grow mild and economies can always be rebuilt. Now Eusebius does not perceive the world as a whole and, through neglect of the mystic practices, has lost its sense that full humanity extends to all people. Though we should perish at the hands of our enemies that is only what is to be expected: for every empire sometimes grows and sometimes declines. And death, whether for an individual or a city, is the normal lot of all who move under the heavens. But the immortality of Eusebius is the greatest evil. Accordingly, whatever our destiny may be, let us turn aside from that path."

As the reading closed, the poet's face signalled his joy at our presence, while the reading he had chosen suggested to us his faith in a peaceful resolution of the island's differences, since the Commendatore was now reaching the limits of old age and a change of government might be expected imminently, that is to say within the next twenty years or so. We thanked the poet and, at a sign from Tetuani indicating the poet's exhaustion and need for rest, returned quietly down the mountainside to a nearby village where Tetuani and Lino had established a modest household. There we passed the night, enjoying a simple yet sustaining feast, making welcome use of the conversation to satisfy our curiosity for more information.

The poet, who is known on the island by his initials as DM, formerly went by the name of Omeros Eliseo. For many years working as a humble teacher in various village schools, DM refused all honours as a poet, saying his teaching was the more important work and if he should be given any reward let it be for teaching, since poetry he enjoyed and it came freely from the gods whilst teaching cost him many a headache and was the product of considerably more human sweat. In truth his patience and humility, whether as poet or teacher, endeared him to the island. Among his most important pupils was a man referred to universally as "the medic" since he organised the extraordinarily dedicated and humane health services of the island, a wonder throughout Atlantis until the arbitrary policies of the Commendatore threw them into chaos.

Tetuani and Lino informed us that, in the opinion of the islanders, the greatest poem of DM's was the short lyric called "Tomorrow", a moving poem in the voice of a very old man facing death and responding with joy to the birth of his grand-daughter. DM wrote this poem when he was 19. Weary of always being asked to recite it, he later said he would have to wait till his death-bed to write his truly finest poem, an inner monologue in the voice of a young boy of 19, filled with passion, violent longings and the incertitude of youth. He said he had not yet decided whether he should call this work "Yesterday" or "Tomorrow", or possibly "I am going to begin what I once was".

In the years of silence, it seemed to Tetuani, he had begun to create two kinds of poems—the ones written down on papyri, and the new subtle genre of gesture poems. She wondered whether these last poems were not, finally, the only ones that would truly endure.

(FROM PAUSANIAS, *Days and Nights on Atlantis*, CHAPTER 14)

XXIV

Tomorrow

Now as always
as the sea scatters
the obligatory decision to breathe

as the palm trees tremble
in the unimaginable winds
that free us and number our deaths

the three walls of the house
still standing
open like a shell

to welcome one more
messenger of hope
the daughter of my daughter

she whose life-cry
echoes in the white space of all whirlwinds
the one who has elected air for her element

tomorrow as always
the new day
this life which begins tomorrow

and sleep
the element of elements
all these five minutes that will become

this day.

(FROM *19 Poems of Life and an Ode to calm temporarily confused ghosts—the Collected Poems of DM*, 25ᵀᴴ EDITION, MACABUKRO CITY, ABUKAR)

POSTSCRIPT: By the age of 30 DM, formerly known as Omeros Eliseo, had published almost 500 poems. After that time he continuously shrank the number of poems in his collected works while still writing new poems. The 25th edition of 19 poems and an Ode represents approximately the mid-point in his career. It is believed that by the time of his death he had perfected the book so that it contained no more than five pages, all of them blank. (W O'S)

XXV

When gold, green and blue dominate the rainbow, with a fine trace of red pulsating delicately in the background,
the day is favourable for lovemaking, giving birth to children and sleeping naked washed by the stars.

When violet and indigo stain your fingers and everywhere is the colour of regret,
it is time to change the world.

(FROM *The Red Book of Ebtesum*)

XXVI

Can the quest for renown go too far? Now, as is well known and stands recorded in Book 2, Chapter 8 of this work, to prevent every general claiming a triumph after each minor battle and so overstretching the Treasury, the Roman Senate passed a law that no general may request a triumph unless fifty thousand of the enemy have been killed in a single battle. Of course, seeking to reach that figure, generals merely increased the scale of their slaughter. In the campaign north of the Ister the Roman generals constantly fought battles of extermination seeking the magic figure of fifty thousand enemy dead in a single day's fighting. Each day the news would reach Rome of the previous day's body count. It was awaited with avid glee—for two hundred days, battle after battle, the count hovered around the figure of forty nine thousand. To achieve these results every man, woman and child was slaughtered by the legions. An area twice the size of Gaul stretching from the Ister to beyond the Chersonese was put to the sword. The teams of auditors who supervised the official body count had to be replaced many times over due to exhaustion. In two hundred days, as the Roman public eagerly awaited the feast of a triumph, the glorious spectacle, the free wine and festivities, around ten million people from Upper Dacia and lower Scythia perished. On the two hundred and first day the quaestor, Aemilianus Decimus, ordered a cessation of the fighting. On the previous evening tiny flakes of burnt human flesh, carried by enormous seabirds, landed on Rome. All the vestal virgins died of a mysterious illness. The water in fountains tasted of the Dacian dead. Bread in the bakers' shops, no longer rising, spread as a thin greasy paste along the walls of houses. A foul air rose from the soil and sharp particles of fire penetrated the skin. In one day nine hundred Romans died in the city. Orders were given for mass burials and purification rituals took place. Across the devastated lands of Transnistria quiet descended on battlefields, on burnt-out villages and poisoned fields. A new law was passed banning triumphs for five years and limiting campaigns of continuous battle to fifty days. The legions returned from beyond the Ister and reports of the campaign were removed from all the history books. Alone of the stories in this volume I have not taken this from any written account but from what every Roman knows. Because of the campaign a curse lingers on Rome. Between Rome and Rome's successors and the vast region of northern Dacia and Scythia eternal enmity exists. This explains in later generations the long centuries of war between the Atlantean Empire of Eusebius, inheritors of so much of Rome, and the people of the Dacian-Scythian homelands.

Let the reader ponder where the quest for renown may take us.

(VALERIUS MAXIMUS, *Memorable Deeds and Sayings*, EXTRA PASSAGE FROM THE END OF BOOK FOUR, TO BE FOUND IN THE GREAT LUSITANIAN EDITION OF 300 AD)

XXVII

To the north
bow low
scatter the beads of water
gently scoop tufts of wheat
let the wind trickle
through emptiness

To the east
bow low
scatter the grains of dawn
may your hands be open
kneel
let where the sun is
know you
Speak
"Shame on my head
on my eyes
Shame on my lips and tongue
Shame on my hands
on my walking
Shame of the seed
and of destiny."
Again dip slowly your hand
into the grain sack
scatter grain
scatter what lives
what will live
Speak
"Grain of grains
dew of sea
fire that rises from mist
accept our shame"

bow again
lightly sprinkle the water

To the south
stand firm that the realms
of Four Heavens
may see you
bow low
scatter the grains
let the ghosts
know of your presence
scatter the dew of water
let the beads of water
rest on the lips of all people
let the thirst of the living
and the thirst of the dead
be calmed
bow again
wait for the silence
to give you permission
to stand

To the west
eyeing the west as an equal
eyeing the west as a mother
eyeing the west as your child
scatter the grain
scatter the bright joy of water
kneel
kneel do not speak
wait for the light that rises and sets
to touch you
wait for the winds that come
from the lands of all the dead
to filter around your ears

wait for their voices to enter you
wait till their voices speak
wait till the words
are fierce and tender
wait till the words
tear at the sinews of pain
till the words slice
through forehead and skull
till the heart is open to all words
the earth is struggling to say

Kneel longer
wait till their voices
cease
wait till the silence steadies you
speak
"Brothers"
speak
"Sisters"
speak
"I give back
I give back
I give back"

(*Dawn Ritual of Purification* FOR FAMILIES AND DESCENDANTS OF THOSE WHO
PARTICIPATE IN SLAUGHTER, TO BE USED BY ALL VISITORS WHO ENTER THE
HOLY CITY OF KITEZH)

BOOK III

I

In the feast laid out at Alcibiades' house Terpander posed for us the question "Why is it that time flows backwards?" Discussion continued on this topic for a while till the much-travelled Timon broadened our understanding with his sketch of the Menandroi, a people who live in a region of India that is constantly being invaded by the future.

"The Menandroi see clearly the past and the future but have great difficulty perceiving or understanding the present. To them a deep mist coils itself around where they are and the present is a core of blackness that travels everywhere with them. They spend much time writing letters to people dwelling in the remote past or a long way off. Likewise much of their lives is devoted to correspondence with the future. No sooner is one such letter written than they are busy writing another. Now they live on high platforms raised above the ground to discourage people from visiting them, but equally these platforms serve as convenient resting places for the highly trained pigeons that transmit their messages. From time to time it happens that those who receive their letters make the mistake of visiting them, for the Menandroi cannot perceive anyone who is present, but always fix their attention on elsewhere. In this tribe women conceive with great difficulty and rapidly lose all interest in their offspring. Accordingly it falls to the elderly and grandparents to protect children. For some reason it is only towards old age that the notion of the present dawns within the Menandroi. Sadly, as it has been said, for them the words 'now' and 'here' fuse into the word 'nowhere'.

"The Pravati, on the other hand, live entirely in the present, asserting that anything more than five minutes into the past or future has no reality. Likewise they claim that reality only extends as far as a man can throw a not too heavy stone. In their estimation beyond that distance things turn to water—or rather, so they claim, language ceases to be applicable as all elements merge into a soupy texture they call 'that'."

Socrates said, "It seems, then, if we dwell only in the past and future we lose reality, while if we dwell only in the present we lose understanding and soon become a shadow. Likewise with what is here and what is distant. Must we then spread ourselves like some thin paste so we grasp and clutch tightly at all times the distant, the present and the approaching? Must we be always pouring back and forth the luminosity of now, the diverse hints of then and the steady light of what will be tomorrow? But how can 'here' and 'now' be always different things, never the same for two people? If we had a house like that or a tree or a loaf of bread, what good would it do anyone?"

Proteon, a pupil of the illustrious Zeno, who was visiting at the time, said, "Both are illusions—that is all."

But sitting in the corner all the while was Zamindar, the one sent as a deputy to Athens by the fire dwellers from beyond the Indus. Now he had resurrected sky books from the deep wells where they were hidden and knew how to read what stones say and in his childhood, transfigured by the beauty that lies beyond speech, he had understood the difficult prediction poems spoken by birds. He began then, as if the room was strangely empty, his voice reaching us with the softness of someone very close and very far:

"Where I was born, in the infinite dimensions that blended in my village, were both those ignorant of the present, obsessed only with tomorrow and yesterday, and those who could perceive nothing beyond themselves and the narrow corner of light that fell directly on them. After watching them both for many days I realised they were identical. Since then I have travelled much. The high platforms rented out by those obsessed by what was and what approaches will all be reclaimed every two years as another fashion obliterates them.

The dwellers in only now die out, incapable of sustaining their voice. Yet the not-altogether absent or present, those who travel between places, are real. 'Here' and 'now', 'past' and 'present' are real—it is the gathering that makes them real. They are real because we are not one being but many beings."

(FROM XENOPHON, *Conversations from the last years of Socrates*)

II

Greetings

from the ear that hurts,
the brain that is damaged
and the hunger of all yesterdays
buried in their interminable pomp
and bankruptcy

eagerly to say goodmorning.

(FRAGMENT FROM *Knowings* BY ERYCTHEMIOS)

III

As the grey tide swings
between shingle and sand

what your love might be for me
always

glitters far out:
blue current etched

by the wind of elsewhere.

(FROM *The Red Book of Ebtesum*)

IV

In Africa not far south of Kitezh, only a few days journey from Ebtesum, in several rich and spacious valleys can be found the most beautiful language on earth. The sounds of this language so enchant all who hear them, the rapture is so exquisite, that every year a select band of visitors come from Ebtesum to hear this language. No one can translate what is said and words do not appear to have meaning in any normal sense of the word. It is not possible to order fruit, tidy kitchens or transact business in this language though food appears just the same and houses are built and water is directed craftily through channels and pipes to create coolness and abundance. The men and women of this land are reputed to be the finest, most passionate lovers on earth and loneliness is a concept inexplicable here. The scholars of Ebtesum when I asked for their account of this language said, "The meaning lies elsewhere." And others said, "Think of the human voice as the central music to this planet—the music from which all other musics derive. Think of its curvature as landscape, its clear rippling, its dark forests and sunlit peaks, its harsh pounding and delicate escape. Go deeper into why the human voice was made so beautiful. Go deeper into why it can never be owned by rich or poor, never restricted or confined. We admire beauty of the body. The human voice is the beauty gathered by the breath, the sovereign of the body. Many are struck to silence by the beauty of bird song—far deeper is the beauty of authentic human speech. What sullies it is containment. What blights it is ownership and division. Most people accept that a sound is not, by itself, a meaning, but many believe that a word, a sentence, a phrase is a meaning. In that speech, in that valley, only a life is a meaning."

(from Herodotus, *The Uncut Histories*, Book XIII held in the Gades library)

V

You reached me

You reached me across glass-shards
fragmented as voices from another room
bent through the oracular nerve-endings
that are the chemical of fear in this world

beloved
in dawn's cold nakedness
as in all those moments I neglected to clothe you
in the disintegrating garments of rapture

everywhere
you still speak
the tenderness ahead of me

ghost or lover
in the moment of ecstasy
be the two hands pressed against my back
be the cry of joy
that holds me inside life

(POEM 13 FROM *19 Poems of Life and an Ode to calm temporarily confused ghosts*
BY DM—FORMERLY OMEROS ELISEO, MAKABUKRO CITY, ABUKAR)

VI

Here you slip into the rule of twenty—what happens when
everything is multiplied by twenty. Suddenly where a house stood
there are twenty houses. In a room where two people would have
slept there are forty people. And the rule of twenty works in the
opposite direction with regards to wealth and the ability to purchase
life's necessities. Where a day's labour once earned enough to buy

ten loaves of bread, a basket of vegetables and five fish, suddenly it buys half a loaf, perhaps a carrot and the flesh clinging to a few fishbones.

Demetrios wondered how and why he had entered this land. Was it freshly created? Did it always exist? Each street divided into twenty streets, each household into twenty diminutive houses.

It was, so voices whispered to him, the world created by the Grand Central Lottery of Eusebius, run not within Eusebius itself but in the varied realms of outer Eusebius. The lottery, organized according to the strict principles outlined in the Nicanorean Ethics, was hailed as a wondrous invention by the designated spokesmen of those lands. Each week in each of the separate realms of outer Eusebius one person wins a fabulously large lottery prize and is permitted to leave, passing through the heavily armed gates that lead to Inner Eusebius, bringing with them their twenty closest relatives. Each ticket costs about a month's wages but, through the beneficence of the state, at birth each child is given two bonus tickets.

Now, in order to increase their chances of winning, people have as many children as possible and the game has the effect of constantly multiplying the population. As it replaced taxation the lottery is immensely popular. The inhabitants of outer Eusebius are deeply grateful for this beneficence of the state, constantly comparing their good fortune with those who dwell beyond direct Eusebian control, always facing arbitrary tax demands and the peril of destruction by Eusebian armies.

When the lottery was first introduced a few renegade mathematicians argued that when each family acts in this way, increasing the number of their children, the odds of any particular family winning in fact decrease. Gangs organised by Eusebian agents promptly hunted down these verbal terrorists, much to the approval of the Outlanders who branded them liars and deceivers.

Rumours as to what happens to those who win are conflicting. Some describe them as enjoying wealth and luxury; others suggest they merely become the underclass of inner Eusebius.

But explanations of any kind, whether of the Grand Central Lottery or the rule of Eusebius, were of no help to Demetrios. What he saw went beyond explanation. "It was as if there were two sides to my head", he said. "Day after day, for so many years, I took the right turn and walked up the right side of my house to what I considered a normal street, the street I had always believed I lived in. But one day, inexplicably, I turned left and the other world, the dark one, multiplied itself to infinity. Once I had entered that world, though I retraced my steps with great care and learned henceforth always to turn to the right, I could never be entirely sure in which world I lived."

(LONGINUS, *The travels and tribulations of Demetrios and Zoe*)

Longinus' brief account of life in outer Eusebius, whilst preserving a core of truth, is highly limited, reflecting the narrow purposes of prose fiction and adjusted as it is to a late Roman audience. The longing to escape heavy taxation and the compulsory labour demands typical of Longinus' time helps explain the excess importance given by Longinus to the lottery, an alternate taxation method long proposed but seldom used uniquely, presumably because the rich might be tempted to buy vast numbers of tickets and so contribute to public funds. As is common knowledge, the duty of every state is to ensure that the burden of taxation should fall entirely on the poor.

(MONOCHRASTOS THE COMMENTATOR, NICOSIA, C 709 AD)

VII

Half an arm's length above me
mosquitoes tracing a zigzag pattern,
unpredictable, elaborate,
more beautiful than stars.

Completely still

I watch the grey swarm's
inexplicable drawing—
tiny masters of life and death,
greetings!

(ERYCTHEMIOS, *Knowings*, BOOK IV)

VIII

In Egyptian Dodonia the profound and secret mathematicians discovered the complex numbers that govern the movement of mosquitoes. The sage of the Mathemasis, Anakluphon, observing one afternoon the dance of mosquitoes above him for the period of several hours was able to memorize every movement and gesture. Later, compiling the patterns on rolls of papyrus, he elaborated the formulae of recurrence and change. Over the course of a year Anakluphon developed the mathematical constants that govern time, for just as π has proved indispensable to the geometers and the formula $e^{i\pi} = 0$ was to be of use to the death merchants of Eusebius, so the constants that govern the recurrence of all things mental and physical were invaluable to the designers of the great calendars that hold the history of earth. The possession of such calendars among the numerous enemies of Eusebius was one of the threefold sources of the passing of each of its manifestations.

(HERODOTUS, *The Universal History*, EDITION HELD IN THE LIBRARY OF THE NESTORIAN MONASTERY IN GANDHARA, THE FAMOUS BILINGUAL GREEK-ARAMAIC EDITION, CHAPTER XXIII)

IX

By morning
three women, an old man
with a cart, two children.

By evening
two women, two men,
a young boy with a dog.

This summer,
two years passed.

~O~

Flies zigzag on the air;
a stone lies
where it has always lain;
smoke stirs
in a green space between silences.

Days end.

~O~

Today, looking down on the plain
where three roads meet,
a white dove settled
on my shoulder.

There is only
one journey.

~O~

Rain falls on dark roads.
Behind rough white walls
tears are endless.
In salt brine
olives best preserve
their sharp pure hunger.

~O~

Just above the level of the trees
two lightning bugs flicker their passage.
In the garden a single candle
shows me the path to the sky.

~o~

In the outer spaces of the world
the pure light awaits.

(Irene Philologos, *A poetic journal of ten years in Boeotia*)

X

Grey-lidded dawn that wakes two times—
once on the shores of peaceful islands
and once in the hearts of men.

(Fragment of morning liturgy, Sect of the twice-born, Ragusa,
c 57 bce)

XI

"The blue snail"

It does not offer
an answer
to autumn.

There
where it has dragged
its own sky

everything it touches
shines
with belonging.

~O~

Over a stone bridge
all feet leave their own
residue of mud.

~O~

The vendors of bread and sweet pastries
stalls laden with beads and perfumes
mansions of the rich
sinking yearly deeper into the city's
obliterating mud

And before me
the white butterfly confused by the wind's messages
the plum tree opening its fragrance of coolness.

(*The Green Book of Ehtesum*)

XII

It is well known that in hot countries shape-changers are more common. This applies to animals and to humans alike and can be easily demonstrated by the prevalence of lizards that are green and thin in dense foliage yet grey and jaggedly circular on a dusty road. Likewise in hot climates it is common to see a family of villagers become slender trees when soldiers approach yet float off as brightly coloured balloons on festive days when the sky explodes and music makes it easy for people to transform themselves into eye-catching shapes. How pleasant it is on hot days to sit back under a tree at sunset and watch the neighbour's children, brightly-painted and distended in the shape of griffins or unicorns, drifting between us and the lower clouds.

Herodotus who observed this phenomenon in lower Egypt considered that, as the particles of which we are made warm up, they more readily shift into different shapes. Xantipater of Miletus, using such observations, reached the conclusion that humans are a kind of speaking water: smooth-flowing at times and easy to find their way among all things, but a torrent of destructive violence, inexplicable to themselves, blind ones.

(TIMON OF ALEXANDRIA, *The Book of Observations*)

XIII

In last night's dream
you had married a second time
and again not me.
Even in old age our timing was wrong.
Practical as always,
you had chosen a wealthy lover.
Yet the room in which I saw you,
young, naked, with teasing eyes,
was so much like the old room we once shared.
Filled only with your fragrance
it opened on a small courtyard
a few yards the other side of death.

(TERPANDER OF COS)

XIV

The poems of midday
have little time to be written.
The sun, the fierce one,
melts the wax on which they are inscribed,
the papyrus bursts in flame.

Few words can match a steady shining.
Dark places favour elaboration.

(*The Green Book of Ebtesum*)

XV

Outside they were burning the blue-veined leaves of the balikbo plant whose smoke clears the air of mosquitoes and the earth of fire-ants but, if once inhaled, its breath fills a man with loneliness, a subtle but disorienting loneliness for which there is no cure. Whoever has tasted deeply of the balikbo plant wanders far from all family. The ants disown him, the mosquitoes shun his presence. As the balkibo's blue-veined breath uncurls within him, he feels the universe take a small but infinite step away from him. He sees his apartness as incurable, his irrelevance to the flow of the world as absolute. Offerings made for him at the temple consume the fire that is lit for them. His name erases itself from all language. Truly the world forgets him.

(SALLUST, *On African curses*)

XVI

In Kitezh and the kingdoms nearby, though they know of stone and timber and partly use them as conditions require, they prefer to build with water. The most prized houses employ three or more interwoven waterfalls for their walls and the roof is generally left open to the night sky. In inclement weather sheets of a certain plant painted with invisibility are used. Sleep, they say, is always deepest when surrounded by flowing water and the stars glitter with most tenderness when seen across a ceiling of shifting water. When a couple seek privacy they divert a waterfall around themselves—"to draw the curtain of the waterfall" is the common expression in their language to refer to lovemaking.

(MACROBIUS, *A journey through Ebtesum, Kitezh and central Africa*)

In periods of history when Eusebius has been on the wane or recently disappeared, following the cyclic collapse of its manifestations, alternate forms of wealth developed. For too long historians have neglected the lively trade in water and advanced water technologies that flourished in Africa. The export of such knowledge from Africa to regions of Europe, Arabia, and Southern India was crucial to the flourishing of the twin kingdoms of Kitezh and Ebtesum. Also worthy of further analysis is the fact that, when Eusebius triumphs, those parts of the world richest in water become the poorest—a direct punishment, many hold, for those eras when water regulated the affairs of men. Vast water distribution highways, of which the aqueducts of the Romans are but faint memories, linked many lands that the blessings of the fruitful clouds might be known to all. Likewise the craftsmen of Kitezh and central Africa knew how to use the power of water to run all manner of machines, to transport goods, to lift heavy weights. Many have written of the music created by special water machines, the criss-crossing melodies of water especially prized in Kitezh.

(DIOGENES LAERTES, *Commentary on Received Knowledge*)

XVII

He is coming,
the great poet of African silences.
Water is in his steps,
the great torrent
of water crashing though rocks,
water that slips and glides
through the locked fingers of children

dreaming of sunlight.
He speaks the soft rain of all seasons,
he speaks the fragrance of fruit,
the drawers and porters of water,
the skilled craftsmen
who shape and guide water
to accomplish all the longings of men.
He speaks the unspoken abundance,
the full granary's ease, the floor laid out
for the ritual greeting.
In his speech lives the woman whose soft voice
tames all beasts,
who feeds doves and scorpions alike.
He knows the secret name smoke carries in its own language.
He understands night and speaks its infinite epithets—
he knows the twelve words for waiting,
the three hundred diminutives of sad.
And through his voice
flows great calm
and the five tones that unite
thunder and raindrop.
His voice is the child at five
and the woman at eighty.
He comes to renew our world.

(THRASYMENES, POET AND ARCHON OF THE GREEK COLONY OF PHOS IN
MAURETANIA)

XVIII

The Essene community of Qomqwarresh in central Africa developed
books of water. The book made of water has numerous unique
properties and the Essenes paid particular attention to these in
their painstaking creation of water books. In a book made of water

it is possible to see several thousand pages simultaneously. Even for those not adept at mystic reading, whose attention generally focuses on a specific line or phrase, a shadow or background glow will appear as if below each phrase every other word of the book was quietly swimming. To those who read these books, gazing at a specific line, it seems that everything ever written in the history of mankind and everything yet to be written surrounds one, the depths opening beyond the depths. Trained scholars of the Essenes will read a book of several thousand pages in about twenty minutes, though they sometimes confess the practice does tire them a little. "Only a book carved in water," the Essenes say, "can hold the mirrored flow of the One behind time."

(MACROBIUS, *A journey through Ebtesum, Kitezh and central Africa*)

XIX

The rivers descend to sleep below the cities.
In those deep caves
stillness glitters
where the mountains float inverted in the dark.
They have closed the roads
from respect for the dead.
They have redirected the birds
who come each day
to clean the fields of grain
and the foodstalls of shadows.
They say great Rome has fallen,
the Empire is over
and only memories cling to doorposts,
gone with the old who go.
For us who knew only injustice
little's changed—the air
perhaps clearer, the sky resting

in a corner where bread is gnawed,
where water tastes of stars.

(FROM THE SABINE ANTHOLOGY OF POEMS WRITTEN DURING THE 3ʳᵈ
INVASION, AUTHOR UNKNOWN)

XX

Only by walking across water is it possible to know the true calm
of homecoming.

(SAYINGS OF EUDOXAS, LOWER NUBIA, 310 BCE)

XXI

What is that noise in the night?
A frog? A drunkard?
Or a small lizard who's just swallowed his own death?

(FROM *The Black Book of Ebtesum*)

XXII

At puto puto parties held in upper Egypt and lower Nubia, while
sipping on the nectar of the delicious puto puto plant, those invited
participated in learned discussions based around the improvisation
of stories. Participants at these parties came from many lands and
spoke varied languages, though Greek was generally the agreed on
means of communication. Each member of the group told a story
or parable or improvised a poem based on certain jade emblems
that had fallen to his lot according to the roll of sacred dice. Now
following the traditions of the Essenes, after each story the other
guests had to develop a *peripateia ton logon* or interpretation of the
story. The Essenes held that by gathering the greatest diversity of

peoples and encouraging the free trade of the *peripateia* an approach might be made to the presence of the divine. Records of many such parties were in turn kept by the librarians of Alexandria and later passed on to the other great libraries of antiquity.

(NEOPTOLEMUS, *A brief Account of Life in Alexandria and other Egyptian cities*)

A breakaway group of Essenes founded the colony of Qomqwakum beyond the southern reaches of Nubia. There they fused knowledge of the Platonic canon, Jewish wisdom and certain practices brought back by those who had participated in the Embassy to Annam and the Kingdom of Silk. The practice of the *peripateia ton logon* or *interrogatio fictivo* attained its highest development among them.

At the same time they made contact with the philosophers of Kitezh and Ebtesum.

(MACROBIUS, *A journey through Ebtesum, Kitezh and central Africa*)

According to practices from the Kingdom of Silk the emblems are finite but the interpretations they give rise to are infinite. The essential emblems of the universal dreambook as known in the Kingdom of Silk number perhaps sixty-eight or perhaps one hundred and sixty-nine. Disordered in appearance, they are represented by images cast in jade that they may glitter in the hand, uniting the openness of man to the justice of Heaven.

(FROM DIO CASSIUS, *A true account of the Embassy from the Emperor Antoninus to the Kingdom of Silk*)

XXIII

(Jade emblem chosen by the dice: Boy and dog)

"The boy with the dog traversing the city.

The boy with the dog traversing the city never growing older, unchanging over many lifetimes.

The boy with the dog traversing the city writes a book, the book that will take many lifetimes. Winter and summer it grows. It traces the dimensions of the city, the dimensions of the sky in which it floats.

The boy with the dog sees all who live in the city. Sometimes those who live there see them—at nightfall, at the flickering of dawn, when the full moon crosses the water. Those who see them say: 'it is moonlight on the white houses of cemeteries; it is the city recording itself in fire'.

The boy with the dog traverses the square city, the city whose four corners are sun, moon, fire, water, the city whose secret name is 'Dawn is rising', where the streets run north-south, the wide boulevards east-west and the circle is the shape for all the sculptured water, the lagoons, canals, looping rivers and lakes that bind and divert the city, protecting it that no demons may enter, blessing it with the joy of water."

When Nestor had finished his story Athanasius began the analytic discussion, the *peripateia tes anabasis*.

"Clearly many layers are involved in this story and our analysis must be careful to balance all its elements. The boy with the dog is the pairing of soul and body, mind and emotion, reasoning spirit and instinct. Yet it is also necessary to consider the city through which they travel which, although it might be the material world, is obviously the world as consciously organized by state power. Its repressive force tolerates the pair only by reducing them to a ghost-like indifference. Yet the city is officially tamed by the presence of water. What could be more transparent that this desire to mislead the repressed through the ruse of feminine beauty as compensation for rigid militaristic structures? The core to the entire story is the "white houses of the cemetery" for here the spirit of prophecy enters. The true message of the story is the eternal doom awaiting the builders of the great repression."

The turn now fell to Cyrene, daughter of Memnon, to take up the second thread of the peripateia:

"Sun and moon are shelter; the curve of water and the straightness of the road are shelter. The city is balanced, folded over itself, as betokens those who have grasped reciprocity. So why is there any need for the boy with the dog? Why did the dreamer of this story feel the need to add these elements to the sum of perfection?

The boy as wandering consciousness, inner spirit, is clear enough, yet the dog is the key element. The dog enables the boy to exist outside time—it maintains his innocence. For the story in its deepest shadows speaks to us of time and its transcendence which is only possible through the acceptance of the natural world. The dog does not write but enables writing, does not speak but enables speaking. In all lands he is fidelity, the one who recognises us beyond the changes of ageing, the one who perceives good and evil through smell alone, the one no argument can confuse.

Without the dog the boy would merely age, become engrossed in the daily commerce of the city. The boy with the dog has a secret name. He dwells within. He is the one who writes. He endures."

"What you say," Timophoros interrupted with the bad manners typical of those who overvalue their own travels, "reminds me of those who dwell on the island of Surinayma south of India. For them the stones on the seashore of their land hold the most absolute sacredness. The stones define the steps of an elaborate dance performed each month at full moon and dictate a unique music structure that, in their belief, gives continuity to the earth. All their way of life, it might be said, is given to them by the curved resonance of their coastline."

The turn now fell to Mariam, the great mother of the Essenes of Qomqwakum, to continue the *peripateia:*

"To my way of seeing this story is about stories. It speaks of those times when stories arise, cross-over points between night and day, houses white as vacant space that shelter only the dead, the ordered world of the polis remade by the disorder of wandering, seeing and being seen, the distorted mirror.

To return to Cyrene's paradox, in a perfect city why is there the need to add these witnesses, this boy with his dog? The story tells us little of this. Yet the need to speak unites all men and women—from Homer for whom the Greek letters were invented to the sages of India and Bactria, the great anonymous poets of Ebtesum and the numerous poets and storytellers of all lands."

As Mariam closed her thread of the *peripateia* a silence fell on the group, a lingering after-echo of inner peace, as is the way when a true Essene utters a comment, however slight it might otherwise seem. After the lingering moment needed to savour this radiance, the *peripateia* continued.

"The sign of the dog worries me," Alloromorph began. "Unable to grow, the dreamer of this story images a dog, a caricature of a castrated companionship. If the boy does not grow it is because he does not know how to make the dog transform into the lily pond, the all-seeing sky, the marrying maiden, the waterfall of surrender. Like this boy our world for so long cut aside woman, seeking to represent wholeness through abstractions. The city with its feminine curves of water suggests what the boy needs to grow. The boy is the false story-teller, the one who cannot take action, who cannot free us. He does not engage with the world but drifts across it, a spirit alien to his own footprints.

"But even more layers of this image are worthy of our meditation. The boy with the dog is not seen, or scarcely seen, mis-seen as one might say as moonlight or fire. What does mis-seeing mean and why this insistence on the imbalance between the vision of those who dwell in the city and the vision of the boy himself? Only what is true can be mis-seen. Like Cyrene I sense that the boy with the dog is the unconscious self, the divine spark confused by the world of appearances. The unconscious inner self writes a book that takes many lifetimes, a book that can only be contributed to in so far as one dwells neither in day nor night. Clearly the boy as a child does not write but merely accomplishes the miracle of walking. His writing is his walking, his writing is his presence in the book. Those who dwell in the city sense the necessity of his existence. By intuition they know of his passage. For in some way he is a part of each of them. He is the journey of the enlightened one, the one truly awake whose story can be contained in no book, not even the wondrous books of water. The uttering of the true book will only happen when all awaken, when the boy's wandering is reabsorbed into the city that dreams him."

(*Conversations held in the Essene community of Qomqwakum, southern Nubia,* RECORDS WRITTEN ON NUMEROUS PAPYRUS SCROLLS HELD ORIGINALLY IN THE LIBRARY OF ALEXANDRIA, LATER STORED IN THE NESTORIAN MONASTERY OF ECBATANA)

XXIV

In the language of the Tano Tano people all things are divided into those which are either awake or asleep and those that are either open or closed. Houses, shops, doors, the hands of people, the eyes and lips are awake or asleep. Water is open or closed but a flower is awake or asleep. The sky at night is said to be open yet closed during the day. Above all open and closed is used for the human heart and the inner eye, as for the sky, water, the mirror and the body as it gives itself to the raptures of love or to all-destroying death.

(MENANDER OF GANDHARA, *Treatise on the diversity of languages,* 250 BCE)

XXV

NAUSICAA: You have come from far, and love
is a stranger's right. But first
speak to me of the journey, of what news you bear
of places known only to exile.
For from strangers all seek a name or a word,
a presence, a gift brought back.

OSIRIS: Many wonders mark the earth.
Small fish that climb the sky and race across water—
I have seen their wingbeats dazzle the sailors at noon.
Or an old man bent above a blue lute
out of India, I've watched his worn hands
threading time,
making the horizon at midday tremble,
settling the shape of sunset in lands
where the water-craftsmen dwell.
Beauty is the one word uttered by earth—
it is beauty I bring you.

(FRAGMENT FROM *The Handmaidens of Persephone* BY XEUXIS OF ANAGOGE)

XXVI

The Amanostoi who live north of the Hyperboreans crave originality. Accordingly they destroy their houses each dawn in a mellow fire they call "beginning". What occurs next is difficult to describe. Being obliged to impress the word "novelty" on the surrounding air they gaze dumbstruck a while at the poor effort made by the sun. Water, stone, earth and fire all seem predictable building blocks. They shift from one to the other, listlessly craving an effect that forever evades them. Each morning seems the same. How they long for the old cultures when each breath was prescribed by fixed rituals.

How they yearn for those ordered times when, instead of destroying their houses, men simply destroyed each other.

(FROM DIO CASSIUS, *A true account of the circumnavigation of Europe from Lusitanian Gades to the Chersonese Bosphorus*)

XXVII

We see the emblems in the land:
the south side of the city
where trees die off,
where a boy with a dog wanders far
along paths between sunken rice fields,
where a hot sky rains flakes of salt.

On the south side
puddles meander where roads die out.
The knife-grinder and the collector of rags
bend the horizon, distorting the world with their cries.
Myopic girls gather small coins for a sad time
and, if love comes, it must take its fragrance
from the racks of fish drying on the pebbles.

Birds desert us.
The swollen belly passes from the mother to the child.
On the south side when a life begins
a life ends.

(POEM WRITTEN DURING THE SECOND GREAT HUNGER, ERYCTHEMIOS, *Knowings*, BOOK II)

XXVIII

Where we are the longing for water is holiness.

(TEXT FOUND INSCRIBED ON AMPHORA FROM THE ESSENE COMMUNITY OF QOMQWAKUM, NUBIA)

BOOK IV

I

In those long periods when books vanished, when memory was the only way to record that the earth went back to the time (almost legendary) of one's parents, when it seemed possible that cities and roads, villas, harbours and fleets, marketplaces and farms were the product of some beneficent magician, springing into being somewhere around the time of one's birth. In those vast eras when the companionship of trees, the profound critique of flowing water and the wayside stone's almost haughty refusal to comment seemed perfectly adequate as a guide to the perplexed. At the time when night was never sure that dawn would come to interrupt it and not some other event like a shower of burnt-out meteors or perhaps afternoon would reappear and play itself backwards through the previous day. To be human meant to breathe, possibly to eat, have sex, feed a baby. To be human meant always to be heading backwards, towards less and less, towards zero. Rain fell and entirely unpredictable things flashed across what might be the sky or else the dreamscape of one's closed eyes. Forests grew down into stillness. Lakes appeared like hollow hands offering the soft petals of extinction. And always at the edge of sleep came the voices: "You have ten minutes, ten days or ten years before the vanishing of the world in death—what is it that is worth saying?"

(FRAGMENT FROM *A paraphrase of certain writings by Leonidas the self-exiled*, COMPILED BY OMEROS ELISEO)

II

… and from the depths of the water rises the fragrance of music. It is the Kingdom of Siripech—alone of all lands it accepted its vanishing. Massive as inverted pyramids reaching towards the earth's centre, chambers of imaginative space soar downward into the blue chasm of the waters. Vanished from earth, its music resonates everywhere. How often Pharaohs have come to this shore, have gazed into the stillness and wept. Its people never sought eternity. No one hungered that his name should last forever. The Kingdom of Siripech never cared for architecture with its straight lines and blocks of stone. All it built were thatch huts, simple shelters against rain, and truly its people were happiest living outdoors and sleeping wherever weariness or love's tenderness overtook them. Music was their passion, whether produced solely by the voice or by various plucked or blown instruments devised from shells, crafted wood or the tensed strings of certain vines. Only after they had vanished was it understood that their music was mankind's one hope for survival. Without their realising it, the music they created could control the oceans and winds, restore order to the seasons and, in rare moments, set limits to the evil in men's hearts. Rival tribes, extraordinary poverty, Eusebius, the Pharaohs themselves destroyed Siripech and its people, all but wiping its name from the annals of history. Sensing that the final hour had arrived, its leaders retreated below the sea, taking their knowledge with them. Siripech is the name given to the music that drifts some mornings almost audible above the waves, and Siripech is the name of a high-browed woman with sharp jet-black eyes, a face beneath the sea visible from certain cliffs where the Pharaohs gazed, understanding too late how what is overlooked and despised alone blesses and saves.

(FRAGMENT IN GREEK INSCRIBED ON A CLAY JAR CONTAINING PERFUME, FOUND IN THE RUINS OF EL-BAKRI ON THE RED SEA COAST, DATED AS AROUND 720 BCE)

Siripech, in the name of the wind
you come to us, tenderly
we hold you, with tears
we cover you.

In a poor hut
where music is about to be invented,
teach us to love.

(SONG FROM *The Royal Songbook of Amanate*, YEAR 12 OF KING MEN)

When the Nile did not rise in the customary way for three successive years and famine threatened to destroy all the towns and settlements, an expedition was organised to find the sacred kingdom of Siripech which was held to lie somewhere within the sea dividing Egypt from Arabia. Flowers were strewn on the waters in the hope that they would reach Siripech. I have seen the flowers. I have heard the weeping of the people. The old have said to me, "If there is hope there is hope in Siripech."

(HERODOTUS BOOK XXIII, THE ECBATANA EDITION)

III

The apparatus to construct the world is put together in unlikely places. On evenings like this, a sad twilight in Clazomenae after a storm, with ships laid out on tressles above the turgid water—how far away love is, how delicate the sensation of stumbling forward in a haze that blurs Clazomenae, Aegispotami and the hills shining above the Bosphorus. Words grind their way towards stillness; earth and air stand motionless, and I imagined myself an architect of the true speech of the world.

(IAMBLICHUS, PREFACE TO THE IONIAN EDITION OF *The Soul's Journey across Eternity*)

A unique alphabet was developed for writing those elaborate calendars that are left on walls in abandoned houses or secreted in nooks of common inns that the dead might read them and so orient themselves as regards all that has happened in the missing years, the time since they last visited our earth. Texts and readings prepared for the dead carry a special importance as the dead have no other way to acquaint themselves with recent events. We should always spare a thought for the dead. They do not have our ability to immerse themselves in idle gossip or frivolous purchases of gaudy novelties and so blunt the terrifying sensation of time's passage. The intolerable dullness of being weighs heavily on them. No wonder the dead stoop—no wonder the script used to write messages to them glitters, arrests, is striking, loves sinuous and tempting corners. It is necessary to woo the dead back into a forgiveness of life.

(MANETHO, *Commentary on The Soul's Journey across Eternity*, THE BILINGUAL COPTIC-GREEK EDITION OF HELIOPOLIS)

IV

It is over, as trees are over and stars.
And yet it has not yet begun
like a loaf of bread that we plan to make
when we buy the flour when we find the coins
when life reinvents itself.

(FROM LEONIDAS THE SELF-EXILED, *Enigmata*)

V

There has always been abundant writing in the more far-flung regions of our Greco-Roman world—whether in the prosperous South Indian settlements, on the Cinnamon Coast, among the Hyperboreans or on those islands that border Atlantis. Yet prejudice has always demanded that writers in such places be suppliers of local colour, curiosities and vivid travelogues. The educated elite of Athens and Alexandria have long scoffed at the idea that a profound philosopher could emerge in such places, let alone be content never to visit their renowned cities. To them it is unthinkable that a serious writer or poet might choose to remain on an island so far removed from the traditional Greco-Roman centres that it lies indeed beyond the Equator. Yet such was the case with the Greek philosopher Leonidas the self-exiled. Leonidas lived his entire life on the tiny island of Phokaia, some two months sailing south-east beyond the busy East African port of Zam. Resisting numerous entreaties to journey to the renowned northern cities, he always said that truth was never a property of north or south. His writings were later collected by the disciple Nikephoros who brought them to the Greek port of Marsilia, from where they were soon transported to the island of Abukar, just off Atlantis. In the days before the rise of Eusebius on Atlantis the teachings of Leonidas the self-exiled guided the Philosopher Kings of that realm.

Whilst the principal volumes of his work have for the most part disappeared, a short précis of his sayings was in the private library of Omeros Eliseo (later known as DM). Many critics have traced Leonidas' influence on Eliseo. The critic Monochrastes, for example, aptly remarks, "The notion of the essential, the quest for the absolute minimum in life as in art, the belief in universal reciprocity, the preference for silence over ornamentation and the delight in artistic removal—all these elements Eliseo found in Leonidas the self-exiled, as well as the strongest confirmation of his own choice of a small island as the summation of human existence. Separated by immense distances all but unimaginable to the pre-Socratics, the two maintained a dialogue beyond the chance dictates of death and geography. It is as if two oceans were talking to each other."

(Dio Cassius, *A brief Compendium of the Philosophers from Heraclitus to Pseudo-Dionysius*)

VI

When my daughter appears
in the space where my head was,
I understand her gaze, so fragile,
so distant.
The enormous clock used to say:
"It is still four o'clock.
It is always four."
My breath goes on without me
in certain glances, certain
tensings of the eyes.

Trees break apart, leaves
cover the paths of my garden.
I am looking for the daughter
who lives far ahead of me.
Blossoms sway on high branches over the walls.
Laughter tears itself free from the world's chill fabric.
I have fallen asleep inside my own life.
From somewhere deep within the restlessness of her eyes
quietly the future goes on speaking.

(OMEROS ELISEO, LATER KNOWN AS DM, POEM 7 FROM *Nineteen Poems of Life and an Ode to Calm Temporarily Confused Ghosts*)

VII

The lottery seller of Cumae

Where roads dwindle into twilight,
huddled under dry leaves,
he offers us his whisperings—

> *to you a child, to you death,*
> *to you great fortune in the fifteenth year,*
> *to you illusory fame,*
> *to you happiness, to you pain and fire.*

The two sides of names were folded over
to let the world be invisible.
A fish that had swallowed a star
was migrating towards the West.
We came hungry for knowledge.
We stayed on in the dark
waiting for the wind to utter our thoughts,
to tell us at last who we are.
One day they will all file past our window—
the bald man who auctioned sleep,
lovers with glass hands and eyes of burnt silver,
the leaf-gatherer who returns to each leaf
its dream of becoming fire,
the one whose small voice was the ocean,
the one who forgives.
While words go on sleeping in books,
the pebbles of our mouths
fall in round silences.

To feel loved the sky needs only its shadow,
the tree its branches.

(Omeros Eliseo (DM), Poem 17 from *Nineteen Poems of Life and an Ode to Calm Temporarily Confused Ghosts*)

VIII

Poetry could be a type of imaginary furniture—
a sofa setting for a feast in the villa we have long abandoned.

Or it might be an extension of being,
the wing of an imaginary house
dominating the bay where two oceans meet.

It could be a lightening up in the weather
where the unexpected shines from a stagnant pond.

Its path crosses the mountain range and deviates along the shoulder
of an ocean where the dead come closest to speaking to us.

Waiting for poetry to catch up with us,
it is easy to believe poetry must always be the same,
as if the habit of what had become easy
was the right way to live.

Poetry can appear to belong to words
yet it always ends up coming out at a different angle
into this thing called life.

The true poetry of an age may leave words altogether,
seeking refuge in the silent hostility of those who resist the
    conquerors' blandishments.

In poetry the nostalgia for beauty must learn to accommodate
    horror.

The pure line of a poem must learn to bend according to the
    confused
perplexity of our efforts to be at least in part honest.

Not knowing who we are, we go to poetry as to an oracular surgeon
    of the soul who does not interpret our dreams but only leads us
    to dream more deeply.

In poetry as in parenthood we have to be stronger than we really are—we have to pretend to a strength which often miraculously appears, so that the line between well-intentioned fakery and sincere ineptitude blurs and endlessly remakes itself.

Poetry carries a small sampler of blessings. They cannot halt the tragedies. But like walking with the steadier eyes of someone who has taken up residence inside us, poetry helps us to keep our balance.

It is no good asking for a poem to be this or this. Life deals only what it deals.

In poetry the quest to be beautiful and the quest to be truthful sabotage each other, merge into each other, remake each other.

Poetry seeks to make sense of life through the gift of indirection.

(LEONIDAS THE SELF-EXILED, SOLE REMAINING FRAGMENTS OF HIS BOOK, *On Aesthetics*)

IX

The inhabitants of Phokaia are quite clear that their ancestors came from places far to the east, arriving in long ornately carved boats propelled by oars and a single sail. Yet the Phokaians possess no boats and had no knowledge of the winds before Greek traders came among them. They say their skill in making boats was taken from them when a great monster arose from the sea. Likewise they assured us that their ancestors possessed a wondrous music, using golden disc-shaped objects arranged in a line to produce the most varied and exquisite tones, yet their present music consists of a few rudimentary tunes delivered with no great dexterity on ill-made clay pipes or tapped out on small metal drums. One possession they retain from their ancestors is a secret calendar that can be used to chart the location of all the fish on earth though the few elders who knew how to read the calendar have died.

The most remarkable achievement of the Phokaians is their language. It is said that, having reached the small island that would be their home, following the instructions of their holy men they burned their boats on the shore. That evening the ashes lodged in their throats and the next morning they found that, though knowledge of sea-craft and music had deserted them, a new almost intolerably complex language had taken possession of them.

The language of the Phokaians could be regarded as the extreme opposite of our languages. Not only do they constantly add to the beginning of words, producing the most intricate precisions of meaning and weaving extraordinary connections between all levels of experience, but the purposes for which they use language are hard to explain to those who are not Phokaian. The prefixes to words, the preliminary change-notes, as their grammarians call them, indicate, among many other things, the degree of formality, the time of day, the state of weather at the moment of speaking, whether causality in the word is to be perceived as flowing forwards or backwards, the degree of longing the word experiences to rejoin the things it describes and (most importantly) the five residencias or realms one might be talking of. Their words become extraordinarily long. In part because of this they do not use language to converse about everyday matters that are at hand or to issue instructions, but rather language to them is a kind of parallel universe, which flows alongside other activities, a music, a tapestry, a mirror that all attend to while going about other unconnected tasks. Their island is small—two days walk suffices to trace its perimeter. Their language brings the universe into their presence: from stars to sea monsters, from the delicate quivering of fish to the listless ripple of a desert wind. Humour and grief flash in jagged splices across their language. They have lost everything and they have gained everything. At times they wish they could forget language and simply hammer objects as other people do, accumulating women and making money. At times they regret that their ancestors fixed upon such a narrow world, a tiny island generating endless verbal complexities. Yet their speech is beautiful and silence, they say, gathering in the space where the voice fades out, is the strongest word in all language.

(MENANDER, *Travels in Zam, Phokaia and the great ocean of the South*)

Leonidas knew the language of the Phokaians, passing entire months living in their presence and their speech. During the busy fishing and farming seasons he would withdraw into the private world of Greek to write. Undoubtedly the intricate language of the Phokaians entered all his thought, along with their paradoxical relationship to time.

(FROM MONOCHRASTES, *A brief biography of Leonidas the self-exiled*)

It is sometimes misleadingly asserted that the Phokaians forgot their ancestors' knowledge and even degenerated through living on a tiny island separated by immense seas from all neighbours. Those who have listened attentively to their stories know that nothing was forgotten. Choices were made to abandon certain practices which, however convenient or beautiful they might seem, lead to terrifying consequences. The Phokaians had fled a disastrous cycle of civil wars, an era when the quest for trade goods and luxury led to an explosion in the traffic in slaves. Cities were destroyed, wars waged that women and children might be captured and sold. All this was done that silks, perfumes, rare foods and wines, statues and glittering entranceways might grace the ever more sumptuous houses of the rulers. The long-debated decision to renounce the use of boats was the Phokaians' way to ensure they would never return to that violent archipelago. It also served to protect them from chance meetings at sea, whereby others might be alerted to their existence and come in search of them.

The court music of their ancestors' archipelago relied on a peculiar gong-like instrument requiring very precise combinations of gold, silver and other precious metals. Not only were such instruments too difficult to bring with them or manufacture, but the music itself was always associated with the taste for luxuries. It had long been used to mark off the *atheremonistanika*, the caste of those who believed their refinement, their ancestry, their lighter skin colour, entitled them to despise and enslave others. However beautiful the music, the Phokaians told me, it always whispered of superiority.

The language the Phokaians discovered on their island became, in effect, their supreme music. Running alongside everyday life it also rippled and curved to its varying rhythms—the arrival and departure of friends, the preparation of food, children's games, the flicker of rain on the dry brick of their houses, the trembling of the sun above the sea. Their language binds the Phokaians, joining old and young, abolishing every artificial difference, diverting, informing, sustaining them with its humour, its shifting tones of a finely registered tenderness.

(XANTIPIDES, *My year among the Phokaians*)

X

If our journey leads towards the source of the wind, we are travelling also towards the place where music first arose and began weaving its intricate shelter around the chaos of the human heart.

Far underground in the city's sacred caves the wind is born. A high priest and a few followers tend the caves, having taken unto themselves the custodianship of music. There for a long time they fasted and held vigil, trusting their dreams were in some way necessary to strengthen the music. Wasting away almost to death, the high priest trembled as enormous white birds fluttered through the hollow of his chest. Wildly spinning leaves curled over his eyes as the wind held him in its embrace. A single pure sound sustained the walls of the cave. Soon what had been merely wind rushing through the twisted rock chamber was no longer one confused sound but an interwoven composition of voices, an immense articulated language located safely outside human control or intentions yet not altogether indifferent to the fate of humankind.

The first note of true music, curled over itself, prolonged, repeated, had begun its interminable journey.

(Nicola of Narbonne, the twice-born)

XI

If an arrow could speak it would always find reasons to reject the target.

Water matters more than words.

A change of religion coats the tongue with opinions. A heavy rain squall washes the mouth with the sky's clarity.

No one can count the number of people we have been in a single life. One death is never enough.

For each of us the edge of the universe lies exactly where we sit.

Stone crushes us with the weight of an eternal demand. The ocean heals us by listening.

Bees gather minutely, sea-turtles drift slowly, spiders dwell inwardly.

To form a just image of truth, walk inside the silence.

The fish that never reaches the water's surface has already translated the sun.

A pier can no more lead you to the ocean than a gravestone can enter the land of the dead.

Do not hunger for explanations. The language of the earth is dust.

If the ocean wanted to count the sandgrains it would have to empty itself.

A single breath is enough to demonstrate the truth of heaven.

(FROM FLAVINIUS OF ILLYRIUM, *In response to certain proselytisers*)

XII

For the Phokaians it often seems as if time scarcely exists. In the farming and fishing seasons days go by in strenuous activity without speaking. Everyday life on Phokaia passes in familiar routines nudged here and there by gestures, a flickering of the eyes, an inclining of the head or a sudden settling of the body into the posture of welcome. At other times talk circles incessantly, vast interconnected, self-interrupting cycles of stories and legends. Time shifts slowly, haphazardly around these people with little attention being paid to its contours. They use the word "yesterday" to indicate the time of their ancestors, the great sailors who guided their boats over wide hostile seas to reach the island. But "yesterday" is also all the time the island existed alone with its animals, its stones and clouds, and all the time before humans first breathed on earth.

It may be that in some remote era people other than the Phokaians once lived on the island. On the roof of a cave near the island's mountainous peak are paintings of spiral circles, the same spiral design that can be found on certain seashells washed up from time to time on the beaches. According to the Phokaians these paintings have existed since the earliest days of the world, left there by spirit beings. A certain family or clan among them bears the responsibility for maintaining the vivid colours of these paintings—no one will say which family. The Phokaians, without knowing why, also took it upon themselves to perform a ceremony from time to time near these paintings. Leaves of certain plants are burned and the smoke wafted over the paintings while weeping spontaneously breaks out among the spectators.

For the most part the Phokaians only speak in the present tense. Their legends, epics, stories of animals and trees, anecdotes about vanished people, and their famous saga of the archipelago, all are narrated in the present. Sometimes one can feel as if the stories will never stop. Yet there is a certain kind of silence among the Phokaians which requires a careful analysis.

Apart from the physical activities required for the provision of food and the general necessities of daily life, on the one hand, and the elaborate legends and stories that inform, divert and bind the people, on the other, families, groups of people and individuals are from time to time gripped by the special silence cast by works of art. Lightning, thunder, particularly heavy and sudden downpours after long months of dry weather, all these phenomena the Phokaians experience as works of art. They gaze intensely at the jagged, chaotic and brilliant patterns of the lightning. For them there is no doubt that this is the art work of their ancestors. No one here feels fear or anxiety as they hear the crash of thunder. The rare individual who dies struck by lightning is considered to have rejoined the spirit world. United in silence on a hillside or the warm sand of a beach, whole groups of families watch with breathless intensity these immense instantaneous drawings splashed suddenly on a summer sky. The profound stillness and pleasure that touches every nerve of the body suffices for the Phokaians as proof that they are in the presence of their ancestors.

*   *   *   *   *

On days when clouds speckle the sky with intricate and delicate patterns the Phokaians will rest for a moment in silence, glancing upward and letting the gaze linger there, taking in the fineness of the art work. Occasionally in the movement of the hand or the trembling of an eyebrow I have caught them saying in gesture-speech "They have done well", meaning of course the ancestors who, no longer among them, communicate ceaselessly with them.

*   *   *   *   *

My life on Phokaia has led me to question what is art. Originally, it seems, art might refer to any experience, object, phenomenon or presence visible or audible that triggered and focussed a specific intensity of experience, an intense concentration, a vivid awareness, the sense of reading into the inwardness of things themselves, as well as that edge of aroused well-being and rightness appreciated in the texture or thisness of a thing. Much later, in eras when money had been invented to provide a kind of universal quantifier of experience, such aesthetic experience was limited and localised, confined to a play that might last two hours and be performed three times in a given year, then never again for five years.

The Phokaians brought with them to their island a highly developed concept of art. Numerous testimonies have reached Zam, Alexandria and India of the exquisite court music to be found on the Phokaians' ancestral archipelago. Reaching their new-found home, the Phokaians renounced the social and human costs of the technology that generated that art. Instead they discovered, somewhat to their initial surprise, that the artistic experience recreated itself, only strengthened now by the absence of musical instruments or elaborate materials for sculpture, painting or craft work. The Phokaians are right then in saying that their ancestors created the vast spectacular displays of lightning that transfigure their night sky, for it was their ancestors who passed on the ability to see the lightning in this way.

*   *   *   *   *

Let us hypothesise, then, that art exists on a continuum. At one extreme are the intense, all-absorbing, anonymous art works of thunder, lightning, cloud structure, or rain storms, cultivated by the Phokaians. In the mid-point of the spectrum are the great tragedies written for performance in the sacred festivals at Athens, works where the artist can be named, yet for the most part the characters, stories, values, are not inventions of a particular playwright, but rather the common inheritance of a people. And, at the reverse extremity, is art (if it can still be called that) as it exists or will come to exist in Eusebius. There, under the supervision of the entertainment cartels, plays, stories, music and paintings were produced in great number. Yet emptiness invaded everything. Extraordinary novelties of effect were attempted. One year feats of complexity were tried, another year feats of simplicity. A listless indifference multiplied itself across the teeming variety of the rival schools. Nothing could be found in Eusebius that resembled a correlative for the emotion of wonder.

(LEONIDAS THE SELF-EXILED, *Philosophical Investigations*. FRAGMENTS FROM BOOK ONE)

XIII

In the region of Niqali on the west coast of Africa medical practicioners use the contemplation of various aspects of nature or times of day to cure a wide range of illnesses. For the discomforts of pregnancy and preparation for childbirth they recommend the contemplation of dawn, especially when seen over a river or across marshlands. For the anxieties of old age the contemplation of trees in autumn or near the edge of winter is advised, provided the patient is strong enough to put aside all self-pity and observe with minute attention the topmost branches and leaves twisting in a steady wind, detaching themselves painstakingly, divesting themselves of layer after layer while becoming each moment more beautiful and gaunt against the grey sweep of the sky. The ocean at sunset is the recommended contemplation for anger, while a swift flowing creek is held to be a good tonic for the early stages of depression.

It was noted in the curers' conference held in Alexandria under the supervision of Hippocrates that the irresistible rise of anger and random warfare as undiagnosed epidemics has coincided with the great turning away from nature. In Eusebius they carefully followed a policy of destroying nature wherever possible. Relying on the Nicanorean Ethics the rulers of Eusebius saw it as their duty to multiply inequality to ever greater levels, in the process stripping the earth of forests, replacing rural areas with urban conglomerates and leaving deserts where farm land once existed. The Eusebian armies of devastation, those enormous though temporary shapers of human history, were made up for the most part of victims of the great anger epidemic.

(FROM PLINY THE ELDER, *Notes towards a universal history*)

XIV

Waiting for dawn at Aegispotami

In plain daylight startled by a city
nestled on a small flat mountaintop
the size of a leaf.
To wake almost holding it
on a camp bed by the marshes and the dawn
that hasn't come.
And only darkness,
the wide enfolding circles of water,
myself sole surviving general
of a vanished army, the would-be Emperor
Antoninus Marcus Gnaeus the First.
Mosquitoes drone their threnody.
Wounded in the soft tissue below the rib cage,
the barb twisting tight,
I thirst but will not fill the pitcher.

A few more breaths and dawn will come

with the cranes rising, their wingbeat
in broken sky.

(PTOLEMAEUS OF CYRENE, FROM HIS COLLECTION *Elegies*)

XV

Buffeted by the brackish tang of flesh,
the sweetness of salt,
I stumble towards beginnings.
Where to buy the difficult and true essences,
the blue wine, the oil wherein nothing dies,
round slivers of perch, the exact everydayness?
Through what impossibly mellowed cheese
will I trace the fragrant line of the future?

Underground amphorae
store the harvests of the earth and their sleep.
We will all rest there soon enough.
But where to find
what has not yet been invented,
what the eyes of the woman I love
tremble towards?

No one can speak for me, least of all
myself.

(OMEROS ELISEO (DM), POEM 5 FROM *Nineteen Poems of Life and an Ode to Calm Temporarily Confused Ghosts*)

XVI

Well after midnight I am walking through rooms flooded in a
mellow clouded light quite unlike that produced by fire or candles
or any form of illumination I have known. Everything sways slightly

as I cross the house, careful not to disturb any of the several sleepers here, family or strangers. I sense it is the reflection of a troubled sea that has come to take up residence at the foot of certain nearby hills. For several days I confess I have felt a sea was moving towards the house, perhaps drawn by the sleepers who crowd the alcoves and corners or by the softness of the wood. So close to us now, the sea's milky light is already glowing on my hands and my breasts. From room to room of the house I don't know what preparations I should make to welcome it. I have little knowledge of seas, other than the legend of the curved and intricate shells they leave us, tiny objects that fit in the palm of a hand and may be used as a sealed horn to summon immense sheltering waves when death enters the cavity of the skull and the lonely wind tries to tell us that we were always alone, that there is truly no one.

(ANTIGONE OF ARMENIA, *The book called exile*)

XVII

To use a name we must have some idea of what it would be like for that name not to apply. I say "Crow" and I have an idea not only of what a crow is, but of birds that are not crows, of a sky, a garden, a tree in which there are no crows. But, when we say "time flows" and "time is irresistible", what idea do we have of time not flowing, of a successful and permanent resistance to time?

Is time only an extravagant invention spawned by our awareness of change? Children turn into adults. The new-planted tree grows tall, produces fruit, the fruit ripen. We see these things. We call them change and we take them as evidence of a miraculous substance— "time".

Many claim powerful herbs exist to send the elderly back into their youth. Most often a people begin with the simplest tools and over generations develop sophisticated measuring rods, fine-crafted boats and many-storeyed houses, yet the Phokaians moved in the opposite direction, simplifying existence. In all these cases we do not generally say time flowed backwards. So it seems time is not dictated by the content of change. Yet, if changes did not occur, would we even have the concept of time, for what use would we have for that word?

Consider also: we believe it makes sense to say "Time passed though nothing happened" yet, if we did live in a universe where truly nothing happened, we would have no use for the concept time.

If the name time is in itself an empty shell, what does have reality is our attitude to it, our perception or inward experience of it. In Kitezh, in Ebtesum, on the archipelago whence the Phokaians originated, and in many other places, it is agreed that time is circular, an elaborate interlocking system of many cycles, capable of being grasped and studied by the numerous calendars that have passed always between peoples. In Kitezh it is often said that time flows backwards since events undo themselves, the flow of cause and effect that seemed inevitably to move in a certain direction reversing itself. (Remember that the rivers in Kitezh reverse the direction of their flow when the moon and stars are visible.) Likewise in Kitezh it is assumed that knowledge of the future is already available to us. So the fall of Rome, the circumnavigation of Africa by Europeans and the subsequent collapse of Africa into poverty and oppression, have all been prophesied and known though at the time I write this none of these things have happened. Adepts of the Mathemasis in Africa know these things not merely in a general way but can specify the year according to their calendars.

In Eusebius and, for the most part, within the Greco-Roman world it is held that time flows in one direction only, that it is all-powerful, that it weighs on people. For the Eusebioli, though time may initially mean growth, it flows always towards dismemberment, disillusionment, death.

The Phokaian conception of time does not concern itself with such vastnesses. It is protective, benign. Time for them is almost timeless. It wraps itself around the present. It provides for renewal more than loss. In worlds of systematic destruction, like Eusebius, time becomes heavy, oppressive. Yet such obsession denies the truth known to the Phokaians that every moment opens on a universe that is both familiar and entirely new.

*　　*　　*　　*　　*

Each of us believes he lives in a world darker, more closed over than any previous age. Thus those who lived in Athens during the Great Plague, or in the future those living in Rome immediately before its fall, or those in Eusebius during those dreadful hours when their enemies finally close in, all believe their case is unique. Yet the cycles are merely returning.

Consider the wisdom of the Phokaians who shed luxury and voyaged, one might say, across time to find a just way to live. Of them it might be said, "They decided to reverse time".

*　　*　　*　　*　　*

It was observed that the musician and philosopher Parmenides did not change in appearance or physically age at all from his thirty-fifth birthday to well over seventy, during all the intense years of his greatest compositions. Only after renouncing music did he rapidly enter old age and death.

*　　*　　*　　*　　*

If time is tied to change, time is equally tied to language. If there were no language there would be no time.

*　　*　　*　　*　　*

It is often said that children possess a different conception of time, but is that a question of age or rather of a certain openness towards the random blessings of the moment?

*   *   *   *   *

Art and justice free us from time.

(Leonidas the self-exiled, *Philosophical Investigations*. Fragments from Book Two)

XVIII

On Corrosion

Just a slight nick and an entire being bleeds into a brownish puddle. And to think as simple a mix as air and water suffices to eat one away from the inside! One might have once been a hammer, a battering ram, a sharp brooch or the frame of a chariot before the painters got to it. Salt adds to the ferocity of the consumption and what is dry like vinegar promotes this everyday refutation of the adage "You can't get blood out of a stone".

If the very things we would rapidly die without (air and water) can so lethally inject death into these ferrous beings, does it mean the human and the ferrous are eternally stranded at opposite edges of existence? Does it mean we must resign ourselves to perpetual incomprehension? It appears so and yet there is no avoiding the suspicion that we are brothers.

Is there a purpose behind this constant war of the familiar fickle atmosphere on what appears changeless? Is it perhaps a way of restoring all to an eternal dialogue? Do the stars come to us by such a process of remote bleeding?

(Lucretius, "Notes towards a further book of *De Rerum Naturae*")

XIX

How does the earth know
which of us will die first?
Of the five petals on a bough in late spring
which one will live on
as the cool blush of a young girl's cheek?

~o~

Fish may well regret that they chose water to live in.
The sun has to bend its back
trying to reach them.

~o~

Of all things
the inwardness begins somewhere.
The moist underbelly of a stone.
Of a stunted tree
the forward tilt of its shadow
almost touching the absent water.

(FROM ERYCTHEMIOS, *Knowings* BOOK TWO)

XX

The Lake

In dwindling sunlight this flat grey-brown sheen of interrupted
ripples and bird-calls is a presence that keeps moving beyond its
own limits. If I turn to walk away, it is a hand beside me almost
holding me, almost soothing the narrow earth.

On the island clustered entwining gums, a willow, and a goose
sleeping folded up into itself, closed over its own raw helplessness.

Look how a few waterbirds go by, paddling, drifting, inventing new sounds, and one of them has donned the draped mask of a red beak rolled down over its blackness. How just to feed off stillness is a grace I think I could almost know.

In a text of Awakenings a group of boys dive at nightfall into a muddy canal to bring back the wished-for sun, and nearby it says how what is patched onto the eyes to reproduce the glitter of light on distant mountains, what might be given the approximate name "hope", rests always to be found under large pools of water, and may be carried into simple human dwelling places in the gaze of those we are learning to love.

(FRAGMENT FROM LEONIDAS THE SELF-EXILED, *Reflections and Meditations on the Natural World*)

NOTE: From this passage in Leonidas it appears that the landscape and flora of Phokaia belong to the Australian continent. It would seem that the tiny island is a fragment of the southern continent that broke off and travelled across what is now called the Indian Ocean to somewhere not far from Diego Garcia or perhaps La Réunion. It is likely that Phokaia vanished below the waves during one of the world reversals triggered by the Eusebiolan magicians.

(W O'S)

XXI

During his last years of terminal blindness the musician Demetriades learned to see through music. No one can otherwise explain the lightness and fine shimmer of touch all feel in his final compositions. Everything becomes visible: a lone bird gliding over dark sea, the curve and smooth syllables of waves, the splash of a bird's gold-black feathers in olive foliage, a grove of orange trees rising from the valley floor, their shine of early morning trembling in his fingers on the lyre.

But most of all he cherished a certain still and windless blue that is visible only when the deepest water at the base of a cliff is suddenly lit up in midsummer by a sun so careless of its ferocity it doesn't notice how everything is blazing with its sparks, even the black wounds in a tree's bark, even the worm-riddled eyes of the all-seeing dead.

(MENANDER OF COS, *Lives of the great musicians of Ionia and Cyprus*)

XXII

In the Orange Grove Ampitheatre above Halicarnassus they erected the twelve statues of the Nicanoreans. It was something unique in Greek tradition. First to consider was the space itself, neither temple nor theatre, neither gymnasium nor agora—seats where no one was to sit, a view of the sea the statues do not look towards, the insistence on a high ceiling made entirely of music, the ban on clouds passing overhead, the requirement that one walk around the statues without gazing too fixedly at them, for it must be remembered that, according to the Nicanoreans, the statues were made not that we should look at them but that they should look at us.

And next to consider the statues themselves—each represented one of the twelve cardinal virtues praised in Nicanor's Great Testimony: frugality, severity, self-righteousness, ferocity in warfare, filial piety, astuteness in money making, submission to authority, chastity, avarice, the calm banishing of pity, the cultivation of true terror and reckless bravery in the face of extinction. The statues were generally held to resemble more those to be found in Persia, in the lands of the Shah-i-Shah, colossal monoliths whose eyes curdled with the might to reduce others. Yet there still lingered a decidedly Greek feel about them. For all their monumentalism there was no mistaking the imprint of the individual human form. Especially moving and impressive were the five female figures. Paradoxically no statue in Greece was so tender, so breathtakingly feminine and soft as that representing Eleomachia Galiniste, the Calm Banishing of Pity.

Copies of these statues were later erected above the harbour of Marsilia and in Marsilia's twin city, Naurimia on central Atlantis. The copies on Atlantis were of gigantic proportions. Fifty-five stories high, they guarded Atlantis, filling all who entered its port with awe and dread.

Yet profound ambiguity has always clouded mankind's response to the statues. With the consolidation of Eusebian power on Atlantis art became a banished concept and the status of the statues was for a time much debated. Were they part of the education system or did they belong to one of the three entertainment cartels? Would it even be preferable to tear them down altogether? Eventually it was decided to label them "exempla" and to accord them the role of supervisory presences.

The destruction of Eleomachia Galiniste by a deranged student from Outer Eusebius was the single event that heralded the onset of the great collapse.

(MACRONIUS OF ILLYRIUM, *Chronicle of a Sad Kingdom—the rise and fall of Eusebius*)

Few places can compare for opulent display, extravagance and sheer luxury with the city of Naurimia on Atlantis. During my brief stay there I witnessed a performance in the main arena of the decapitation of Terpsichore, as performed by a small troupe of the finest actors. The entire show was presented in gesture-speech: the pleading for life, the averted eyes, the frenzied anguish of abandoned sacredness, the first incision, the severing of the head with its writhing and terrified locks set loose to strangle random members of the audience.

I remember most of all the visit by that icon of the entertainment cartels, the ageing Aglaia—her breakfast at the Saltmines Taverna where the sky is condensed into chips of portable metal, the sadness of her last salad by the dockside stalls where the fish were still frying, her spectacular entry into the Museum of Modern Theft. Impossible to imagine it but at the same time an obscure Outlander, Haroldus Negrus, originally from the tiny island of Nova Hibernia, entered the central vestibule of the Museum, using the black arts of his native land to stage an illegal protest. Erecting an impenetrability shield to resist the Eusebian Guard, he performed his play *Why?*, a solo performance depicting the massacre of the Megarans, at the same time reclaiming his banishment name of Borun Borun in Erd-speech. Resisting arrest he closed his performance with the immolatory rite of invisibility.

(PAUSANIAS, *Days and Nights on Atlantis*)

XXIII

There was a long silent bleeding of those who lived in the hills and were never accorded a name. They bred and were killed, bred and were killed like a supply of nightmare we kept feeding ourselves. When the first Empire fell they imagined they would be given freedom—an absurd illusion. Power may change but not its nature. It was not even as if anyone wanted their land which was all barren forest, all waterfalls and snow and bleak mountains. What was wanted was the killing. Thinning them down we felt almost alive. It was necessary that we should have a land to feel proud of, the more of it the better, and the constant chipping away at the great task of killing reassured us that we were not, after all, the lowliest country.

(FROM *The Annals of Phearcus*, LOCATION, AUTHORSHIP AND DATE UNKNOWN, FOUND AMONG DISCARDED PAPYRI IN THE LIBRARY OF TARSUS)

XXIV

The nights that summer passed slowly in the phantasmagorical loneliness of Capri. Old and embittered, a prisoner of the Empire he was condemned to rule over, Tiberius gave orders that the poet Erycthemios be summoned into his presence for he had heard the poet's name uttered by the wild thunder that lashed the battlements of his palace one evening. Terrified of appearing in the Emperor's presence and desiring only obscurity, Erycthemios at first thought of refusing and accepting the death such impiety was sure to bring. Implored by friends to save his own life, Erycthemios could only obey. Bowing to the inevitable he let himself be taken by ship to Sicily and from there to Capri. On the boat as it sailed from Alexandria Erycthemios felt his powers desert him. Unable to speak, much less write or compose poems, he gazed in mournful solitude at the vast sea.

Now Tiberius meanwhile began to dream with ever gathering ferocity of his own death. Night after night images of death haunted him and, as the boat carrying Erycthemios entered the harbour of Capri, Tiberius woke startled as if a knife had been plunged into him. He commanded that the poet be brought immediately into his presence and at his entrance exclaimed, "Who are you that you bring death to me?" Erycthemios then bowing and approaching whispered something at which Tiberius laughed. It was a laugh that saved both of them. After that Tiberius regained calm sleep and Erycthemios the power of speech.

In Alexandria it was said that only laughter could save a poet.

(SUETONIUS, *Lives of the Caesars*, THE GREAT LUSITANIAN EDITION)

XXV

The blind horse knows the scent of the world.
Walk with it slowly.
Rest your hand on its mane
so you may know that nothing is endless.
There was a river that restored the tracks it erased.
There was a pebble not touched by any journeys
left behind for you alone
forgotten in the hands of the sky.

(ERYCTHEMIOS, *Knowings*)

XXVI

I write this to you in my poor and stumbling Aramaic. It is many years since I have spoken it, a lifetime since my adolescence as a student in the monastery. Gandhara is far and if I write now, feeling death move closer and closer, it is tenderness for the past, for all of my pasts and the souls I have been or might have been. I do not believe I will see the mountains of Bactria again from the citadel window or strain my eyes squinting at the cramped script of the Yavana poets tracing Greek finery into Sanskrit letters. Or pause once more before the fire worshippers taking their dead to the heights of the towers—all that once seemed strange now coming clear—to be torn apart, to be free. If this letter reaches you, know that Eudoxis seeks peace, dying now in Rome where everything shrinks to the stench of vegetables rotting in the courtyard, and the first sun of winter's leaving rests on a small pot of flowers. Greetings and peace to all who cross your threshold. I believe now only in emptying oneself of all belief. A heretic, the sect here would call me, yet I too dwell with the silent ones.

In my mind I walk with you again along corridors, past the bend of the river where the women feed their newborn babies, the elderly hoard the wood to cremate their meagre frames when their time comes, and thin snow, almost invisible, numbers the eyes of sheep. It is not to ask forgiveness, much less to forgive, that I write, not even to renounce forgetting. It is just some obscure presentiment that all must first be gathered, that destiny has set me the trifling, all-consuming task of holding this small fragment of being, of turning it slowly in the space of all spaces, before it too plunges through oblivion into the stillness that remembers us all.

Your servant, fellow sufferer and friend,

Eudoxis.

(LETTER HELD IN THE NESTORIAN MONASTERY, SAMARIA)

XXVIII

Several days journey east from Trebizon, along the route that leads towards the Kingdom of Silk, we rested by the edge of a mysterious lake. Hovering high in the air the lake confronted us with its delicate and fantastical sculptures of ice. The local high-priest of Hathor told us that not long ago in this very place the moon had visited earth, sheltering in the waters of the lake. For many days men walked about stunned, as if existence had taken on a profound intolerable weight that also, paradoxically, charged them with a fine airy lightness. The skin of men and women glowed with the lustre of the moon. Few could resist the power of attraction. Lovemaking which had once been confined to the night now took place at all hours and in the most inappropriate places. It is a strange thing that in the writings of the Chaldeans it is foretold that, when all the world drowns in the great changes brought by the Eusebian Exchange Mechanism, these mountains and the people who dwell here alone will survive.

My Imperial instructions urged me to go forward, to continue across the numerous mountains and deserts that lead to the Kingdom of Silk, there to confirm the agreement between the two Emperors dividing up dominion over earth. Yet I determined at that moment to slip away, to leave to others the sealed documents, the solemn treaties that would soon be scattered by the winds, lost forever in the confusion of deserts and interminable mistranslations. Here, where the moon had dwelt among men, was an ending place. Stones that shone with the light of arrival.

(FRAGMENTS FOUND IN PAPYRI PRESERVED IN THE NESTORIAN MONASTERY OF TABRIZ, AUTHOR UNKNOWN)

BOOK V

I

Hanging upside down
perched in its own
Heaven
the cricket sings:
"I have eaten and am full.
This
is good."

Does it sing for us?
Possibly.
If we too have been touched all over by fire
If we have balanced for hours
on the infinite porosity of earth
and know what it's like
to be the casket of a time-beat
ticking away at metamorphosis
If at times our head and arms have wavered
like a delicate carapace flooded
by all the sky wants us to take in
If we can imagine the dryness of wind
caressing our black shell
all through the hot days
all through the fire of nights
when our eyes are beads of hard blackness
and our frame
breaks open to the homeless language of wind
If we can imagine ourselves
an assemblage of shell and flesh

scattered by the serene indifference of life

If we can call all this
happiness.

(FROM IRENE PHILOLOGOS, *A poetic journal of ten years in Boeotia*)

II

In the village of Ervan among the Oromati I was invited to a house where one room is possessed by the force of absolute silence. In this room numerous birdcages hang and inside them are pale, almost transparent birds that have gradually shed all their colours in the journey towards the invisible. The birds have lost all song and, from the hollowness of their eyes, seem to have forgotten even the memory of what song is. Only from time to time, in one corner of the room, a bird beat itself against the bars of its cage, as if sensing an ancient instinct that pain is the origin of sound.

(PORPHYRY THE YOUNGER, *A journey from Ephesus to Nineveh*)

III

The child fell asleep in the tree, the tree in the world

Growing requires more lifetimes than the great fire.
The tree asleep in the world
spread its branches over the sun.
Days came and went,
and all that was far
made its nest of daybreak in his hair.

Light swarms.
The branches go on forking
budding, giving birth.

The child's closed eyes tremble
as the tree curves its sleepy leaves
around his waist.

Drownings, abandoned cities,
thunder ringing the sky,
an Empire restoring
the kingdoms of grass—
all swirl around the silence of his sleep.

In this gossamer web of breath and longings
snared birds whisper the true languages
into his ear.
Olives, forever almost ripe,
leave the scent of weeping on his skin.

OMEROS ELISEO (DM), POEM 12 FROM *Nineteen Poems of Life and an Ode to
Calm Temporarily Confused Ghosts*)

IV

Know that everything continues.
Know that your breath is not yours,
that the ocean returns to you,
that you have no more self than a wave has.
If white birds come to you on the shores of the Aegean
know they are reaching you also
on a beach of the Great Ocean
where the girls of Atlantis
have waited a lifetime to greet you.
For you a kestrel hovers and dives
above a river that wanders out into the sea.
For you rain streaks the grey of the olive trees;
the shingle on the shore
sighs the same way at dusk as at dawn.

When the currents meet out in mid-ocean
all the water underneath you
could no more end you
than a dream could end you.

In Pergamon they do not let go of beauty—
over and over they let it collapse
only to build it anew.
Know that everything is a wave.
In the core of sleep
its echo travels the great circle of ocean,
answering to the sun.

Not in the husk that shatters,
worthy Lysimachos, seek your image,
but in song that stumbles always
into a higher resonance,
and in clear-sighted action
embracing its double, the consequence,
across the ten thousand worlds.

(ONE OF THE FIVE REMAINING FRAGMENTS OF *The idea of ending among the simple singers of Pergamon*)

V

Among the Mountain People II

And it was a tiny hand reaching out of the soup,
the tender grasping cry of a flying fox
whose bones the old men were crunching—
and the bitter chill was still
around the oil-doused cauldron.
The fire blazed its monumental resistance to night.

How they laughed, the women,
seeing our startled gaze,
our lips dropped in disbelief—
they knew that even children of the forest rafters
don't begrudge the passage of their still budding flesh
into thin broth.

This gliding that goes on when the last skin dissolves,
the tenderness of wild faces.

(IANNARCHUS, *Poems written while travelling with the embassy of Antoninus to the Silk Kingdom*)

VI

The next episode in our story unfolds during one of the many periods when books vanished, either because of the high cost of papyrus, disruption among the class of scribes or due to certain Imperial edicts aimed at halting the drainage of money to purchase frivolous novelties and distracting libels that lead people away from the one true state religion. At a time when the ban on books was being most strictly enforced Demetrios was travelling across the marshy swamplands of upper Hispania towards Gallia Narbonensis. Stopped and searched at a municipal checkpoint, Demetrios found himself in deep trouble when a small slip of papyrus was discovered in the seams of his saddle bags. With terror the soldiers stared at the small torn fragment, their minds reeling with the enormity of what lay before them, the tangible presence of all the sorcery and black magic they had heard of so often. The slip of paper, a fragment of a letter from the previous owner of the saddle bag, read in fact "Do not forget to tell Marius that he must", but there was no one there who could read and the soldiers refused to accept his version of the words. Demetrios was accordingly arrested, hauled before the local magistrate and sentenced to slavery for life in the gold mines of Agrium.

Many months had passed in the mines and Demetrios was beginning to lose hope when, through a change in work gangs, he came to meet Drusus Zamorias, a trained aidos and rhetor, one who preserved in his mind the better part of the library of Alexandria. For in the long periods when books disappeared the preservation of knowledge depended on such men.

Now it happened one afternoon, after a long day of hard labour, that one of the aquaducts chanelling water to the mines was destroyed by a rebel attack and so the workcrew were able to enjoy a few hours rest. Taking advantage of the quiet Servius, the oldest worker in the group, asked Drusus to recite a speech from the secret edition of Sallust's *Bellum Iugurthinum*. It was the famous episode where the Numidean king, once an ally of Rome and then its fierce opponent, sent envoys to Ebtesum and Kitezh seeking to make common cause throughout Africa against the expansive militarism of Rome.

Drusus began at the point where Astariomorph, the ambassador of Ebtesum to the King of Kitezh, speaks in reply to the entreaties of Jugurtha's envoys:

"Eloquently and not unwisely you have spoken of the danger posed to us all by the designs of Rome. With great concern we have watched their progress for many years, first devouring the territories of Carthage in Sicily and Hispania, then destroying that city entirely, leaving not one stone standing or one life spared. And now Roman legions seek to impose their will on the African littoral from the Atlas mountains to Egypt.

"You propose a common alliance that Rome may be met with force and driven from these shores. Such an alliance sounds most reasonable yet it is necessary to pause here, examining all with due care before lives are lost. For once war is started it is hard to draw back and few can then fix their minds on the simple questions that underpin strategy. Now, therefore, we should consider the question: how is tyranny best overcome? What is the most effective way to defeat an Empire that in the name of pretended virtues and to maximise private gain imposes misery on others?

"Leonidas the self-exiled, the philosopher who in the isolation of his remote island has pondered the human condition most deeply, states there are three responses to an evil regime—open warfare, invisible warfare and what he terms the third strategy. Open war, such as you have proposed, requires the creation of military machines even greater than those of its opponents. Inevitably new military leaders arise, gaining power through conquest, much as the Roman leaders did in defeating Carthage. And those who attempt the way of open warfare must likewise generate and monopolise wealth, for war breeds inequality and, as Thucydides remarks, vast armies require vast injustice.

"Invisible warfare may seem a better choice yet it too merely wages war by conspiracy, turning to random violence and symbolic destruction. Long generations of time are needed and, for those fanatical bands who direct it, such warfare breeds fierce hatred and the thirst for absolute power. In all such contests who can say which regime will prove the worse?

"The third strategy is the hardest of all courses—patiently to exploit the tyrant's weaknesses, to become oneself empty and invisible, reading the subtle contours of time to await the completion of the circle, to let evil implode. Likewise we should not forget the superstitious nature of the Romans who fear to venture beyond the Inner Sea, ascribing a divinity to the Sybil's advice not to expand the limits of Empire. Wisely exploiting such weaknesses and encouraging the belief that Africa is empty apart from a few coastal cities, it seems to us that much may yet be made of the poor grasp of geography among the Romans and their taste for inexactitude. Like many Empires their very self-centredness ill equips them for extensive conquest in confusing places. For such reasons we believe invisibility is a strong protector. Moreover, as

Adrianopoulos rightly observes, every Empire of destruction starts and finishes by destroying itself. Though we may be slaves in a mine we can direct the fall of our enemies."

(LONGINUS, *The travels and tribulations of Demetrios and Zoe*)

The twin figures of Nero and Jugurtha circle around each other, pursue each other across the centuries. Neither of them seemed capable of a definitive death. In the two hundred years after his supposed assassination nine messianic figures arose claiming to be Nero. In Egypt and Cappadocia monstrous sadists performed all manner of abominations believing themselves to be the true Nero. The most serious threat to the emperors at Rome was the Nero-impersonator in Greece. Emboldened by the popular acclaim that greeted him in Athens and trusting in certain prophecies, he raised a powerful navy and planned to sail against Rome.

Likewise not long after Jugurtha had been incarcerated, starved in a pit outside Rome and strangled by soldiers, he began reappearing in numerous places across North Africa. The one Sallust had tried to dismiss as a malcontent hungry for personal power was seen by his African contemporaries as the almost successful liberation fighter betrayed by Roman treachery. According to secret calendars held by the Coptic monks, the appearance of a new Jugurtha in the wilds of Bactria was one of the signs that the collapse of Rome was imminent.

(DR NEUGEBAUER, "COMMENTARY ON SALLUST'S *Bellum Jugurthinum*")

VII

In Ebtesum the children weep for Jugurtha
blind man with no name
starved and strangled
he could not find the consolation of death

In Ebtesum the children weep for Jugurtha
the black pit was the final maze where they penned him
his spirit kept wandering the roads
the dogs in the camp knew his presence
from the world of the dead
he brought back the pure fire
he gave us the word Justice
In Ebtesum the children weep for Jugurtha
   If there is evil in the sky
   If water is locked away from our lips
   and salt is sown for our food
   If the oppressors deny us the one true name for horizon
In Ebtesum the children weep for Jugurtha

(FROM *The Black Book of Ebtesum*)

VIII

Steadily central Africa, unsettled by Roman occupation in the north, fell into chaos. Terrified by the threat of imminent destruction, people fled the city in large numbers. One morning the water stopped flowing in its daily rotation through the numerous canals and lakes. The magnificent houses of water that formed the glory of Kitezh disintegrated, rough ledges of rock being all that remained of their legendary beauty. Yet the core of the Holy City was intact—the elders, the royal family, the librarians, the ambassadors from the Essene communities, all gathered in the many-storeyed library where the sacred books of papyrus and of water were stored. Mist and sunlight wove an intricate halo around them as the city and its remaining guardians evaporated like the passage of a rain cloud across the sun. At that precise moment Kitezh, its towers and minarets, its palace and library, appeared on the plain outside Kiev. It was a spring morning in 1505 of the Old Calendar. The elders woke as if from a slight nap and began to be at home in their new language, rejoicing in the edge of caress in its sounds, its extraordinary fondness for the diminutive. As the peal of a nearby bell rang faintly through the early morning chill, they resumed a conversation on means to preserve their scriptures during the approaching Tatar invasion.

(FROM *The Chronicles of Kitezh*, HELD IN THE NESTORIAN MONASTERY, SOGDANA)

IX

In the writings of Memnon sand was held to be even more sacred than water, for water suggests life which it always serves, having no place in its translucent flowing being for the withdrawal of life, whereas sand signifies the willingness to scatter, to dissolve, to be no more. When the sages of Ecbatan decided to write their sacred books only in sand they accepted that everything would be lost. They wrote not to preserve their words but that the act of writing might simplify their restlessness. Sand has been called the material of death. In reverencing sand we reverence the fate that has made us limited, acknowledging the right of every other being to replace us. After the collapse of Kitezh the art of building in water was lost. Sand became the favoured mode of construction as if to signify that henceforth man would make his home inside death. Sand is the marker of absence. Placed over the eyes of the dead, it prevents them seeing themselves in mirrors.

We know water is sacred—that much is easy, but to experience the sacred as most truly embodied in sand is the hard beginning. We must first accept the water's right to refuse to cure us.

(IRENAEUS THE OBSCURE, *The Book of Emblems*)

X

The village by the lake
has mist rising at its centre.
Two houses,
their roofs laced with the sun's gold,
curl into a chill vanishing.

~o~

everything difficult
is dipped in the sky's purity

~o~

The white scavenging of the birds—
perched in olive green dawn
they will return when the patched scar of the cliff across the lake
burns red with homecoming.

(FROM IRENE PHILOLOGOS, *A poetic journal of ten years in Boeotia*)

XI

Know then of the Illustrious ones for, being furthest away, they seem
closest to the true path. Rome they have never heard of and even
Syria is only a vague memory, too far to be imagined as any more than
the invention of a traveller's tale. The Cross for them has become the
emblem of totality, its four extremities reaching all corners of earth
and measuring the inwardness of man. Compassion, generosity,
selflessness, are what they are renowned for. They have long shed
all concern for theology or the self-righteous exclusion of others.
Discarding all quibbles over names for the unknowable, their speech
has reached the purity that comes from dwelling in the Spirit.

(SIMON THE MUCH TRAVELLED, *Report of a journey to the Kingdom of Silk*)

XII

He will cultivate his solitude
on an island called Bitterness.
There he will gather the flock of his brothers,
the clouds,
and know the thirst that comes
from contemplating the sea.
He will learn how trees writhe upwards
into the bleak interrogating
stillness of midday.
Whatever journeys his life held,
he has plotted all his lifetime to return here.
On some rocks above the inlet
a child's kite is left loosely tethered to some bracken:
no one would steal what can never escape.
The only temple where offerings are made
is three jagged stones
abandoned like the blind eyes of the sky.
A dog sleeps in the shade of a wall;
a fig tree guards the island's single well.
He is happy breathing in
the still clear lines that mark his limit.
No immortality, no transmigration—
the earth's harsh dryness
guarantees he will dissolve utterly.

("Eudoxas contemplates his return", Anaximenes of Cos, *Elegies*)

XIII

Responsibilities

to nightfall, always to carry an anchor bolted to my leg to make
    sure I will drown if thrown off a bridge by a wandering gymnast

to accept transmigration on whatever terms, even if as a patch of
    weeds used as a receptacle for kitchen slops, or as an orphaned
    duck crying his incontinence through the house, or the open
    hand of a leaf blown onto the path at twilight, its intricate web
    of veins receiving the entire weight of the sky

to the bricks that burn in the fireplace, to the kindling scattered in
    the yard, to the re-invention of warmth

to the road beyond Paestum where the absolute chill ensures every
    traveller will be lost

to the pure openness of your gaze even if in the faces of other
    women

to beds shared for a night or for years, and all the hollow places of
    the world where there is no one but rain and time

to mice that congregate after nightfall, to the meticulous otters,
    pigeons and a stork who stayed behind, wading through a river
    that comes from the first days of the earth

to the spikes of the prickly-pear fruit, to appleblossoms

to an old woman dead now in a brothel on Samos

to the stones of the road, to a wooden bridge that slanted beyond
    the furthest mountains, to a certain tree that measured the
    halfway point from the village school to home

to count stars accurately, to avoid quarrels with birds, to leave the
eagle his right to distance and unpredictable vengeance

to make bread before dawn, to wash the feet of wanderers, to leave
a portion of each page blank that the Invisible may write their
messages to us, to each other

to the blazing fullness of midday entering the harbour at
Alexandria, to the fortress of Sardis where the walls glow pink
with the last of light failing

to a dark-eyed widow from Tyre and her three children, our few
shared days on the caravan to Yezhd, her listless silence louder
than the snorting of horses, to whatever became of her

to the simple naming of losses, the grammar of obligations and
the wordless empty languages scattered in all places by beauty

to the wheat with its hunger for one more day of sun, to the grape
grown clouded and chill as mist across the fields at daybreak

to the crows of autumn, at all times to scan the shadows in the
sunlit pool, to know how gold is the last moment before brown,
to scavenge life from the bleak edge of survival

to the port of Agrigentum, to the olive groves on the hills around
Malea

to my sister who carried her three brothers across the roof of the
collapsing city

to the dead that they forgive us, to the unborn that the road be no
more broken

to a certain map of the world that showed how every place is infinite

to daybreak, thin trees and the winter sun

(Anonymous, from texts found in the Nestorian monastery in
Bactria)

XIV

Ringed by a wall of mountains, all heavy with snow, the lake was in every season bathed in the brightest light. Cherry trees mirrored themselves in the slow drift of water while various ornamental bridges crisscrossed the numerous canals that wove their intricate circles through the city built between lake and sky. Houses, temples, palaces, as well as the renowned factories for the making of silk, woollen cloth or elaborate tapestries, all floated above the canals like shadows before the water-soaked eyes of visitors. Each day, on falling asleep in this city, I woke towards twilight in the same flat-bottomed boat being punted towards the Prince's Palace or rather that office of the Palace where vast menageries of messenger pigeons were kept—the chief means of communication between this valley and the outside world.

Sometimes it seems to me that the rest of my life, my journeys, my time in the cities of Fars and in the villages along the great river of India, have been only illusions, that my whole life has in truth passed here. I try to tell from the perusal of my skin or the scrutiny of my face in mirrors how many years I have been by this lake. But nothing is conclusive. The great circular tapestries record perhaps the many layers my life has travelled through, as much as they image the expanding rings of mountain barriers, rivers, lakes, forests, not to mention seas, currents of air, split directions of time that enfold this centre where my breath is poised in the moment before expiration.

Sometimes I believe I am a child who died very early but stayed on in his parents' house—a few feet above the quiet patter of their comings and goings. Other times I am a man of almost fifty five who has wasted his life in selfish and vain endeavours. Only, as reward for some small deed of kindness, the gods who wander this earth have permitted him to dwell in a parallel life, gathering the threads of the most beautiful place on earth, the place from which all images have their origin.

Twilight everywhere summons its own confusions. It may be that of the entire city only the messenger pigeons are true. That, or the sound the water makes as it twists with all the depths of stillness against the oar. It may be that the two dreams—of early death, of wasted life—are the same.

(PTOLEMAIUS [EDITOR], *Anonymous writings from the Gandhara Diaspora*)

XV

Everywhere nowadays writing about painting and sculpture abounds, and not a few of our authors have attempted brief studies of music. Yet dance, that most intimate and philosophic of arts, has had few commentators. There is indeed much need for a scholarly study of dance as practised on the southernmost island of Atlantis. There a dancer is not esteemed for standing upright in some contorted posture or for twirling around a given space with or without a partner. Rather they consider the chief interest in dance to be the final moment of the inevitable fall. Dance, so they say, is the delayed stylization of falling. Hence on that island all dancers carefully study the rules for falling, as in how to fall to one's death from a fast-moving chariot, how to fall holding a drink while the continent on which you are standing is reversed below the waves by spiteful magicians, how to fall while convincingly impersonating someone who is still standing. There any average dance competition can count on at least a few hundred spectators, each with a highly developed aesthetic of the differing modes of collapse, from plummeting through trees from a raised platform while peeling a banana to imitating the polar sun in its ability to elongate the horizon. Dance has sometimes been described as mirroring the water's quest to lie down and sleep, but that seems an inappropriately gentle image. Clouded by desire and terror, far back in each of us lies the point where consciousness first grasped how the earth under one's feet is only an illusion of stability. All dance, they say, seeks the clarity of that moment. Flinging pain and failure into one's collapse into catatonia is at most a beginning. The body memorises the mathematical sequence of the trees, and so the ability to let one's being descend from branch to branch towards death. A true dancer always inhabits the space left spinning when a world disappears.

(STEICHEMONOS OF TAGUS, *Commentaries on arts ancient and modern*)

XVI

In Laconia, as in Eusebius, harsh punishments are imposed on all paradox makers for such individuals they consider the most pernicious of mortals. Speech, they argue, must always be controlled so its significance flows in one direction only. In this way alone, their lawgivers maintain, can transactions unfold in a smooth predictable manner and all reality attain the comfortable invisibility of agreed upon truth. Accordingly, paradox makers are at first imprisoned, then—if they can make a convincing case for their innocence—stoned to death.

During the harsh era of the Diocletian persecutions the city of Edessa granted refuge to the paradox makers of many lands. Likewise many paradox makers took up residence in the Gandhara Diaspora. There the city of Kunopolis was one of the masterpieces of the paradox makers' art. Each room opened into another room though no room could be visited twice. The stars and moon and sun were at all times visible in the central courtyard though outside day and night washed over the surrounding landscape. Entering this palace it was possible to see the entire universe and yet see no one. Of all buildings the palace was renowned for its quality of permeability. It was possible for birds to fly through it without noticing its walls or, should an individual so choose, a fine mist of rain would fall only to be converted during its descent into sunlight. On occasions flocks of birds reached the walls of the palace, disappeared, then re-emerged at the far end, exiting into a night sky, while during the time of their invisibility their song, bouncing in all directions and echoing from wall to wall, traversed simultaneously all the chambers of the palace.

In Gandhara other paradox makers perfected a language of the second order—that is one specially designed for elaborate humorous responses to other remarks in the same language. It is impossible to be the first to speak in this language or to use it to say anything directly about the world. It is a highly useful language for mathematicians and poets who suffer permanent amnesia.

There can be no doubt but that the world has long been sharply divided into those who enjoy and admire paradox makers and those who hate them with a religious fury. It is not surprising, given their education, that the citizens of Eusebius view paradox makers with intense revulsion. In Eusebius children spend from five to seven years learning off by rote long lists of the visible. They are then given random exams with unpredictable questions like "In 5000 words explain which is the morally superior colour—grey or green?" or "Oceans impede the progress of Eusebian armies and suggest the ludicrous idea that trade might take place in two directions. With accurate mathematical charts outline a strategy for removing the world's oceans." The results of these examinations are tabulated according to secret formulae and used, in conjunction with ferocity aptitude tests, to assign the Eusebioli to a range of positions from mind management to death quantification. For those who grow up in Eusebius the heady combination of superiority and humiliation throughout childhood ensures a timid anxiety. Whilst the maximization of inequality is the political goal of the Nicanorean ethics, its devotional emphasis is well captured by the chant uttered in ancient Vedic "Make me narrow, narrow, narrow."

(MACRONIUS OF ILLYRIUM, *A brief history of Eusebius—the rise and fall of a sad kingdom*)

XVII

"In honour of our foreign visitors", Trimalchio continued, "we should have something suitably elevated. Let me recite, then, the learned poem of Philemon the Mauretanian—there was a man who knew how to turn a phrase. I have it here in the latest expensive Alexandrian parchment:

Look at them, after all, these messengers
in whom there is no room for regret.
Perched on the lintel of a house
or simply standing on the red spindles
of their legs, it's enough to squawk and squawk.
Food and seeing have scooped out all their being.
Their surveillance is absolute
and their message, what is it?
A scrap torn from the earth's whirring.

But no, a host must not always be a jester and let no man say that Trimalchio can't be serious. I'm a trader and trade has made me rich. Let me propose then as first item for our cosy little symposium the topic of trade. And you, Gorgias, just because your parents sent you to some fancy place in Athens, let's not hear you whining that trade is a dull or slight matter."

At that Trimalchio turned the lead in the conversation over to Lychas who bored us all for a while with his painstaking account of the pepper trade. Next Pyrrho gave us a racy run through the ins and outs of the trade in gladiators from Asia Minor. When these two had finished their stories and a vast platter laden with Syracusan wine and magnificent truffles had gone the rounds, Emiranier, the mage from Parthia, spoke:

"Our generous and esteemed host, Trimalchio, is most perceptive in his choice of topics for surely trade has shaped our world. And I am referring not only to the trade that all know but to that secret trade that forms the origin of all other commerce. For so many generations, back far beyond the first Pharaohs or the building of Troy or Nineveh, this world has been governed by the concept of trade as a conversation of magical correspondences. Birds, plants, signs, rituals appear and disappear across the checkerboard of the world. So gold-crested cocks bred for sacrifice were moved from the Kingdom of Silk to the southernmost island of Atlantis. At the same time a different species of rooster, all fiery red and used only for fighting, was mysteriously transported from a village in Sogdana to the westernmost port of Naurimia. In exchange a light sea-blue colour used to purge grief and seen only in children's dreams was shipped back to the Silk Kingdom. Obscure instruments that carve passageways through the sky moved from the Sea Kingdom of Knossos to the Great Southern Archipelago which, in reply, answered with the hidden dictionary for the language of bees. In such ways endless permutations in the exchange of magic augmented the world. Consider, then, the extraordinary novelty of those merchants among the Eusebioli who first ventured across great distances to trade in life's necessities. They developed the idea that, by depriving people of food, shelter and other basic needs, trade might be vastly extended so that all might buy from far off what once each made for themselves."

(A LARGE GAP APPEARS HERE IN THE MANUSCRIPT. IT IS PROBABLE THAT EMIRANIER'S IDEAS WERE DEVELOPED AT GREATER LENGTH. THERE FOLLOWS THE INTERLUDE BETWEEN ENCOMIUS AND MENANDER.)

"You have spoken a great deal", interrupted Encomius, "of the trade between distant lands. A significant topic, doubtless. But that is nothing compared to the trade between the living and the dead."

"Yes", Menander, Encomius' lover, chimed in. "We've heard a lot of unsourced anecdotes about the trade in magic between certain Silk Weavers and Atlantis. But the strangest model of trade I've ever encountered was in a village barely twenty miles from Apuleium. I stayed there one night when thieves had driven me off the road to Brundisium. To cut to the plain of the story, a family had put me up in their cottage at the edge of the village and I had just fallen asleep in a backroom when I heard an enormous ruckus on the roof. Pots and pans, rain catchers, wind imitators clattering back and forth. By signs the owner of the house and his wife bid me say nothing. Finally we heard the boom of a deep voice pronouncing the words "Yo wa sakasama"—a chant that echoes still inside me. No sooner were these words spoken than a deep silence gripped us. We waited till we were sure the visitors had gone, then clambered up to inspect what had happened. Our mysterious intruders had taken old crockery and kitchen items and left a blue flag painted in magic signs, a handful of strange mushrooms and a fish whose name is death but whose flesh, if one lives, cures impotence. I learned afterwards from the owner that, every month or two when the moon reaches a certain phase, the dead of a distant Island Realm appear on the roof, trading magic items. The words I had heard, so the owner told me, are in a speech that comes from that distant land."

At that moment a large hullabulloo broke out at the doorway as a band of revellers broke in, led by the legendary debauchee Arsinoê. "We insist on making our contribution. We've heard this is the Symposium on the end of the world and there's no way we're going to miss that. It's typical of that tight-arse Trimalchio to think he can keep us out. We're hoping to spot some real dignitaries here, someone who can give us the true word on the fire and brimstone predicted for this town, not to mention the old prophecy out of Thucydides that the earth will disappear below the waves."

(ANOTHER GAP APPEARS IN THE MANUSCRIPT. THEN FOLLOWS THE WELL-KNOWN PASSAGE ABOUT EYESIGHT ON THE ISLAND OF SKRIMORDIA, SEVERAL DAYS SAIL WEST OF HIBERNIA. IT WOULD APPEAR THAT THE RETIRED LYDIAN GENERAL LYSANDER, A PROMINENT EXILE IN UPPER-CLASS CIRCLES ON CAPRI, IS PRESENTED AS THE INITIAL SPEAKER.)

… "Now these people suffer a peculiar eye problem that makes them unable to see the sky. The blue of the sky and the white of clouds they perceive as a vast river of mud flowing over their heads, while the night sky to them is not black or star-studded but rather a crystalline mirror, a dull glow wherein great warts of stone appear. A few among them experience the sky on the horizon as a brown and grey tapestry, ill-formed and badly fitting this globe. A visiting philosopher, on observing their terror of the sky and the ubiquitous depression they lug about with them, concluded that the people of Skrimordia suffer from individualism, whilst the sky, being a collective construct, requires a community committed to happy endings, willing to make the permanent effort needed for colours to endure. On the other hand, the geographer Eratosthenes hypothesised that the sky in those regions indeed suffers an excess of brown, due to the local custom of burning all trees to warm themselves against the bitter cold of those parts. A further opinion was stated by Timon in his much-praised treatise *The idea of truth among the Hyperboreans*. Timon claimed that the supposed blueness of the sky is itself the symptom of an eye disease, that originally all mankind looked directly into limitless space and that day and night were distinguished in a purely intellectual manner, the perception of sky being a symptom of narrowing vision. This same narrowing led to the inability to experience the unity of mankind and a relentless spirit of differentiation. Confining value to one's own group and excluding all value from others lead in turn to greater and greater wars. Only by training people not to see the sky any more, Timon maintained, by restoring that clear sight that in one instant takes in distant space, can mankind learn harmony on what remains of earth. The Hyperboreans, living at such great distances and having no sense of any 'other' whom they might despise, had in effect regained the ability to see into space, only a lingering moral uncertainty still muddied that vision."

When Lysander had finished his account, an old man in the group who had been a long time silent seemed to come alive, as if waking from a trance. Interrupting the loquacious Lysander, he was intent on making his contribution to the flow of discussion:

"I have never heard of that author or that book, *The idea of truth among the Hyperboreans.*"

"Strange, it is very well-known in Cappadocia—perhaps it is too heavy for Italian tastes."

"Perhaps so, but your story of the Hyperboreans reminded me of something rather frightening that happened to me several years back. When my father died the sky lost its colour. Death robbed me of the sky. I would have to wait for it to return. Overnight it had become a brown and grey quilt, an obscure tapestry belonging to some other tribe's way of seeing. It was as if all that stretches above us had withdrawn from me into its own altered space. This happened to me first in a dream but the numbness of losing the sky stayed with me. And if the sky was blocked to me, words were blocked to me—not the mechanical everyday use of words, but the inwardness of words. I lingered this way for some two years till one morning, I don't know how it happened, the sky returned to me."

(EXCERPT FROM PSEUDO-PETRONIUS, *La Cena Fantastica* IN THE MILAN EDITION)

XVIII

He had at last completed his tome, *The Compendium of the Ancients*, and despatched copies to the nine great libraries. His children had long since disappeared into their own lives. There now remained only the essential. He was travelling up into the mountains to find the right place to die. The road, all dust and crumbled footholds, edged its way through stone villages, through the chill verticality of the minimum. At all times water roared underneath him, and from wherever wind-blown spores found fissures of soil between the rock life burst forth. He had tabulated the deeds of statesmen, the sayings of philosophers, what the poets had written of love and the

beauty of snow falling on an empty field when it is almost spring.
Now he was going to find out how a man dies.

(FROM PHILOSTRATUS THE ELDER, *The life of Menander of Brundisium*)

XIX

Terrible things happening in simple words.
They swallow our lives, they spit out children and heavy jagged
    stones.
A year goes by. Five birds go by
seeking warmer landscapes.
Homeless wandering from treetop to treetop
across the kingdom of perpetual rain.

By the doorway of the Emperor's palace
sits a wiry old man whose fingers
are itching to strangle the world.
You can almost make out what he's mumbling,
you fumble for parchment to get it down—

small mad poems to keep the days apart.

(ANONYMOUS, FROM THE SABINE ANTHOLOGY OF POEMS WRITTEN DURING
THE 3ᴿᴰ INVASION)

XX

Condemned to spend the remaining years of his life among bleak
mountain passes, a perpetual exile from the tide's glittering drift,
Aegisthes focussed all his power on summoning the sea. Starvation,
meditation, spells overheard in dreams, the burning of sacred plants,
incantations over seashells given him by a stranger, Aegisthes tried
every strategy.

If a sail would appear
but only wind bringing sand
If the breeze would glitter, salt fragrant on its lips,
but only wind bringing sand

In the twelfth year of his practices a peculiar infection, a scaled
flaking of the skin, appeared. The stain of the ocean began on his left
arm, then spread across all his body. Longing so much for the line of
ships rocking in the harbour at dawn, yearning for the cool waves of
his childhood sea, he could not bring the harbour of his native Cos
into the mountain valley but he could, through an extraordinary
effort, objectively damage himself. It is true a few geometricians
assert that in those twelve years the Aegean moved some few
inches in the direction of Bactria but little evidence supports this.
Undeniable was the rotting odour of salt that pervaded him.

CODA: If a man wants the sea too desperately he cannot alter the
world but may successfully drown himself. It is also possible that the
sea will, of its own accord, visit him. Only it will do this when he is
in deep sleep, when he is unaware of its closeness. How else explain
the salt rot that spread across his arms and chest, clear evidence, the
investigating doctors asserted, that Aegisthes had spent far too long
immersed in salty ocean water though he lived all those years on a
dry ledge of barren mountains.

(VALERIUS MAXIMUS, *Memorable Deeds and Sayings*, ADDITIONAL PASSAGE
FOR BOOK 9, CHAPTER 12, "UNUSUAL DEATHS", FOUND IN THE LUSITANIAN
EDITION)

XXI

She is numbering the memory stones and the bright objects fall
towards her—shells of the red-footed octo-crab, the small chip of
an itinerant storm cloud, petals of flowers in search of a homeland,
the knotted bulb of the giving tree that holds the dead inside life.

And her wrist is a delicate place where kisses swarm.

All that is incomplete, all that is separated from life craves her presence: trees that wander the earth unable to blossom; the wind where the spirits of the unborn and the suddenly misplaced cry out their loneliness.

How lovely when she appears to us in the darkness and we pronounce her name.

Girls whom life has damaged too early will find her in meadows or where rivers dip under moss-stained rocks. She will leave them golden fruit and repay their kindness. They see clearly how her hands have been woven out of grief.

On a terrifying road where the ground has been stolen, if you feel a presence folded around you caressing the back of your hand, know that she has taken charge of you and no ill will come.

In sun-blighted land she is the waterfall; when the firestorm passes she is the one child saved, sheltered by invisible whirlwinds.

Bees crossing a swamp feel the dazzling light of her garments and know which of all the trees she has shaped as home.

On the crumbling wayside path she is the orphan girl who, given food and a few silver coins, indicates the line where the earth ends.

Those destined for extermination have seen her on balconies high up, weeping uncontrollably that she cannot altogether enter this world.

In childbirth, in lovemaking, in death she is the doorway; her hands bring us strength and the great unquenched light.

Let her presence among us be unspoken, unsullied; let the tenderness of her breasts linger for ever on our mouths.

(APHRODITE OF SAMOTHRACE, *On invoking the Goddess*)

XXII

I hate you but I love you—
why the fuck do I do this?

I dream of those dying slowly,
poison frothing from the mouth,
eyes jerking.
To me that peaceful ice
across the forehead,
that scream that cannot find the air,
is heaven.

~o~

If you seek Catullus,
look for him far away
in the coiled smoke rising
from a pyre by the Ganges

or right beside you
in that garrulous wounded bird
who's forgotten all those days
when the birds passed freely between us.

~o~

This black doesn't suit you, Catullus.
Put some bright red,
some glittering brocade
on your shoulder—

the divine is in everything.

~o~

This glittering, this lake polished by the wind

longing inscribed on the stem of a boat

too much death in the bones

I have done with smart-ass love poems

a butterfly explodes in a warm gust of petals

by the lake at Sirmione

(FROM CATULLUS, *The Sermione Notebooks—drafts and sketches*)

XXIII

HERMOCRATES: I must start by asking for your pardon. Yesterday before returning to Critias' house I had promised to conclude our discussions today, presenting my own view on what the ideal society might be. I went to sleep with my thoughts, my reasonings and exempla all stored neatly in my head. Yet the wise assure us that the gods are all around us and that openness to them alone can lead us to the true path. This morning I rose early and, obeying what I took to be some god of the summer wind, walked down to the harbour to see what the waves or the birds of the shore might have to tell me. There I saw, emerging from a stretch of the wavebreak, my lost soulmate and dear wife, Hermione, dead now these seven years in childbirth, but I did not see her as she was in her thirty-first year, nor as when we married and she was eighteen, but as a child of nine or ten, her wet hair streaming in the dawn wind. I trembled and the tears welled up till the goddess who answers all prayers spoke softly:

When you come among us our hands are open.
Your hair falls free and we are gripped at the heart.

I thought of what our friends Timaeus and Critias have taught us of

Atlantis and good governance, both how a city might be constructed and how its citizens might best be organized. Yet, after the visitation of Hermione, a restless sense that my discourse must lie elsewhere overcame me. For beauty is feminine and what existence worthy of humans could there be without beauty? And what use is an ideal society if we do not know how to live within it? It struck me that in reasoning, in planning, in wanting to formulate and establish systems, we have hacked too much of ourselves away. Timaeus and Critias have spoken of cities. I want to talk of hillsides and open sea, of the loneliness of a camp of warriors who wait for death to come with the dawn, and of a young woman who swims upstream against the current so that her unborn child may know the fish as his brothers. The rules and the numbers are important, as is the measurement of borders, but I wanted to speak of the spaces between what can be measured, of life as it flows between us in its own wordless space.

Rightly it seems to me, Leonidas asks the question, "What is it that is worth saying?" For each of us lives in the last days of the world. And it is as if we were to eat and trade stories and make love in a graveyard with the dead all around us, like the chill breeze that came this morning from the Piraeus when months of hot sun had made us believe that summer was forever. On my first night as a guest in Critias' house one of the poets who is yet to be born spoke to me, Irene of Boeotia she said her name was. On falling asleep I heard her whisper these lines:

We think we are breathing but the birds see farther than we do.

And then she spoke again in a brief poem that felt like a prayer for me:

Whatever it was that loved us into life, a hunger,
a tender instinct to shelter,
this presence still enfolds me,
solid and frail like your feet stepping down

onto the tiles where the water splashes,
close as a ray of light falling across our skin from a gap in the curtains.
My dear one, my lover,
your gaze has no knowledge of years.

SOCRATES: Truly there is blessing in your speech. Your words remind me how the distances thin us down. Days turn, clouds trace their trajectory across the sky. In childhood who hasn't visited a swimming hole and seen arms stroking against the water's placid lapping? And yet underneath that stillness wasn't there always a current dragging everything into remoteness, into this everyday oblivion? By all means let us, for a moment, leave aside our talk of the ideal polis and pause to ask what truly merits our attention.

CRITIAS: If I might join in here. I should not wish any to think me overly bound by what I said yesterday. A grain of sand may teach us as much as any lost kingdom. Thales of Miletus stated that all things are filled with gods and this may seem strange yet the evidence is all around us. Recall the story of Hyparchus who was deprived of a body as punishment for shunning the love of a woman. The gods first deprived him of that manhood by which he might please women, then gradually over many years his shame turned him into a withered claw, then a pile of dry leaves. After many years had passed, the nymph Astarte fleeing the wrath of her father and abandoned by her lover, the thunder god, sheltered in a deep forest where the cold seemed absolute. There Hyparchus in his shape as a pile of leaves warmed her body and eased her pain in childbirth. He it was who preserved mother and child and, when a tear formed in the oldest leaf along the vein that had marked the beginning of his death, he released that song which Astarte took with her to her home in the skies. So even in his lowliest, most despised form, Hyparchus proved the dwelling place of a god. Rightly, then, is it said that the least being is impregnated with divinity and that no one knows what their true portion of existence may be.

HERMOCRATES: In the current manifestation of the cosmic cycle, when this particular Athens sends its ships to invade foreign lands and the agents of Eusebius proclaim the universal commodification of all gestures visible and invisible, it is worth recalling the sayings of Leonidas the self-exiled that "what lies outside alone utters" and his dictum, ridiculed by many, that "poets should be free to write outside the human". Of the latter the story of Phineas may well serve as an example. Now Phineas had been stricken by paralysis as an infant and was brought up by eagles. As is well known he bypassed the walking phase and moved straight into low-level soaring. By this means he was able to articulate a perspective on human destiny quite distinct from the more common wisdom. When human speech descended on him in his eleventh year, he grudgingly condescended to spend more time on earth. By twenty-eight he was an accomplished poet. Indeed a small selection of his poems was transcribed by Leonidas before his withdrawal to Phokaia.

If the soaring incantations of eagles are one direction, one limiting case, of earth-wisdom, the dog choir of the Montagnards is a complementary example. In the mountains south of the Silk Kingdom the clanspeople set up a chant, aiming at a subtle harmony that will let all the living creatures of their valley open up and nominate which of their number it is acceptable to kill in hunting. Now what is remarkable is that the true moment of harmonisation cannot be reached by people. For though they instruct or tilt the universe in a certain way, by itself mankind can do nothing to see its work come to fruition. As humans sing in harmony slowly the dogs join in—first one or two, then dozens. Inspired by the human modulations, the precarious journey they trace from dark to light, the dogs' voices strain in a sympathetic yearning. Where the human voices cease the dogs' voices continue, awakened, as it were, by a longing to resolve into harmony this smallest portion of the universe. (Leonidas once remarked on the discrepancy between the power to destroy which, by all accounts, seems innate and limitless and the ability to bring to a harmonious perfection, a far rarer gift that always requires something outside the human for completion. "By so much more", he comments, "does the capacity to destroy outstrip the capacity to build lovingly." Yet in a lesser known treatise *Reasons not to despair altogether of mankind* Leonidas argues the case for the possible survival of earth.)

(FRAGMENT FROM THE DIALOGUE "THE HERMOCRATES" EITHER BY PLATO OR BY HIS PUPILS, AS GATHERED IN THE LOEB EDITION, *The Socratic Diaspora: previously uncollected writings by Plato*, LONDON, 1933)

XXIV

When all that dreadful predictability
comes trudging up from the depths of the universe,
pleading "Say me. . . give voice to my long life",

how beautiful to hear the waterdrop
and its great tumble
from the broken gutter to the wooden floor.

What lies below us, what lies above us, suddenly the one sky.

(FROM IRENE PHILOLOGOS, *A poetic journal of ten years in Boeotia*)

XXV

He wandered far out into the sea to find her. He had never guessed how deep the world was. A shimmer of lost birds raced past him, piercing tiny holes all over his body. Below him the ocean kept shifting, as if it could never quite decide all it wanted to say. There in the depths, layered one above the other, the traces and echoes, the disembodied yearnings of every creature that had lived on earth. Wherever he looked trying to see her, more and more eyes, more and more questionings and silences, appeared.

He knew that certain fish create their own light. No one had told him that the smallest particle circling in the ocean's depths bears its own distinct name for tenderness. Wavering there along a surface that slanted steadily towards the almost graspable sun, his gaze descended the tree of the depths, a richly carpeted stairwell of spinning worlds and subworlds. Receding below him were fragments of sound evolving into new languages, trees that resolutely refused to be withered, and, drifting like soft-veined arms that cradle the universe, mountains on their way to shelter the sky.

The cries of the gulls wheeled round him, sustained him as he spun towards the world's centre. Unable to find her in any one place, he realised she had left part of her presence in everything.

(JULIAN OF NAURIMIA, FRAGMENT OF THE NOVEL *Theophanes and the Merwoman of the river Isis*)

XXVI

From all the unbearable
uncertainty of Heaven
softly you enfold me.
I have no sea,
I have no space,
no sky to give you
trembling and wide enough.
Beloved unlooked-for,
the gaunt houses with the fear windows
are only as large
as all the days before now.

Three shadows cross your face,
three shadows trail
the soft curves of pain
my lips are stroking.

Frail
as if the air no longer held me,
I am the last leaf spinning
in an autumn sky.
Beloved all around me,
is this what happens when we enter
life's stillness,
is this the true knowing?

(ERYCTHEMIOS, *Knowings*, THE FINAL POEM)

XXVII

Jacarandas in Macabukro, almost spring

The tree of infinite veins,
though it blocks the sky,
gives us hope.
All its swirling outgrowths of bright yellow
are too fine for any destiny we know.
The wounded repetitions of its lowest branch,
however darkened, however it stubs itself out
in winter air,
are a rhythm the heart knows,
more beautiful than cherry trees
or the pale shade
of pink blossoms against snow.
For this is the god's shining
so high and endless
along the line of death.
Ungraspable—
but how could anyone imagine grasping—
this thin gold,
these fresh outbreaks of a denser

more fragrant pollen.
Under this canopy
ending anywhere
would be beginning.

(OMEROS ELISEO, POEM 19 FROM *Nineteen Poems of Life and an Ode to Calm Temporarily Confused Ghosts*)

BOOK VI

I

Poem to be sung on the river that encircles Kitezh

Serenely and slowly
the shore slipping by
the great heavens riding along the water
and nightbirds interrupt, break the flow
of images, of mirrored letters
whatever is fierce
whatever is loss
the palm of the hand on the drum's white belly
the long lute's stem summoning gazelles
and a white-haired unicorn that grazes all day
on the pastures of forgetfulness

When the conquerors come
let the river defy their arrogance
When the merchants and arbiters of possession
unpack their dividing scales
let the river rewrite all equations
When the limiters of Eusebius
seek to measure my beauty with their codes
and sell me back my own name
let the river speak for me

You do not cross this barrier with weapons
You do not buy this abundance with gold
nightbirds spreading and scattering
the amulet of light-traced

sky-shaped letters
the great heavens riding the flow of the water
the shore slipping by
serenely and slowly

(ADAMA THE NUBIAN, POET IN RESIDENCE AT KITEZH, C. 750 BC)

II

In the small dark

The woman I love feeds me with stars.
They grow in the small dark
of an immensely open hand.
Walking towards her
I don't realise I have no legs.
Where a great plain awakes on a narrow floor
my head, however broken,
sets out to find her.
Wandering the wrong side of every river
I still am closer to her
than every one of my days is to the dredging of days.
If my life ends in the joining of two gaunt
all-dominating walls, I will sleep always now
somewhere beyond them.

(FROM A MANUSCRIPT ASCRIBED TO CATULLUS, *The Sirmione Notebooks*)

III

Facing the pond the first time
I am startled into silence.
For the wind, caressing it each dawn as a lover,
this simple habit of teaching ripples to speak.

~o~

Five years in the company of these worn cliffs—
the sacred clear as stone
where nothing is reflected.

~o~

The intricate web of the world
led me back to where I was.

~o~

The earth is its own litany.

~o~

At the quarry where I would bring you bread,
some tablet of darkened earth, cast aside, unnoticed,
held all the words your life was missing.

~o~

On the bare floor
grinding the wheat for three cakes of bread—
a handful of olives,
a pitcher of water.

So many dawns stretch out before me.
Father of bleak spaces,
must my arms be so narrow,
never to catch those hills
where the sun has yet to travel?

~O~

Surely it is still there in this unfamiliar village—
the bend in the road where I stumbled as a child
gathering luck flowers, intent I would never marry.

Here among strangers,
awaiting my fiftieth year,
the road can never be straightened.

(IRENE PHILOLOGOS, FROM *A poetic journal of ten years in Boeotia*)

IV

It was somewhere in the grey hour between night's waning and true dawn when I began the process of leaving the dinner party at the Archon Menippus' house. I stopped to say a few words to the two yawning sisters who had come along by chance hoping for the all-night talking-cure for insomnia. Sleep has always been a problem for me, especially when the fear takes over of those altered states I enter through sleeping. How easily I might yield to the brittle shelter of permanent wakefulness, a well-known formula for madness. I had just bid them farewell when a knife appeared in the air before me. Suddenly asleep the sisters began talking with a shared voice:

"He takes the measure of daylight. He stumbles always against the door we will not name. What the wind writes will last longer than his mumblings and, though he soars, there is no place small enough for the burial of his bones."

(PSEUDO-PETRONIUS, *La Cena fantastica*)

V

Born into the influential Chrysostomos clan, at nineteen Irene married her second cousin, Dimitri Philologos. Bitter feuds between rival families dominated the Empire on the death of Theodosius and Irene accompanied her husband into exile, following the machinations of the Blue court faction. Fearing a wave of popular support for the young Princess, the court faction renewed the edict of banishment after the death of her husband. Accustomed since childhood to wealth and prestige, in Boeotia Irene learned to live on millet soup and wild herbs, grateful for rain water where once she drank the finest wine. In a mountain village hearing only a local dialect incomprehensible to those from Byzantium, Irene displayed a tenacity undreamed of by her court enemies. Her writing, as she confessed, saved her inwardly, for there no imperial edict could destroy her. In an age addicted to theological disputes, dull treatises and sycophantic histories, Irene's writing stands out. "A woman writing poetry in the middle of nowhere—how boorish, how monstrously antiquated—at best it will supply some paper for birds to nibble on", scoffed the Archbishop of Constantinople who presumed Irene would die soon enough, an exile in an uncouth mountain village. Her writings survived and were discovered in the eighteenth century in a monastery outside Deka Aghia. "Soon I will be dust", she wrote, " but the ants and the insects and the small things of the earth will remember me."

(PREFACE TO A PLANNED EDITION OF THE POEMS OF IRENE PHILOLOGOS, FROM THE PAPERS OF DR ANTOINE LEMESURIER, ASSISTANT CURATOR, THE SECRET LIBRARY TRUST OF LOWER EGYPT)

VI

Crouched by a lone fire
in the wide country
where the world has vanished.

~o~

Across the lake
they are burning holes in the sky—
tender sparks
twist upward into night.

~o~

Learning to look at shadows
detached from whatever they might once
have accompanied:

scruffy strays
liberated
into the carelessness of beauty.

~o~

In the pure open
a great steady fire caresses each being
with its slowly diminishing touch

from layer to layer
gradually out to the white stars that speak back.

~o~

The small bare table
where the bread has not yet been laid
speaks as a lover makes love:
entirely there.

~O~

The fish have been passed through a net—
sifting their jagged loneliness
into a paste of bone.

~O~

Art, like love,
permits us to fall into it
to discover our own falling.

(IRENE PHILOLOGOS, FROM *A poetic journal of ten years in Boeotia*)

VII

In praise of being conquered

The inevitable processes of history undid my shoelaces.
Without ever opening my mouth, words surrounded me.
A cup from my daughter's hand stood broken on a shelf.
Children and grandchildren
slept in a palm-shaped boat moored to the sky.
Inexplicably
my feet were there on a road
between mist and bad-tempered eagles,
dangling in nothingness.

The inevitable processes of history
removed my connection to the money
I once held in my wallet.
Trees grew in walled gardens,
dogs discovered how the night sky leaves food
in small silver bowls inscribed "Canis".
Meticulously scrubbing the scrawled labels from our eyes,
the inevitable processes of history

removed the names we once gave ourselves
from a place deep in our foreheads.
Evenings were assigned to teach me anxiety,
swallows made off with the bread from my plate.
The more I worked the more I disappeared.
Winters washed over us,
spring was somewhere you travelled to
on any particularly empty afternoon.
Toenails grew; darkness propagated itself
from a single pinpoint to measure the universe.

With no human intervention
fires consumed a thousand villages, poison appeared in waterholes.
The inevitable processes of history
carefully positioned the remains of a few token bodies at
crossroads.
Mysteriously, the length of a continent,
the grasslands stretch wide now, almost silent of people.
An optional attachment to breathing
lingers on in my left lung.

(PHILEMON OF MAURETANIA)

VIII

In the capital my newly-married hand
feared the sun and the swift
shimmer of the colder currents
that fold over each other
in the divided sea.
Here every day of sun is a blessing—
banished from sight
the sea has finally turned blue.

~o~

In the doubled light of breathing
our bodies merged—
death took you
but left me the blossoming strength
of this half-body:
only the insects of the earth
will know me with such intimacy.

~o~

Gold has its distinct flavour—
gold pulp of the opened gourd, golden rice,
the gold skin of a fish
frying in cold air as sunset widens:

as a girl I thought I knew you,
thin paint on high domed walls,
the artisan's fresco-work, what alone could hush
the wild eyes of Authority.

Here as my life folds over
you enter me—
humble substance of the everyday.

~o~

In the village they name every insect
but do not name all the intricate
colours of night—
they name what they talk to,
what answers back —

the beautiful swirls around them
uninterrupted, enormous:
they let it pass.

(IRENE PHILOLOGOS, FROM *A poetic journal of ten years in Boeotia*)

IX

It is easy to believe there is another language always present at the edge of hearing, some slight, altogether bewildering shift in what we thought the finite reality called music, a colour no one has seen yet, familiar perhaps to some other people but hidden entirely from us, words with a nuance another tribe would grasp immediately but, to us, forever incomprehensible, something that could have lifted the whole of our lives into another truth, another intensity of joy and coherence and depth, the lost key that would redeem so many wasted years, so much bitterness. It was always so close and simple, like the fragrance of a certain sweet burnt on windy nights when the temperature drops to a level almost but not quite that of snow and the streets hold sound in a different way. For such things enlist no deities. Their truth is all in their simplicity, the richness they give to living, the richness that assures us living is always just a beginning.

~o~

Made of the softest wood and manifesting at every step how perishable it is, the star-stair winds upwards and upwards from the dirt floor of the marketplace, a crowded chaotic space where pigs roam at random, beggars and thieves are always jostling against wide-eyed strangers, small girls cradle baby sisters. The tower that houses the star-stair is a thin soaring structure of perhaps twenty-nine or sixty-six floors, reaching almost to the clouds. The young child named the Goddess of Dawn is said to live there at the summit and on a few occasions has been seen by visitors. All the tower's passageways are remarkably small, designed perhaps for 5-year-olds while adults need to hunch over tightly to make their way up the stairs. The intervening floors are said to contain the world in miniature.

Every three years the building is first emptied, then burnt to the ground so that a new offering to the sky can be created—either because the wood perishes or because of a fear that magic slips from everything faster than water glides through the fingers of our hands. A new child is then found to be the Goddess. The mysterious thousand rooms that symbolize the world must be shaped once more. In this way the sea that goes away comes back.

~o~

Returning by boat from Egypt and the Kingdoms of lower Africa I felt listless and ill at ease to be once more on familiar Italian soil. Then in the nightmarkets of Brundisium I came across an at first scarcely intelligible treatise on geography. Carefully inscribed on its front cover was its date of publication: MMMXCV: but from what era or what land? Slowly I began to accumulate a library of books from the future. In them I read of a sequence of world devastations, of the disappearance of the human species not once but several times and, connected to this phenomenon, of the philosopher Irenaeus of Chalcedony who taught that the chief error of the ancients from Socrates to Aristotle, from the cynics to the malcontents, was to imagine the ethical word belonged exclusively to man and not to life. "All imagine", he says at one point on page 77 of a vanishing treatise *On the Interpretation of Sand*, "as if individually they would die yet somehow the human species, the human word would survive forever. Let us suppose, instead, it is life not mankind that survives. Let us imagine that the ethical, the beautiful survives forever despite—or because of?—our perishing. Suppose one day in the wider trajectories of the cosmos the ethical, the beautiful will summon back snails, hillsides dotted with yellow flowers and birds with gracious wings, and perhaps, out of a lingering yearning for what passion brings, a young man and woman in their most intense lovemaking, their faces opened entirely to each other as if in those hours they could read in one unbroken gaze all that life utters, the infinite scripture of the world there in the tender curve of a beloved's face. In that scripture is the totality of surrender, a rippling outwards, what does not seek to clutch but to give."

~o~

We were on the highest terrace where the image of the sea glittered in a wide endless sweep. I do not know how long it was since the last flight of birds had gone, tracing their way beyond the horizon of the visible. Certainly for what seemed an immense trajectory of time nothing stirred or changed beyond the narrow world of the terrace with our few movements of the head or an arm, our slight leaning towards or away from each other, perhaps the momentary gesture of touching a plate of food only to draw back from it. The woman who sat beside me moved forward at one moment as if to kiss me only to draw back, just as our hands, though exquisitely shaping the same air, remained separate. I do not know her age exactly but she seemed very young and kept slipping backwards into the unguarded instant of being an adolescent, almost a girl, ready to love and go on to marry, have children, while I, whatever my real age, drifted steadily into being an old man, half paralysed, my face creased and life-worn, with only a few brief years left. It was a transformation she sensed in me over which I had no control. But a delicacy of absolute longing and stillness held us enraptured for those hours that were at once, though neither our words nor our gestures said this, one unbroken outpouring of love and leave-taking. For so many years, the long years of bitter aloneness, I hated myself for this shame, this desertion by life when life had summoned me. Now at the ending of days I sense only the beauty of her face, the mutual truth of blessing.

~o~

Facing the dark and naming it, I remind myself, doesn't mean wanting to live there. The beauty of the earth is seamless and obeys no logos. It prepares its own remedies—the dream cure, the writing cure, restoration through music. So the return of the sea follows the charter of the moon and tenderness lets life flow back. Inwardly we walk the earth as many people. Outwardly in dimensions visible

and invisible our speech, when it has left demands and grievances
behind, continues.

(FROM LUCIUS OF OCAMPO, *Interrogating a lost life—notes towards an autobiographic philosophy*)

X

On recovering from an illness

I think somewhere I am arranging
a small puppet show on a tiny altar,
the right size to slip undiscovered
past the guardians of my convalescence.

Mushrooms, asparagus, bread, a reliable mop:
such are the ordained necessities of the day—
these simple orders that exhaust me.
I peer up towards the spare
walrus suit hanging in a corner of the room.
It is necessary to keep some defences.

To disintegrate undetected requires more planning
than a sparrow brings
to a lifetime of foraging.

(FROM A MANUSCRIPT ASCRIBED TO CATULLUS, *The Sirmione Notebook*)

XI

The House of Abandoned Gods

All those household gods which are abandoned, left on hillsides
or discarded under bridges after nightfall, gods that have become
unfashionable, chipped at the edges or wanting a thumb or the hem

of a dress, gods whose names have been forgotten or whose power bled long ago into the fields that surrounded their rain-bedraggled gaze. There is Anunka, god of lost plates, and Bibi, the blind god who grasps the world through the slight sounds the sun makes as it filters down on objects. And there are the gods that protect sleeping children from walls that shift at night, forgotten now in abandoned houses or found years later by new tribes who know nothing of the perils of shifting walls and floors.

He began the task of bringing them home. The shed he built for them was little more than a shelter from the rain, constructed on a hillside overlooking the harbour so the gods might enjoy the company of the waves and the cheerful commentary of seabirds. As the shed started to overflow with gods, he took to placing them on vacant lots between the coast road and the sea. Little by little anonymous offerings arrived and life returned to them.

The man who collected the gods had been a ferryman but was forced to live on land when his ferry sank in a freak storm. As is well known, the Imperial cult of Zeus the Awakener holds no sway over water and those who entrust themselves to rivers or seas must find more ancient, more obscure gods to invoke. When the ferryman began to live on dry land it was the abandoned gods that spoke to him. Seeing them in ditches or rubbish heaps at the back of houses or left to decay on sidewalks, he felt the need to bring them home.

In one place, just south of the main harbour, the road divided the bluff where the abandoned gods sat looking out at the sea from an immense temple built to honour Zeus the Awakener, the official state divinity. Despite the monumentalism of his surroundings, Zeus began to long for the simplicity, the unmediated carelessness of the abandoned gods. They had all day to savour the play of wind and weather, to taste the minimal varieties of impromptu offerings, while each day Zeus had the same carefully regulated quota of oil and animal fats to reach his nostrils.

Gradually it became clear to him that true gods need to be abandoned to regain that openness that connects them to the numerous worlds through which we move, visible and invisible.

(MANETHO, *Collected Syrian Fables*, TEXT STORED IN THE LIBRARY OF ALEXANDRIA)

XII

A wolf is talking to me about my fear of becoming trapped in the borrowed pantomime suit of a cat. My paws are barely strong enough to cup a few mouthfuls of milk to my insatiable lips. The wolf listens to my anxieties. "Only when you find happiness," he counsels, "will your fears be strong enough to destroy you."

*

My father's face, becoming alive in mine, understands what fear is. We both look clearly into the small space inside the palm of a child's hand. At any age, when you have lost the way, death is the first but not the last thing that opens.

*

Let me know the gifts you leave behind you. The rat people are hard to understand—tiny scurriers who pass along the edges of dwelling places or store their meagre gatherings in roofs. Endlessly they converse about the observed and the unobservable. Were they rats who through long observation became people or a different tribe of hominids who chose to maintain their kinship with rats? How they grieved over death, and every death made them smaller and stronger. Ferrying nuts from trees and scraps from tables, they paused at the sound of another creature falling, falling and dying, while their own eyes opened into the thin grey shining of one more dawn.

*

The black wall is lifted into place among the furniture of the tiny one-room house of the unembittered heart. Rain falls through the head onto a white page. The whiteness laps up the rain as if it could never have enough. Two people make love with their lips searching the ceiling for undiscovered erotic tremors. Their bodies have merged into the beams of the house which rocks and pants furiously under the warm blanket of rain.

*

Do not underestimate the track carved by a dissident numerology. Out there it shines towards you. Its names have been lost but keep recurring in signs along the main highways. Memory guides you so strongly in the damaged world, the open unsheltered zone where you thought you could not live. The alignment of the most remote planets glimmers in the tilting cup of wine you balance against the night wind. Maybe it is a prayer whispered into oracle bones when the word "love" was first invented in China, maybe that is what saves you.

Leonidas the self-exiled, a guest that evening with the Essene Community of Qomqwakum, began the commentary, the first *peripateia*:

These are indeed a strange selection of texts that the dice have chosen for us—all found as they are on the one papyrus copied it seems from a scroll originating in the great deserts of the north. I shall start with the first text, then proceed immediately towards the last, according to the principle that opposites are always joined.

The wolf in this story comes towards us across an entirely domesticated landscape. Violence and evil have left only a light dusting on his pelt. Of all beings the least to be trusted, it is he who utters truth. Is it a truth intended only to destroy, an anticipatory curse aimed at that moment when happiness within the world seems for once possible? Who can be sure? I also note that this wolf has abandoned the outward strategies of kill and consume. For him, true destruction comes from within. And what savagery in his caution that human fulfilment, that simple longing called happiness among mortals, should create the fissure through which death comes.

"The gifts you leave behind you", "fear", the "white page" and "alignment"—it is this configuration I would like to hold up to our scrutiny for a brief moment. Hearing these words I was cast into the remembrance of a certain cave I visited, the resting place for one of those blank walls most revered by the Phokaians. Perhaps because of the intricate layers of its language, or because of the interminable journey that opens for those who venture into communion with its being, Phokaia is rightly called "the smallest island but the largest continent". And this is because the Phokaians have learned how to value. No creature there is considered beyond the realms of kinship.

In our text the rat is the double of the wolf, an inspirer of dread, yet here again the rat becomes an exemplar of attentiveness, diligence, compassion. At the point where the rat enters the story we pass through the great transformation—fear gives way to eros. And how curious that the text should end with that most ancient dispute—which people, which language first developed the word "love"? For duty, power, control, responsibility exist in all languages, yet "love" carves a slower trajectory across the human sky. And yet our text bestows the honour on China, far back in that legendary time when words first inscribed themselves into the bones of all things, at the moment when the great symbols arose to hold the Four Heavens in balance, the moment that is co-temporal with the hour when the Sun takes back the earth.

(AT THIS POINT THE MANUSCRIPT RECORDING THE LONG CONVERSATIONS OF THE QOMQWAKUM GATHERING BECOMES TORN AND ILLEGIBLE. PAPYRUS NO 4759, THE SECRET LIBRARY TRUST OF LOWER EGYPT.)

FOOTNOTE: Would Leonidas the self-exiled have visited Qomqwakum? At first blush it looks unlikely. All the biographies agree that he died on Phokaia, never returning to participate in the intellectual life of Athens or Alexandria. It is possible that he began a journey at some stage to return to the Greek homelands but went no further than the Nubian centre of Qomqwakum before abandoning the idea.

The desire to include famous philosophers in late antiquity dialogues is notorious. However, the fame of Qomqwakum as a place of open interchange between all traditions and all peoples may well have inspired Leonidas to a brief visit. It may help solve the riddle of how his writings came to be disseminated across the ancient worlds, arriving quite rapidly at that other island, Abukar, off the shores of Eusebius where Omeros Eliseo responded to the thread.

(W O'S, AMONG HIS LAST PAPERS)

XIII

Small as the sky folded over,
sheltered
from wind and time:
our two bodies
as we love.

~o~

There are people laughing in the darkness,
an ancient laughter
full of stars and stones.

~o~

Small bits and pieces that wear away the infinite—
this greyness that wears it away—
anxiety that rubs it thin,
rubs it to nothing.

On a bleak day when even pretences are too far,
how they mock us
coming to us over the waters,

invisible whispers of bone song.

(IRENE PHILOLOGOS, FROM *A poetic journal of ten years in Boeotia*)

XIV

Twelve parasangs north of Armenian Rum lies the city of Mirdek and its inhabitants, the Arebatoi. Their language contains only half the vocabulary of other languages since they regularly use one word to signify the contradictory extremes of a singular endeavour. Thus in their language to advise is the same word as to ignore, to long for could also mean to shun, to admire to loathe. Likewise for them terror sounds the same as worship, joy as despair. Certainly misunderstandings and confusion abound in their discourse yet they consider such experiences merely a normal part of existence, the guesswork that enriches a life.

Living in an extended haze between trust and distrust, always threatened by a collapse into wordlessness, for many generations the Arebatoi depended for their inner security on landscape and, chiefly, their sacred mountain. The mountain ran alongside all the windows of their life. Every room in the city looked onto it. The inhabitants glanced upwards to its slopes to read off the coming weather, the hour of the day, the stages of their life. To live without the mountain would be to feel such loneliness, such devastation, water would no longer taste like water and your own face would wander off, no longer able to find its way back from the depths of mirrors.

When magicians arrived wanting to buy the mountain for an undisclosed sum, the Archon of the city and his advisers were soon persuaded to accept the transaction. With much talk of "progress" and "unlocking the wealth of the land", they quickly constructed the semblance of a majority to support their plans. Promises were made that the wealthiest ten percent of the Arebatoi would reap unimaginable financial rewards, yet the payments were all in Eusebian currency, committing those so paid to buy back, on a ninety-nine year lease, the intellectual property right to breathe air, now classified as a distinctly Eusebiolan invention. One morning the inhabitants awoke to find a hole in the earth where their mountain had been. Grief, anger, bewilderment overwhelmed them.

"Look", the Archon said, "how our people rejoice in their new-found freedom."

(FRAGMENT FOUND IN PAPYRI PRESERVED IN THE NESTORIAN MONASTERY OF TABRIZ, AUTHOR UNKNOWN)

XV

Equinoctial

painscapes and lovescapes
rounded together—autumnal, almost.
All over the wastage
beginnings,
iconographic—
a child's game with broken bricks,
a bird singing over a drainpipe.

Across the jagged Empires
one by one they commit to their truths—
great compounded decisions
of a thousand small minds,
how much ruin can you bring?

In two open hands
the universe pours.
Sandtime in the fingers' clutching.
Small face with one tear,
how much blessing in your gaze?

(PHILEMON OF MAURETANIA)

XVI

You liked the music from the wrong side of the city, the side we couldn't visit because of the war. You brought back from there a long-fluted gold horn and we had to take it apart carefully, bit by bit, to make sure there wasn't any magical destruction hidden inside it. I was both your border guard and your lover, drawn to the shining whiteness of your breasts, the glittering forbidden parts into which you had been. You knew how to get past all the borders and road blocks, your serenity untroubled by the rigid Imperial pronouncements that governed our lives. To see you was to see a nakedness that shone to me, this dazzling you had no say in that lit up the world.

(FROM *The Annals of Phearcus*, LOCATION, AUTHORSHIP AND DATE UNKNOWN, FOUND AMONG DISCARDED PAPYRI IN THE LIBRARY OF TARSUS)

XVII

The boat that is all leaks
still rows us across the river into Paradise

There at the edges of earth,
in a space where the knotted, the twisted
becomes all openness,
simple as hands signing on silence

we wake in these empty rooms,
transfigured,
discovering how the palms of our hands
fuse in tenderness, giving off light.

Almost the house of a single sigh.
Twins now, death-joined,
folded into the shape of the forgotten,

the small pure leaves spin over us.
How little of the world we clutch after all,
this half-inch of air grasped by our mouths.

Going,
taking not even the leaves that fall against the window
and still saying:
"Your eyes, your eyes,
your beautiful luminous eyes."

~o~

The lightning in the orchard

Applelife we shared it
the halved and pitted
shedding white decades between us
cautiously you picked its syllables
off the faultlines in your teeth
from the black and speechless
stump-hole where the mouth
begins its hesitant
lean into death

Fragrance my nostrils gulp
like the last of air
humanly
be with me
tenderly
nuzzle my wounds

Tongue me with applescent
press the ripening of your breasts
against my lips
kiss me into blossoming

Let the spirit dog whose pawprints mark your left shoulder
burrow his saddest eyes
into the hollow where the collarbone sleeps

Trace in your fingertips
the stargod rising
the torso's desperate swim
to live beyond the skull

~o~

The scar-sky

Hiding under tables, curled up in corners,
blunt as a stitched thumb and singing among stars,
my wounded double, the scar-sky,
you are deathless and could be horror
if I didn't name you and walk with you.

When my lover folds me delicately
into the curve of her breasts and side,
you are there as old wounds in the palm of my hand,
as the twisted arch of an ankle resting under her thigh.

Vast dark tapestry of past and future loss,
you are the faint line a single hammerblow
makes in the stone pavement,
intimate as an eyelash falling
against my lover's infinitely tender face.

~o~

If at nightfall

If a man
If at nightfall a man
If a man at nightfall should turn
    should turn into a jug of water drunk by unknown lips
    in houses where the dawn is about to set out
If the dawns reflected in the eyes of those who have drunk
    a man's silence, a man's helplessness
    decide it is time to set out
If what sets out
    is already moisture and drinking and unlit houses waiting

If a man at nightfall
If a man at nightfall should stop before he turns
    before he turns away into distances that do not know him
If the sweetness of drinking should pass silently across walls
    in the tremor of a star
    and stand in a different house unlit as yet even by the future

If a man breathing softly should speak into the water at nightfall
    in the tremor of a star
and the three steps of walking should pass into the brimming
    water
If the water should carry not only moisture
    and drinking and unlit waiting
    but a word-thread trailing backwards

then ...

(PHILEMON OF MAURETANIA, *Four Poems*)

XVIII

… they will stand at a window suddenly gazing at the line of darkness over nearby hills, enthralled as if the sky had never taken hold of the earth before. Other times groups of them will engage in elaborate high-pitched conversations that cease as mysteriously as they began. Their camaraderie is intense and touchingly stylised, though briefly a look of dejected aloneness will assail them. For in fact this club of dedicated banqueters is only a random assemblage of those visited by a gift or curse peculiar to this land: years, decades before it happens each knows already the precise hour and manner of his death. Sometimes a young man of twenty will awaken with the knowledge that in fifteen years his head will split open in a fall from a chariot. Every detail is present to him: the watching crowd, the angle of the rock, the blood seeping from the wound, the hours of delirious fever, the steady rotting of the flesh—all are visible so exactly that there is no doubt of the reality he has stumbled across. And such knowing comes to him not once but day after day all those fifteen years till the moment of his death. Of course people have tried changing the course of their life this way or that to avoid the end foreseen. Occasionally they succeed in bringing it forward a little, substituting perhaps a fall from a very high building for a fall from a chariot but mostly this does not happen. Suicide is an elective many discuss but very few take up. Depression might be considered the natural state of mind of this group and yet the determination to place one brick on another outweighs gloom.

Now it happens that within the numbers of what may be called this club a distinct group possesses an additional gift. They foresee not only their own death but a collective event in which city by city, village by village, all of mankind vanishes. Discussions abound as to the likely remedies. Some propose anchoring the earth by strong cables to the moon and replenishing the earth each month with the moon's reflected blaze. Others advocate the abandonment of all previous activities and the practice of the deepest psychic withdrawal. What they see damages them yet they channel this damage into a glow of purposive contemplation. If the avoidance of world collapse is to be possible it must start from this group.

(FRAGMENT FROM THE ETRUSCAN EDITION OF PAUSANIAS' *Days and Nights on Atlantis*)

XIX

In the shrieking forest
a branch breaks off—

in your hand
it grows calm.

~O~

A fire burning in a field of sand.
On all sides night draws close.

~O~

Little misplaced animals
wandering a road lit by stars—
two steps along the way
you are already past your end-point.
The puddles of darkness
wash strength into your feet.

What is hidden
forgives.

(IRENE PHILOLOGOS, FROM *A poetic journal of ten years in Boeotia*)

XX

Changing house

They need a small bus to carry the bones of all the fish
that have been eaten in this house.
When a house moves
it must bring all its detritus with it—
the ash of all the wood burnt in every fireplace,
the grease of the five thousand chickens
broiled in the memory of the dynasty.
Chains to hold the boat by the river must come
along with the light garland of leaves
that greeted a homecoming,
the marriage sheets, slippers woven
for the infant feet of the princess who now
wonders where her grandchildren have vanished.

In the slow train
of carts, covered wagons, winding files of bundles
strapped to the backs of mules and servants,
small objects must be placed.
So many presences must feel at home in this journey:
the boy who gathered the names of all the insects,
the father in his wicker chair still presiding
over his dream of ownership and giving,
an old lady wrapped in a whispering shawl of fire.

And there are doors that have fallen into long-collapsed rooms,
doors that must be found now, their frames restored
and brought back to form a passage for the sun.
For a house flows out into the trees that surround it
and the fragrance of pollens caught by a spring day
becomes a part of the invisible cornerstone—
like the dust settled in the space between ill-fitting bricks,

like the open hands that found other hands
in rooms that are now
all sunlight.

(FROM DIONYSIUS THE FORGOTTEN, *The Book of Odes*)

XXI

They buried him far down so he could see a long way up, through grasses that looked like bubbles of air, through layers of soil and clay, this shaft where light fell on him. The further down he was the more powerful the light. During all those years of his living on the surface, the ocean that dominates the planet had spoken to him in its wave-breaths. Now, deep inside earth, how beautiful and simple to feel the sun penetrating all beings to their core—the pebbles, rocks and clusters of forgotten seed all moving like fish through the transfigured emptiness of soil and stone.

(FROM "A CONVERSATION BETWEEN DION AND THE SYRACUSAN ELDERS", PAPYRUS FRAGMENTS FROM LOWER EGYPT, IN THE LOEB EDITION, *The Socratic Diaspora: previously uncollected writings by Plato*, LONDON, 1933)

~O~

According to the learned account of Xantipater of Naxos no difference exists between land and sea when seen by the angels sent by the Ens Soph. Alike both kingdoms stretch downward through many layers of floating elements—two porous fragilities into which time vanishes. Across millennia we swim through earth and the rhythm of the waves attunes our breath to the pitch of a sheltering inner sea. There the turtle, the stone, the glittering hands of lovers, the eyes of young girls wander in the perpetual newness of all that awaits them. Now, just as the ocean has its own purpose, so the earth speaks to the sun and welcomes it deep into its being. On

every side vast wells and pathways lie open, visible to those who see
with the vision of angels.

(FROM FRAGMENTS ATTRIBUTED TO THE PUPILS OF PLOTINUS)

XXII

In the quiet space
between autumn and autumn
whose face hasn't sometime
woken into the purity of strangeness,
a white mask that takes the measure of clay?
Among sacred scraps, the ants' scattered nibblings,
suddenly to stop, almost catching a music
always there at the edge of hearing,
the guessed-at rising single-mindedly
into nowhere.

We could have lived in the tiniest kingdom
nursing a tenderness
the size of two leaves joined.
Coming down forest paths
on any ordinary day we might meet
the god of the summer rain.
There (had we known who we were,
how the sky goes)
we might have asked for the small golden flower
whose touch heals
this inner winter.

(OMEROS ELISEO, POEM 16, FROM *19 Poems of Life and an Ode to calm
temporarily confused ghosts*)

XXIII

For some time now the stars had been moving away from their usual resting places. Less and less of the known world remained to gaze into his bewilderment, to speak to him, to answer back. During the long months of silence, the tree opposite the window where he would sit had leant further and further into the secret sky of burning water. Inextinguishable strangeness drew closer to the roots of the green budding world that had since childhood been the backdrop to his writing. Every gesture towards speech, towards writing, fell aside, abandoned before it started, a useless endangering of all he loved. Words as they appeared to him read simultaneously as a curse in the mirror language that lay behind speech. And while he was silent the world left him. Stones found paths that led deep into his hand. He remembered the river that had lost its way on earth, its faith that it would continue in some other place on the far shore of the desert or all-circling ocean that had erased its name.

(Manetho of Alexandria, *On the final silence of Virgil*)

XXIV

One day soon the trees will look at me
as I once looked at them—
the first opening, the last closing of the eyelids.
Returned to the first simplicity
of stepping beyond me
what it was that moved in me to see their gaze
echoes out into the wide
comprehension of leaves.

The years have spliced me, my face a stone
fallen through too many rings of water.
In the eyes of the trees it will be clear

that time was always jumbled—
the earth that holds me then,
bone or ash or shadow,
will as at the first moment
receive all their gaze.
This blessing from beyond us that flows through us,
life opening onto life.

(ERYCTHEMIOS, *Knowings* BOOK III)

XXV

A true Emperor has no need for extensive domains. When the Hung
Nu invaded, the Emperor Sartorius redefined his boundaries so they
corresponded exactly to his shadow. All night his kingdom remained
a mere possibility. By day it crossed the landscape of a devastated
realm, bringing to all those it fell on the blessings of good governance.
Even today among the Armeniani there are those who by chance
have stepped into the late afternoon shadow of Sartorius, their lives
forever transfigured and made straight. Well known are the numerous
Emperors who, following betrayal and defeat, re-established their
Empires within the sacred space marked out by stones on a mountain
top. In the annals of Enobius it also states that true Emperors do
not require their rule to last for prolonged epochs. The Emperor Wu
Li's Kingdom covered the entire earth but lasted only the time it
takes for a leaf to fall from an oak tree to the soil beneath. In those
few moments his decree on the irreversibility of truth was recognised
somewhere in the deep recesses of all stones and water.

*

When a windmill wishes to travel (to visit her cousins in Egypt for
example) she must first ensure several weeks of stillness across her
chosen corridor of sky. Pitching in high seas on moonless nights of
polar blizzards will never do. The sails of a windmill were not made

to slice through oceans of madness or to maintain balance when the earth has lost its centre. A thin maiden of salt feels understandably squeamish travelling five miles on horseback. How much more conspicuous a squat windmill must feel having always a blank-faced infinity before it and only its love of repetition to sustain itself. If it could be lowered into the ocean at the right angle then perhaps it might discover the art of swimming, its muscular arms propelling it into the calm that exists when objects find their own current.

*

On days when the Rituals cease to have efficacy what words will you use when you meet a ghost on the white road?

A true Emperor doesn't need a large country.

Millions of battle-cautious dots will never make a solid stream.

How does water connect us to stars? How does darkness belong?

In the fabled city of Eternal Order the light from interminable waste zones belied the arched bridges of its maps.

All the Iconographies tell us that the mountain is there for climbing. What to do when instead it inverts itself, offering only a laborious descent to the place of origins?

Still, and in stillness, a broken staircase unites.

If you search for medicines when you have pain, what will you do with the terror that comes when you have joy?

(FRAGMENTS FOUND AMONG PAPYRI IN THE NESTORIAN MONASTERY OF TABRIZ, AUTHOR(S) UNKNOWN)

NOTE: For the phrase "A true Emperor does not need a large country" compare Mencius Book One, section 5, "To be a true emperor, even a hundred square miles can be land enough." (*Mencius*, translated by David Hinton, p. 8) (W O'S)

XXVI

Death of the unicorn

The unicorn has found his way into a clearing between terrified stars. Fissures of a sudden unique calamity run in all directions. Darkness and a stiff icy wind have thinned down whatever language is left to the world. Beyond the singing of the river is the gathering bass note of leaves falling. If only he could bury his ivory horn deep in the flesh of the tree called Wandering. If only somewhere still held the strength to welcome an outdated Immortality. The unicorn, fading into the air's white breath, maintains the balance of his singularity, a tremulous attention to all he will never see, that strange inexplicable tenderness being born the other side of the dark.

(GREGORIUS OF LIMOUSIN, FROM *Poems written in summer of the year 1000*)

XXVII

There are words—
we don't know what they are—
and summers—
we don't know if we'll get there—
and doorways left open
into bright courtyards
and an arrangement that looks like life
though the water is rising past our ankles.
Through all the thirteen tiers of the serried hillside,
sleep, we can't find you.

The distances are what they are:
magical.

(IRENE PHILOLOGOS, FROM *A poetic journal of ten years in Boeotia*)

BOOK VII

I

Sandgrains endlessly reshuffling
on the edge of departure,
these wind-shaped gestures:

from the great world chosen
the black space of the poem.

(EXCERPT FROM *The Secret Book of Infinite Space*)

II

Is there no human equivalent for the lifting of anguish and pure seeking and pure addressing from earth to stars that is the howling of dogs?

If the stars come down to us as rain, especially the white dawn rain of frost, earth returns towards the stars in the howling of dogs and in the fundamental pitches of the great grief words, the wordless words that don't refer but simply mirror and are.

Even photographs of our own body, the scar marks, the fissures and abnormalities, tiny specks of light or dark that might mean the irreversible progress of death within us, imitate stars laid out across a night sky.

By bringing the stars into consideration when speaking of dogs, it helps earth and sky recognise kinship. So we *see* in a different light.

Placed in relationship to stars, dogs appear neither our inferiors nor simply our more trustworthy equals, but rather as reaching out beyond where we can reach. The pitch of their howling addresses the stars. In this they move beyond us.

Equally the wordlessness of what they say as they howl may give their lamentation an authenticity our own clumsy grappling with speech blocks from us.

Those species of dog especially who must grapple with the threat of extinction might be seen as simply going before us, reaching a space humanity may enter soon enough, and so they speak from a place we have not yet learned to find a voice for.

(EXCERPT FROM *The Blue Notebooks* OF LEONIDAS, ADAPTED BY W O'S)

III

The route most people took into the village was a simple straight road, only you could not walk it. The surface would not support the pressure of feet or else the earth was simply too sacred to walk on. It was necessary to wait for a spirit being to pick you up and hold you delicately in mid-air and so cradle you into the village. The spirit beings appeared as horses that left no marks on sand. Your body glided onto their back. You fused slowly with their silent and bristling skin. You were at home in your childhood long ago even if you had waited seventy or a hundred years for a spirit horse to appear. You were somewhere enclosed within the air and also standing already in the village we call "Arrival".

No one can say exactly why this village claims us so deeply. Sometimes a man would be untangling his socks in the morning as one does and a great cloud would roll across their milky grey surface. He would notice sheep and tiny sheep dogs bounding across his ankle and, if he listened closely, he could hear shepherds calling across rocks and a lost river plummeting into darkness. In this village it was an everyday thing for time to just open, for fullness to appear in an empty basket on a blank floor. No one dies here—there are just different degrees of sleep, each of them familiar and safe. But the strangest thing is how in kissing one person all others feel that kiss, a tenderness that redoubles and extends itself, flowing through all the dry, so long invisible sand of the earth.

(MANETHO, *Commentary on "The Secret Book of Infinite Space"*)

IV

Nightmares

From the high gatepost the severed horse's head dressed in its small lace underwear, torn and fouled with blood, went on talking with her. To live among corpses seemed the most that she deserved. So many children were playing on the other side of the fence. They had voices. Their bodies easily and comfortably floated up into the clouds and yet would come down again just in time for supper. When she felt the grey sharp-beaked bird walking inside her and noticed that her chest was missing, it seemed the most natural development. For so many years she had lived with a small glass body. She had to carry it so carefully from the tiny shelf in the stable where she slept at night to the riverbank where she washed the mistress' clothes. They called her "the little child whose home is darkness".

(MANETHO, *Collected Syrian Fables*, TEXT STORED IN THE LIBRARY OF ALEXANDRIA)

V

Ballad of the Three Marias

This little turtle has no sea—
place him gently in a cart,
let the cart set out

into the land where there is only stone and sand,
let it roll over dry earth, across boulders, shattered ground,
out to an open space
where the sky will take pity and send him a turtle-sized sea.

Three Marias appear on the road,
three Marias out walking
looking for the river that was.
Where the river should be
only stone and dry grass.
They say, "Where is this river?
Where are the fish that swam here,
the reeds that wrapped and twined around our feet
when we came here to wash and taste the coolness?"

One gives a handkerchief to the other—
it passes through the third Mary's body.
One gives a comb to the other—
a butterfly flutters out
from the opening in the forehead.

The three Marias are sitting on three stones.
Each has forgotten the name of her lost son.

Above the sand
spirit fish spin in the rivers of air.
A fish knows how to carry coolness deep inside its body,
how water glides
even when it can't be seen.
The spirit fish are whispering the names of all the stars.

A stone shines where the water goes on living.
The son travels the bright skies
towards the birthplace of names.

(from an Armenian songbook found in the Coptic library
at Erzerum)

VI

How do you live in a country that is travelling backwards? Each day it loses more of itself. Year by year its leaders strive to remove whatever elements of justice or compassion its people had slowly acquired. It prides itself on destruction and believes every reality can be renamed. So the great vanishing grows.

(LEONIDAS THE SELF-EXILED, *The Grey Notebook*)

VII

Is there a single word for infinite space? τὸ ἄπειρον maybe, no line. But it must also be very small. Your hand goes around it and what strokes you back, what enfolds you, what reaches you instantly through the pores of your skin, draws all you are, all your past into limitlessness. You go through a first door, then a second, then a third. You know where you stand is infinite. There is no need to move at all.

Sometimes we have called it the vast, the all-seeing, the starting point, or else the falling into place, the space waves make as they collapse on sand, the tree just there outside stirring slightly in afternoon breeze, teaching us all this.

(ARISTOBULUS, *On the Nature of Being*)

VIII

How much precious care of days, of weeks, of lifetimes do we need to give us this brief wordless space of lovemaking?

(INSCRIPTION ON A CAVE WALL, CENTRAL CAPPADOCIA, C. 32 AD)

IX

Naked and shining, cleansing yourself under the waterfall,
you leant me a beautiful song.
I do not understand a single word of it.
I will have to invent the wavering line
that carries me across the darkness.
In your new-given speech
skies explode all along their torn edges.
Fears travel the jagged curve of my veins.
Each place I stop
is moored to the sky with small nails.
Daylight threads itself from your glances.
I have seen how hesitantly you move forward
bringing each foot
into a space of blessing
from the god of each new twist of earth.

(FROM ERYCTHEMIOS, *Knowings*, BOOK III)

X

All roads, even the most inward, the invisible, disappear in this
place. Every means of transport is useless. It is necessary to *become*.

(INSCRIPTION ON THE EASTERN GATE TO THE HOLY CITY OF KITEZH)

XI

Definitions—symbols left out from the Imperial Dictionary

the concealed path that attracts a forest

graceful chaos

to release dawn, the blessing-curse of a leaf falling

a fatal disease that offers inextinguishable happiness

to impersonate birds that have a disdainful attitude to ponds with a reddish tinge

to let one's hands soak in paint all night before dampening the brushes, to interrogate blank walls on where the heart should be centred, to accept sunlight as the most delicate of murals

a trio of strangers who agree to admire sunset together

a howling at the edge of darkness to remind the sun that earth still has kept readied for it a pillow and a soft bed

on a path where thistles wound the traveller, to touch the hem of a woman's skirt that her heart may free itself of bitterness

(FROM *The Fragmentaria of Posonius*)

XII

To understand this troubling book, we must suppose a people for whom it is common knowledge that God exists. For them it makes no more sense to say "Is there a God?" than "Is there a sky?" or "Does water exist?" They walk around, they live, they see God, he talks to them, they answer back, he comes up one hour, goes down another, they go to a pond and scoop up a mouthful of God because they need to drink. And though it seems to them God only entered their world quite recently, it also seems that God was there stretching back to the time when landscapes were made. Coming from outside strangers often asked, "I see the water and the sky and the earth of your land, but what is this God you keep having conversations with?"

Over the course of long stays strangers observed that the conversations with God became more intense, of greater duration, when things went wrong. When lightning destroyed cattle, when flood washed away part of a village, when a plague broke out or a child died, the conversations became ferociously sharper or vanished altogether. What was this presence, harsh as the blighting sun when all water sinks far into the land, what was this being that arose above all at the centre of tragedy?

Suppose God is a synonym for Life, but Life understood and experienced in a very specific way, with extraordinary intensity, with a dazzling inability to do anything but surrender before its power. And, when understood as God, Life becomes a person, a voice speaking to us. It locates itself in the depths of the ocean. It whispers as a breeze opening doors.

Within this world to say God does not exist is like saying Life does not exist, a perfectly intelligible proposition but difficult to live with. And so, pinned down by the inexplicable wave of suffering that descends on him, Job faces a choice—to curse Life and die, or to continue praising Life. Job clings to the belief that Life is good, and Life allows Job to come close and talk with him. From the depths of pain Job speaks to Life and asks what this suffering means. (The transition between God and Life is perhaps most of all a matter of gender. In the languages I know the word for "life" is feminine, the word for "god" masculine.)

Job must speak to God in some language and God must answer back in some language—but which language? It seems reasonable to suppose that God has no intrinsic preference for Greek over Latin, Hebrew over Aramaic, Sanskrit over crypto-Nubian. The language spoken by the aboriginal inhabitants of the trans-Bactrian oases would seem as close to his heart as Homeric Greek or old Etruscan. It would be difficult not to assert that God would be equally at home in the elaborate grammar of turtles as in the speech of finches, that the soaring discourse of the eagle carries no more and no less charm than the meditative vibration of hornets.

Most importantly, God must exist just as comfortably in languages where there is no word for God, where the possibility of

God cannot arise even as the remotest object of thought. Perhaps those are the languages closest to God's heart, the languages he casts spells in when he speaks from inside a whirlwind.

~o~

At certain moments, perhaps when accidentally in some altered realm, I have felt a white softness enfold me. For those moments nothing can touch or disturb that enfolding, and perhaps each thing that is beautiful enough endures within us, in a way that no anger or violence altogether destroys.

What was it that Job touched that gave him such freedom from inner destruction?

To be Job is not only to suffer unthinkable cruelties. It is also to be connected in some indestructible way to one's own inner heaven, the only one that matters, the one that is here and now and outside of time all at once.

For those of us who don't know how to say the word "God" but who also intuit that Job addressed a reality that spoke from whirlwinds, what is that reality?

~o~

It is one thing to write about Job from the outside, but from his Book it is clear that Job was a poet and the poets that follow him, like all good poets, want to write from the inside. For a poet to write about Job is like inviting all the forces that bring death and tragedy to enter one's life. Knowingly even to begin a mere two-line epigram on Job is to ask plague, possession by devils, death from avalanche on a mountain pass, the sudden appearance of Hittite archers in an overcrowded agora, a worm invasion of the veins behind the eyes, to enter one's being, to snap the hinges of the door and take possession of one's house. For it is not possible to write a poem about Job from other people's sufferings. And the cunning wisdom of the prophet requires that it is not enough to take on the suffering that comes to oneself alone, the lonely man's pain, the transient one who has had many years to get used to being cursed. It is necessary that death seize one's children and that the pustules of blighting erupt along the skin and in the eyes of those you love. For these good reasons no poet should wilfully try to write about Job.

(FROM LEONIDAS THE SELF-EXILED, *Reflections on the Books of the Hebrews—the Book of Job*)

XIII

Burial Chamber

They come drifting towards us as stars come drifting across skies. They illuminate and darken at the same time. They perceive the blackened, the eradicated portions of their bodies. They perceive an earth where blackened, eradicated eyes and voices speak, answering each other across the curve of night. Above, a few stars, stubbed-out, abolished, still travel their own space, counterbalancing the earth's weight.

Our speech is a babble, a false summoning, wordshapes erected as an anti-tombstone over the great killing.

Two chairs sit opposite me—it could be they are waiting for the King and Queen of the dark—they look almost Minoan. The head-dresses that grace the absent shoulders will come later. Behind them a window looks out on our small share of the infinite. I assume that sooner or later the occupants will arrive. I am not sure, though, that any person could quite replace the luminous power of emptiness. No matter how strange or how monstrous, they would look too much like ourselves.

(FRAGMENT FROM *The Secret Book of Infinite Space*, OLD PERSIAN TEXT FOUND IN THE NESTORIAN MONASTERY OF TABRIZ)

XIV

Why does your sea not resemble mine? It seems to have an old soul. The rings under its eyes are too deep. As you speak a chill bleakness of shoreline and sky widens. My sea ripples and casts spells. Young boys are always diving into it from high wharves:

Reaching it from any angle of the world, I pause to catch its blue and delicately rising intonation. I stand breathless, accepting the blessing it offers. My sea does not believe in death.

(FROM LUCIUS OF OCAMPO, *Interrogating a lost life—notes towards an autobiographic philosophy*)

XV

There are many different kinds of water
only some of which it is comfortable to walk on.
When you stand motionless in many-layered water
you must be like a hummingbird, vibrating
with great energy to move forward.
If you turn altogether into a hummingbird
be sure to let the strips of different coloured water
know how at ease you are with their merely standing there.
They have every right to ignore your quest to move forward.
It is your choice, after all, to go once more
naked into the veins of earth
at the expense of your frantic heart
and all it imagines of space.
Healing yourself is why you came here with your daughter,
seeking the water that belongs to the underworld.
Where the red sky echoes with tiny blue finches
you will sit under the driest of trees,
your face suddenly stunned

by the thousand invisible insects spinning
great circles across the journey of your breath.

Life has so much more blossoming to do.

(APHRODITE OF SAMOTHRACE, *Approaching the source*)

XVI

The river divides him from himself.
Alone it understands
our hunger to vanish and endure.

(FROM *The Black Book of Ehtesum*)

XVII

There is no doubt that the hado-hado bird lives in a flurry of light.
Restless it paces the shadow cast by its own impatience to live always
at the zenith. Sometimes a lone bird will, through misadventure,
hasten the gathering darkness and the sharp edges of isolation and
despair will dangle jaggedly into its throat and eyes. Stunned it
does not understand what it is to be both living and dying. Its cry,
gathered in tiny bottles of exquisite slenderness, would surely cause
the world to stop if anyone should thoughtlessly shatter the glass.

(PLINY, *A Natural History of Atlantis*)

XVIII

Delegates were invited from among the country of the woodcarvers
to build a platform suitable to receive the greater and the lesser gods.
How should the beams be set and according to what alignment
would the participants in the ritual stand? When the woodcarvers

arrived they brought with them a wholely new set of questions. They assumed the gods would arrive in full daylight with no need of stars to orient their entry into the world of men. In their view everything about the platform would need to express openness to the universe while existing unremarkably at the intersection of infinite layers. Dignity must go hand in hand with the utmost simplicity. Arrogance as much as indifference blocks the gods' presence, for no title or status, no skill or elaboration can influence the gods to visit or to stay away. How then through the grace of design, through the bizarre richness of curves and shadows, invite that trance in which the complexity of the world is shot through with blessedness?

(FROM LUCIUS OF OCAMPO, *Interrogating a lost life—notes towards an autobiographic philosophy*)

XIX

Curled over himself as if his mother hadn't conceived him out of love, even his hands keep twisting over themselves. Truly he was born under the number 13 in the hour between two days, the hour lopped off from the tree of being.

In the village where he lived as a fisherman all knew him by the secret name Misfortune whispers to comfort itself when the wind's loneliness paces the roads.

In midsummer when sky and water merge, mistaking the reflection of the landing place for the landing place, he fell into the swift flowing river and became an otter. Sleek and rolling in water, he forgot his human shape.

Tumbling under waterfalls, he didn't interrupt his pursuit of wilder currents to listen to discussions of perfection.

The fragments of his smile break in eddies around him while sunlight and clarity stretch on all sides.

How else would an otter read water?

(JOSEPHUS OF ALEXANDRIA, "NOTES FOR AN ESSENE COMMENTARY
ON OVID's *Metamorphoses*")

XX

On arriving at the Nestorian Monastery, Gandhara

Each step is worthy of a lifetime's study—
the hairline cracks, the play of sun and a cloud's passage,
the way grey blends into white
and a shadowy luminosity glitters
intermittently just below the surface,
the weight of a million stones
resting under the guardianship of Heaven.

The foot studies the vertical face of the step,
estimating how it might feel, what it might cost
to master that elevation.
And at once I am transfixed inside my own shadow—
behind me, all the earth that I have known,
up ahead an infinity of steps
and at the top
somewhere
the origin of light.

Seen completely and in all its
nakedness,
one step should be enough.
There is no need to climb the stairs.

(MARINUS OF SAMARIA)

XXI

How did those who wanted to collect doorways, do so across the vast stretch of ancient time? For only recently have image-stealing devices arrived among us from the future, and for millennia to work pictures in clay, stone or papyrus was an expensive and rare luxury of the few, yet surely all people realise how important it is to hold clear in the memory the shape, curve, texture and number of all the doorways one has stepped through in one's life. Each doorway, each frame and passageway, has waited so long for our arrival, our sliding through; each has its own blessing and name. Each one bids farewell to us, peeling away one more invisible false skin that had encased us for so long.

The Pahoi, who live west of the Sarmenians not far from the Carpathian Mountains, carve markings into their arms and cheeks that each doorway should be remembered. One places one's hand on a scar or one looks at a scar and immediately a particular doorway returns. The Treviani, on the other hand, tried collecting sticks that they might speak to them of doors and arches but the infidelity of the broken is notorious. The Ligurians are said to have developed a special language wide and solid enough to hold doorways, and within this speech, it is said, those objects that are also moments of transition readily arrange themselves into easily memorised poems. During my visit to Liguria I made numerous inquiries about this language but none could recall hearing of it.

Strange indeed—all accept the necessity of an accurate account of the door and doors yet no proven method of retaining such knowledge seems to exist. Generally it is claimed that the good fortune of hunchbacks consists in the fact that, from birth, every door and arch they will step through has already been inscribed deeply into their spines. A blessing to others, it is a knowledge they have only one word for: pain.

(EXCERPT FROM BOOK XX OF *The Uncut Herodotus*, THE ETRUSCAN EDITION)

XXII

What happens to a book that claims to say everything? It breaks apart at the edges, like a space where the sky invades a building.

(FROM *The Secret Book of Infinite Space*)

XXIII

In that land each day they set off into the fields to gather colours. Once, long ago, when they first reached this upland valley at the foot of the sacred mountain, they had imagined collecting vegetables, cabbages perhaps or bitter olives, or lemons that might be cut to flavour water. Yet, once they drew close to the broken soil or the branches of trees, the heaviness of objects appalled them. Surely air was enough, they thought, or air and water with the occasional fish or the husks of grains left by others. Suddenly to grasp the substance of things felt like gorging on sadness. Like choosing to be the oversized walrus bloated on tiny fish that does not understand why it will never own their speed, their unencumbered darting between the rounded pebbles of ebb tide. They recalled then how, in certain legends of the Dravidians, the morning star only gained its happiness when it relinquished its claim to dwell on the earth's shoulder.

From remote surfaces blessings ripple. The trembling leaf and the great seabirds of solitude bear the curved shape of what nourishes them. Sometimes, in the arrival of waves, pools of light enter us with their buoyant knowledge. So the sky might have taught us that being everywhere is possible for those who have understood forgetting.

In the valley below the sacred mountain each day the fields stretched immense and unknowable before them. It was the aromas, the colours that dazzled and fed them. A certain shading of blue that had never existed in the world before, the shimmer of gold that plays along the edges of morning—such things travelled far into them, into those small places where death cannot altogether find us.

(XANTIPATER, *Among the Parthians*)

XXIV

(Jade emblem chosen by the dice—the weeping Poplars)

"It used to be that poplars were the most loquacious of trees. Always when a saint or holy man was buried a row of poplars would be planted to guide the weary people of the nearest town to his tomb so there might be shade for them to rest and let openness blossom within them. In this way the saint's spirit might more comfortably converse with them.

"Yet in this emblem the poplars weep. Unable to contain the grief words that for so long had beaten against them, they give way to a surge of inexplicable sadness. They weep even though their heads rest in the immense cool of evening. Now though poplars are straight and narrow, possessing the greatest formal eloquence, their roots spread wide and indeed they have been called in the phrase of Virgil "amicae aquae". Seeking the underworld, poplars aspire to the condition of guardians of the heavenly portal. The precision and formality of their stance may to some degree explain their weeping.

"Drawing sustenance from the secret spaces of earth and being at home in the clouds, the poplars have understood which way the earth is drifting. Each day they lost a word and, at the same time, their images of the world were shrinking. One by one the stars went, then the animals that would come at sunset to drink the deep reflections that curled in the stream below them. The poplars have never had a rigorous sense of self so love came naturally to them. Going outwards has for them become weeping."

With these words Astarte told her story of the weeping poplars, the jade emblem with its spiralling leaves and intricately carved tears resting like the universe, wordless and untranslatable, in the strength of her open hand. Then Nestor, who had lived for many years in the courts of Gandhara and had been among the first to send Vedic scriptures to Alexandria, began the analytic discussion, the *peripateia tes anabasis*.

"What to make of this mediation between earth and sky that is weeping? Somewhere in his lost writings Plotinus said to love is to take up residence beyond the annihilation of days, to lose words and to see the world shrink and yet to grow. For the poplars, those stately masters of decorum, the loss of language and the shrinking of the world were all one. As Astarte reminds us, they have long accompanied people on their journeys to places where stillness is possible and yet what surrounds them now so overwhelms them that weeping has become their voice. When poplars weep the world has surely reached its last days."

Waiting on the edges of speech, Mariam, pre-eminent among the sisterhood of the Essenes, took up the second thread of the *peripateia*.

"Grief and love unite in the dignity that links earth and heaven. So in dark times the poplars exude tears just as they have long been the serene custodians of love-making. We can recall how the women of Gades still sing, 'The cool breeze of the poplars has undone my hair, mother.' Breaking the convention-bound world in the directions of rapture and sorrow, the poplars also bring to mind the journey of the prophet Eanarra, she who announced the way of the lovers: 'We were cradling each other, pressed tight together and still breathing in the gentle swaying of a boat that carried us upstream far into the great snow mountains of the centre. Or else we were simply holding our breath, tiny as a speck of light lodged between the wings and shell of a bee's endlessly vibrating body.' And later

Eanarra, when asked how love could endure the knowledge of the body's dissolution, replied: 'We held each other and were destroyed. Then we returned to be destroyed again. We called this the journey towards sweetness.'

"The emblems we make and are continue endlessly reduplicating. Today, as we sit here conversing, just as the hand of Astarte cradles the poplars, so the poplars in her story are cradling the world that vanishes."

(*Conversations held in the Essene community of Qomqwakum, southern Nubia,* PAPYRUS SCROLLS HELD ORIGINALLY IN THE LIBRARY OF ALEXANDRIA, LATER STORED IN THE NESTORIAN MONASTERY OF ECBATANA)

XXV

The assistant to the Master of Silences
prepares his ceremonial measuring rods.

All morning they have watched evening grow.
The bare spines of the trees
vibrate in sympathy.
The robes wait in the small room with the doves.
Three shadows stand alert
in the narrow place
between birth and its effigies.
How fine the spaces they are measuring.
At the centre
a woman lies on the ground with death talking to her.

Always there is a mark that must be found,
some blemish in the eye's radiance
to instruct the Master on the true alignment.
Soon insistent crowds will arrive
by trams from the suburbs
and families who specialise in grief

will turn up in tall-masted ships along inlets
hastily carved through the desert mesa.
How terrible to be dead
and not know what kind of landscape
your spirit requires.
If the Master of Silences could only measure accurately enough
the smallest gesture would suffice.
Then your spirit might slip out of the body
and dwell in something simple—
a doorhandle, a stone left unmoved
where two rivers meet,
a certain direction between the slanted trees,
what your daughter would know at once
as your true, unmistakable
vanishing.

(IANNARCHUS, *Poems written while travelling with the embassy of Antoninus
to the Silk Kingdom*)

XXVI

What offerings should we make to the plants that they might
understand our intentions and feel less offended by our movement
across the land? The people who live here believe that the plants
do not accept them, that there is no way to bridge the hostility
and incomprehension that have developed over so many millennia.
According to the stories that have been handed down, the philosopher
Leonidas was invited to visit that he might converse with the plants
and establish some suitable rituals. He replied that he could be of
little help since any valid ritual must grow out of the same soil as
the plants and lie within the common ancestry of people and plants.

It is well known that all plants think with their roots, that they
recognise each other more comfortably in the darkness of earth than
the light of day. Rather than think with our heads or speak, should

we not, then, train our feet to show due respect for the authority
that lies within roots? If humans are most drawn to the beauty of
flowers and leaves, would plants not respond most strongly to the
moral eloquence of toes and ankles? Some have nominated clashing
conceptions of time and identity as the chief explanation for the
breakdown in the dialogue between plants and people. Perhaps
the key difference is that, whereas people have long relied on
the application of power to enforce their wishes, plants chose to
become adepts in the arduous practices of an infinite diplomacy.
Wind, rain, birds and insects, all know the delicate entreaties of
plants: the incessant incantations of trees, the listless whispering of
a tangled hedge in spring. Often plants adopt the tactic of making
it appear they have no wishes at all.

When a person desires to travel they gather their baggage,
they stand up and they go. When a plant decides it is time to
move elsewhere, it must first negotiate transit rights, genealogies,
protocols—an entire negotiation conducted underground. It must
plan the sending out of emissaries to inquire of the land; it must
consider the time of the year during which insects carry pollen and
the likely success rate of seeds scattered among rocks. Some have
asserted that with plants, as with people, there are those who wish
to conquer the earth. The evidence is indecisive.

(THEOPHANES, *The Philosopher's Day-Book: Journeys along the East African and
Arabian littoral*)

XXVII

A speck of peppercorn
stuck in the corner of my mouth—
there, beyond the last wine and the sweets,
still tasting of the harsh earth,
offering me the heart of distant pathways
to chew on.

* * *

An implausible winter burrows a tunnel
between your hand and mine.
Beloved, our life-battered bodies
merge in a prayer of white beginnings.
Threaded wands of trees like the hairs of your pubis
tremble in the air's cool wonder.
Beauty like the soft plains of your flesh
lies far away, an exiled land,
lies right here too
under the dream protection of my hand.

* * *

The slowed-down world
glitters carefully in the small stream
where yesterday's mud
puts down roots.
Everything grows in the palm of something else.
Only our wounds face the night sky
with the fierce simplicity of their barbarous tongues.

(FLAVINIUS OF CAPPADOCIA, *The roads of the troubled sky: fragmentaria from
eight years in the slave colony of Neapolis*)

XXVIII

Travelling in a caravan towards the World Capital where the
Great King had invited him to speak at a symposium on the
four elements, the philosopher let his mind drift from topic to
topic, seeking an adequate response to present. Already they had
crossed many lands and for some time now the unbounded sea
ran alongside his meditations. The philosopher wanted to think of
how we are in the world. The words "violence" and "loss" seemed

essential to him, the words "cherishing" and "holding back". The sea the caravan journeyed beside stretched all the way to the island of dogs, the island where dogs cast aside by sailors had established their own community—a space little more than a sandbank where an immense loneliness ranged, for here lived the dogs who had been cast out by humans.

On the sandbank where the dogs lived the wild closeness of the stars generated the music of grief. Eventually the resonances of the music sealed the island off and, like many things that become too strong for human consciousness, it flickered inside and outside time, appearing and disappearing across the void, indifferent to the changing names of the millennia.

He wondered in turn what would become of the people without dogs, those who sailed on to make new lands abandoning everything once cherished. Deciding that speech and closeness robbed them of marketable time, they developed a thing language to replace the old creature languages. Instead of talking, they held up objects and compared one with another, banishing forever from their lives whatever is open or vulnerable.

(FROM LUCIUS OF OCAMPO, *Interrogating a lost life—notes towards an autobiographic philosophy*)

XXIX

Summoning the Angel

I read words jumbled out of Scrabble sets and they speak to me
    absolutely.
The most beautiful poems appear in the tender spaces of marigolds
    left to breathe freely between railway tracks.
I have a taste for the burnt leaves that fall in an autumn of cinders.
In the aisle for lost causes two squabbling children struggling with
    food wrappers perform the most elaborate ballet, the poignant

ferocity of their fingers crumbling the world's textures.
A man examines the map of an exploding tree and walks for five
 days seeking the almond of sleep that is his double.

Across the earth a little light and a little light is extinguished.
I open my terrified arms into a stillness I have never known, at
 home with my cousins the ants and the twenty-four stepsisters
 who address all the stars by their first names.
Brown blood spurts a small voice in the centre of each hand.
The universe invades me.
Breaking waves pass effortlessly through my forehead, their
 uninterrupted surge the kiss that peels me open.
My middle name is "River that never was".

In the estimation of crows all that is blue is possessable, the white
 eyes of the fearful an affront.
Starting from nowhere, a rough sand causeway bends, twists and
 heads off into the distance towards the faint outline of spires.
On this day I am embraced by deer who recognise buildings as
 forests that once went astray.

(AMONG THE FINAL NOTEBOOKS OF W O'S, THIS APPEARS TO BE A LOOSE
ADAPTATION OF THE LOST POEM *An Ode to calm temporarily confused ghosts* BY
OMEROS ELISEO)

XXX

Sitting by a river the Book yearns for its own vanishing.

(FROM *The Secret Book of Infinite Space*)

POSTSCRIPT & APPENDICES

POSTSCRIPT

A Note on the Text

Rescued after his death from the chaos of his Wollstonecraft flat, the above previously untranslated fragments constitute the principal work of the neglected classicist, William O'Shaunessy.

O'Shaunessy called his collection of short texts "Apocrypha" to highlight their position outside the established canon. What we generally think of as Greek and Latin literature is in itself a very small fragment of ancient writings. Homer's epics were written down around the year 800 BCE and authors were still writing in Latin and Greek around the year 1000 AD. We are looking, then, at the history, philosophy, poetry, travel writing and personal reflections of some two thousand years, an enormous literature written by men and women in the widest diversity of places, both within Europe and beyond. O'Shaunessy set out to uncover the repressed literature of humanity across a period more than double the timespan separating us from Shakespeare. In part he tracked down new texts, in part he used the strategy of taking seriously editions of the classics previously rejected as "inauthentic". O'Shaunessy argued such alternate versions often preserve crucial passages expurgated for political or religious reasons, allowing us to construct an alternate way of looking at events.

Undoubtedly O'Shaunessy also sought to select and arrange texts that might speak to a contemporary reader and open wider perspectives on those spaces where the political and the intimate merge and cross over. Significantly the other chief work O'Shaunessy left behind was an extended essay *Thucydides and/or*

Chomsky: Athens, Rome, Washington and how they perished.[1]

As well as Latin and Greek O'Shaunessy was fluent in Aramaic, Sanskrit, Coptic, and the languages of ancient Africa, as well as several European languages. Travelling extensively, he lived at various times in such places as Lisbon, Athens, Alexandria, Isfahan and Herat. Many of these trips were undertaken to track down texts in monasteries and private libraries. At one stage O'Shaunessy was funded to research materials held in Nestorian monasteries in central Asia. On another occasion he was commissioned to translate Greek fragments found at a Red Sea site in Egypt.

Believing that the reader might be interested in a little more background to *Apocrypha* and O'Shaunessy's life and temperament, I have included as an Appendix a selection from several personal papers, as well as four of his own short stories and a sample of his poems.

—*Peter Boyle*

[1] Since writing this Postscript the text of this essay has vanished from the computer file and its copies on the hard drive and on a memory stick have been scrambled or deleted. Strangely no printed copy of the essay was found in O'Shaunessy's flat after his death. It seems unlikely, then, that it will be possible to reconstruct it.

Fragments from
William O'Shaunessy's Notebooks

1/5/95

I was trying to think of landscapes and how they eat into us, how we hope for something from them, of the dream that writing will redeem us. I am seated a few seats away from the place in Northside Plaza where I began translating Leonidas' Investigations—two years work that was finally rejected by Void. Next to me at present an Italian family in animated discussion. The lilt of their voices raises me beyond blackness. Everywhere in the world, North Sydney Shopping Mall or Paris, this hope to begin a new life—couples strolling by with babies and toddlers and trolleys with groceries. I think of my decision to leave Cambridge—of my absurd rejection of Natalie at twenty-one, my shuffling between dead-end jobs, travel and the Clinic, all my inept efforts to win a lover, and then my growing obsession with the Apocrypha, the futile hope that it would be published, that it would justify my life.

17/05/ 95

Writing in Stanton Library, North Sydney. Remembering fragments of my past. Cities with crowded bars, neglected museums and libraries; deserts like the edge of the Sahara I crossed once in local buses; high places like Srinagar and the village two days north of Herat, the sacred rivers that ran past them; beaches and coastlines and islands. Didn't I hope, however absurd I knew this to be, that the places themselves would make me a writer?

What did I mean anyway by the phrase "to be a writer"? It was what I used—not to be a poet, to write a novel, to earn my living by writing books, but "to be a writer", "to write".

30/5/95

Several times in my life I have dreamed of magic books. In the dream I am in an underground cave where a fierce river traps me on one ledge. Near me is a gold-framed book that I must carry across to the other shore. As I wade in, the book gets heavier and heavier so that I sink like St Christopher, the Christ-bearer, carrying the infant (a word itself meaning "not-speaking") across a flooded mountain torrent. And with each step this small silence I carry, draped in the whiteness of blank paper, gathers all the heaviness of life.

5/07/95

I have been trying very much today and over the last few days to decide on a final edited version for Book Two of *Apocrypha*. The papers for at least seven books* are all there, but what order should they be in? And who should I send them to? Who on earth will take them?

* (NOTE IN THE MARGIN)
The books are all to be around the same size as Books in Antiquity, like the books of Herodotus or Homer, the division of a work into easily manageable portions for the binder and the reader. Each book to be inter-connected but diverse, above all in the range of forms, to give prose fiction and lyric poetry their due, even-balanced weight.

8/12/99

For so long I tried to write novels and poems before deciding the translation of all-but-vanished authors would be my mode of expression. What is it about myself that I can only write of my life by turning completely away from it, to texts by lost writers, to languages no one learns any more, to a culture reduced to a blink in cyberspace? I suppose I have at least unearthed my own community. There are people here I feel I have come to know through working so long with their writings—Erycthemios, Omeros Eliseo, the undiscovered half of Herodotus, Leonidas, Irene Philologos, perhaps Irene most of all for I think of the strength it must have taken, going into exile with her husband, banished from the capital and adjusting to poverty in the rural backlands of Boeotia. And I think of the type of poetry she sought refuge in—not the conventional religious piety of the age but an eccentric honesty that left her open to all the pain of living. Then there is Longinus, Cassius Dio, Macrobius. Even the condescending eloquence of the critic Monochrastes moves me. This range of voices speaking to me out of the silence. "This book woven from my life and become my life".

Perhaps it has been good in a way, working with the dead, feeling so little confidence in myself, so much certainty in them, in the necessity that they be given a voice. For, when I see myself or those around me, I see shadows. Of my childhood, only flimsy memories. A year's blindness at four, then recovery, then a series of mishaps, months, half years in hospital. And the loss of my mother at sixteen, but to write these things seems pointless, worse than pointless. I don't believe for a moment they amount to anything more dramatic, more painful than countless other lives. And if real life consists of barbeques and infidelities, children gone astray, houses bought and sold, loves won and lost, I have no more talent for writing all that than I had for living it.

If space and time are equal dimensions of a singular presence on earth, what was written two thousand years ago is as immediate to us, as essential, as what is happening now two thousand kilometres away.

Everything is circular—Thucydides and Chomsky are one.

FOUR STORIES
BY WILLIAM O'SHAUNESSY

Death in another's landscape

Waking in my grandfather's house in the middle of the yellow and ochre plain. No one was about and the broken flywire door leaned open. The wooden veranda creaked. It was overcast as if it had been raining for thousands of years. Black inky clouds settled on the horizon. From the bed I reached for the radio, swivelled the knobs for a while, listless and edgy and unbearably sad. Getting up I went into my grandfather's room. He lay there in his sweat-stained old-fashioned pyjamas, his eyes detached above the white breathless face. I realised then that he was dead. I stood there looking into the hurt little boy eyes of the being who in his unpredictable rages and tender-hearted obsessions had dominated my life for over thirty years. Stepping closer I was knocked back by the smell of someone who has been shitting blood. Driven back by the stench I rested outside on the veranda, bent over the railing, breathing hard.

I could not face my grandfather again but went back to the kitchen for his rifle and began walking towards town. In the confusion of that day I lost my directions and ended up about noon scrambling along a ridge of sandhills when I saw on the horizon a block of shimmering apartments, a sprawling hotel of faded yellow concrete. Years before these hotels had been built right across our country, half of them by the Americans, half by the Russians. Now locked up and abandoned, they lay like sleeping shells, waiting for the invasion.

As I approached the hotel I took the precaution of burying the rifle under a clump of bushes. On the porch of the locked hotel a few soldiers lounged about in half-unbuttoned heavy uniforms. I tried to explain about my grandfather, but they only shrugged their shoulders in a gesture of incomprehension. We both wavered there trapped in the void of having no common language. The soldiers didn't seem to be either American or Russian and I had no idea where they came from. It would not have shocked my grandfather to have seen us occupied by a new force. We had always lived on the margin of someone else's dream.

I walked out the back to look at the pool. In a glaring burst of sunlight I walked the yellow scum of ageing tiles. The wide Olympic pool, empty of water, was slowly filling with spinifex and sand. The diving board was marked by cracks, and green slime grew slowly across it like a blossoming tree. I thought of my grandfather's body floating there in the sweat of his bed, coated in a crust of shit and blood.

Leaving the hotel I found the rifle I had hidden and headed off alone across the desert. After hours of walking I was halfway up a rise of hills when I heard the stone dogs coming after me. I started running, hearing the howling of the dogs behind me. When I reached the top of the hill I looked about: the valley below was swarming like a sea with wild dogs.

At the frontier

Glistening fields of snow. How quietly the sun walks over them. Wave on wave of white debris stretching off into the blue-grey sky. Walking that roadside, crunching the white debris underfoot, my face muffled, hands staunched in pockets, how warm I felt. Mud under my feet. All along the shining roadway thick-jacketed truck drivers silent and idle in the doors of their trucks.

Further up the road a mud building daubed in green paint serves as a customs check-point. I understand there's been a revolution in the capital and the frontier has been closed. I go inside. Most of the truckies no longer bother standing about the single desk where a methodical looking official refuses to do anything as international transport comes to a stop. A team of young boys with armalites monitor the tensions in the room. Morose, overtired, they lean against the walls.

Next door is the shorter queue for private travellers. A young boy is in charge. I present my papers. No, I cannot leave. No, I cannot go back. I must remain on the frontier. Through the opened doorway I see the sad stare of unshaven faces. A young man, one of the soldiers, has taken down the clock which stood on the wall and is playing with the back of it. Some half-dozen truck drivers turn to watch. I walk back outside.

Flakes of snow turn remorselessly in the sky. Women sit on planks in a canvas stall, feeding soup to their children. The children look out into their own space. Their warm clothes, their miniature hats give them the look of elaborate dolls misplaced in an enormous landscape. It is only at an odd angle avoiding their jet black eyes that the mothers slide spoonfuls of soup between their lips. Solid, anxious, these women with black kerchiefs over their hair and drab pullovers and coarse brown coats.

A great orange ball, a beach ball, materializes on the white snow before one of the food stalls. A truck driver has rolled it across to the feet of his son who seems as unimpressed by this intrusion from his father as he is by the spoonloads of food his mother frets over.

I walk back up the road to the bus. Snowfilled windows of abandoned cars; the creaking of iron as it twitches against the breeze. On the horizon white mountains are shifting slowly, drawing slowly away.

*

At the frontier the waiting continues. Truck drivers share their few scraps of food, candy bars, cigarettes. Water is rationed out from a tap they have kept working. The women seem to produce soup out of nowhere and once a day we are given a large mugful. Cigarettes and duty-free liquor are broken open and passed around on the stranded buses. One day it is announced that the old currencies will no longer be honoured and we will have to wait for a new form of money. Most of the men looked rather tense at first but we survived with very little difference as it turned out.

Walking each day for exercise through the camp that has grown up along the roadside, I get the impression that our numbers are increasing day by day. There is no longer the same hostility between the young soldiers and the truck drivers—the isolation and the snow and the waiting are moulding them all into one thread. Only the very small children remain detached, withdrawn, their eyes concentrating on something untouched and invisible.

Snow continues to fall. Men have to work steadily to shovel it away. A heavy immobility presses everything down. Drifts of snow move over the trucks, the stalls, the signposts, the customs building. The older people step about gingerly. We all can guess what it would be like to slip, to fall asleep, to be thrust under the deep waves of snow.

I carry a small notebook with me and a pen. There is only one page left so I don't write, wanting to save it for as long as possible. On the sixth day I mark off a small space at the top of the page and put down the sentence:

"A revolution is freshness and burial."

The Restaurant, the Hospital, Venice

Dinner was over. Coming out of the restaurant they noticed the fine sea-spray curling in slow clouds over the esplanade. A massive grey hospital had loomed up in the course of their evening together. Like a fortress of disease it had taken over the rocky headland. Arm in arm the two of them entered through a side doorway, then moved along the corridors. They passed wards where men lay in traction and pregnant women sweated, cushioned up with pillows. A small girl walked past, wandering the polished moonlit floors in a white nightgown, her head punctured by a red hole.

Their way led through ward after ward of children. Faces peered through the bars of cots. A boy cried softly while the red stain of the wound beneath his plaster impregnated the air with the stench of sweat. Overhead fans clicked and turned slowly.

A few night nurses passed, scurrying by in blue uniforms. Letting go of her hand he stepped forward into one of the rooms. An elderly matron came in, draped in her brown nun's habit, moving about slowly on creaking shoes. Her flashlight circled the room, beaming into the lonely empty faces. He felt drawn towards the dozens of eyes that gleamed there. He knew those eyes. He would always know them: eyes that had ceased to dream of parents or home but saw only immense sky, the clear fine element one could hope to tread one day just as others learn to float in water. Then by night came the terror, the black silence that drew towards them from the central skylight of the building. Over all the wards hung the smell of fear and of stale urine.

His companion watched him gaze about the room in rapture, then, moving on ahead of him, she took a wrong turn and came into a ward of very old women. She could hear the sound of gums sucking. Their bloodshot eyes hung open, terrified of the great black bird of death that would swoop one day or another into their laps. Nervously edging forward she stopped in front of a bed where an old lady, her hair done neatly into a bun, lay back with folded arms dozing. On the blanket before her an opened Agatha Christie, at the bedside a bowl of fruit, a single dying orchid. The stillness, the perfection of the old lady touched her as if she had discovered what she had always wanted: this quiet bedroom, freedom from the need to please others, solitude, the final gathering of the self into a body as shrunken as a thin raft of twigs. Watching the night breeze stir silver threads on the old lady's brow she felt young again and safe, like a child in a parent's bedroom on some hot summer night when a mother's closeness brings peace and sleep.

The wind jolted the door ajar with a screech. She felt suddenly self-conscious being there, staring at this unknown woman. Leaving the room she went off to find her lost companion. He was in a children's dormitory, stooping to pick up a picture book which had fallen from a child's bed. Irritated by so much unfamiliar experience she snapped. "Hurry up, can't you? Let's get out of here quickly."

At last they came upon a wide well-lit staircase. "So that's it," he said. "We only had to move onto a different level. If we go down a flight of stairs we should be right near my flat." They began the descent. From a turn in the staircase there was a last glimpse into an annexe of white-sheeted beds, empty and waiting. About them still hung the sweet scent of ether, lemonade, old buildings under demolition.

When they came out his flat was worlds away. They were standing beneath high old-fashioned tenements on a cobbled lane beside water. He recognized the Rialto bridge across the Grand Canal— to the left umbrellas, tables, large earthenware pots crammed with carnations, a sidewalk cafe. Beyond was the vast architecture and clear blue sky of Venice. He raised his arms, shaking off pain and heaviness, taking into himself the curved blue stillness, the elegant city built out over the seas at the world's end.

He caught the attention of a passing gondolier who, nodding enthusiastically, indicated he understood where a hotel was and how to get there. Then he turned back to fetch his companion. She stood by an open doorway haggling with a vendor of old records. Beneath the bristled beard and dirty clothes the record vendor glowed with youth, fire, sexiness. Ignoring the stranger he walked across to her. "Are you coming?" he asked. "Oh that," she said, "I'm in no mood now. See you whenever."

He walked back to the canalside. His gondolier was still waiting. There seemed nothing to do but climb in, be taken away. Collapsed in the boat, he closed his eyes for a few seconds. Opening them he found someone had slid spectacles on his face. He was now wearing a white hat, a white suit. He looked up at the gondolier. Waves, rippling, broke against the prow of the boat. Along the canalside wavered a glimpse of faces and uniforms, hurrying, unfocussed. Lounging back, sweaty, indifferent he came out with the sentence,

"And how much do you charge?" The gaunt cheekbones of the gondolier flickered in cruel scrutiny. "The signore will pay". For one long moment, shrinking into tunnel vision, he saw himself being punted over waste waters against the vast fading sunset.

Story of the Spanish couple and the girl with the cats

The little girl came across the sand with the cats. There were two of them: a white one and a grey one. She looked all of nine or ten, but she might have been seven or eight. Or thirteen.

The beach was deserted apart from a couple who sat halfway up the sand at the furthest end from the stairs. It was cool now, late afternoon on a day in early spring and the breeze still had a wintry chill to it. The couple sat there in silence looking out at the sea. The woman was fair haired and bright-eyed, youngish but not altogether young; the man squatted thoughtfully on his ankles in a way that seemed Asian though his face was an odd mixture of European tendencies, an aristocrat's face, mournful and worn. After a while he stood up and began taking photos of the woman who was smiling back at him with a touch of irritation.

The only photographs that mattered he had made her destroy. He said they were too dangerous. If the authorities found out they had had a child they would want to know where it was, what they had done with it. He said it would be making it too easy for those in power. First they kidnap your child, then they accuse you of murdering it. Child murderers and child molesters—the world has such a horror of them; agencies and police forces can pursue you around the world for those crimes and everyone will assist in your persecution. So they had torn up and deposited in three separate garbage bins the photograph of themselves and their eight-month old son Paul asleep in his pram while they stood arm in arm, so proper, so beaming with happiness, beside a rose-bed in a public garden on the other side of the world. And not so long after that, when they reached Europe for the first time and he began to realise how crazy he had been, obsessed with persecution, he left Nice station and walked into the first camera shop he found and bought a camera. Now he was a photo-fanatic. He took rolls and rolls of film of wherever they went: pictures of her buying oranges or stepping onto trains, pictures of parks and art galleries and beaches, sunrise off Corfu, Mt Fuji and the Taj Mahal, the two of them drinking Coca Cola at Pukhet and eating a grotesque fan-topped ice cream on Mabini St, Manila. The photographs were dated and placed in albums and the albums deposited in a suitcase until the suitcase got too heavy. Then they would sort through the photographs and argue their way down to the few they would keep. Often they would take a whole segment of their lives and say that no, it wasn't worth it. So they would take the condemned albums and dispose of them. The method they preferred was to drop them off a pier into the sea. In inland cities where there are no decent tracts of water this was a problem. They resorted to soaking rags in gasoline and setting fire to rubbish bins. Thus they consigned either to the waves or the ashes entire eras of their life together: Paris, Barcelona, their two months on Crete, the year 1981, the winter of 1986. And the day after the destruction he would return with as much enthusiasm as ever to taking shots of themselves against the facades of new countries.

After more than ten years of wandering their life had resolved into its own pattern. Each time they came to a new country they would relax on their savings for a week or two. Then she would disappear to find work. It irked him that he couldn't support her—couldn't even support himself. She would say to him, "Don't be stupid. I can earn this way in six weeks enough to support us for half a year. It's not something that touches me. I just do it and switch off. Remember you're a retired revolutionary—what business do you have with bourgeois scruples?" One time when he insisted on working as a labourer he put his back out and cost her a small fortune in medical bills, all for a weekly pay that was less than what she could earn in an hour. After that, though he grumbled a little, he never seriously tried to change her decision.

During the month she worked they lived like Spartans: never touching a cent more than was necessary of what she earned, eating only the cheapest food cooked over their gas burner in some rented room, sleeping in separate corners, barely touching, like monks observing the strictest chastity and poverty.

The sky was turning to sunset. The beach grew colder and colder. Noting the girl's persistent presence they shifted from English to a kind of pidgin Spanish they spoke when they wanted to conceal their thoughts.

—*Que pasa con la niña?*

—*No sé.*

—*Seguro es muy tarde para una niña aquí en la playa. Siempre hay hombres peligrosos.*

—Maybe, *pero tu crees demasiado en la impotencia de los niños.*

—*Cálmate. Es tarde y hace frío.*

He rummaged in their handbag and pulled out a spare jumper for her to look at, thinking of how he might shelter the small girl from the wind. Her eyes signalled against the idea.

—So *sólo.* Maybe is *huérfana.*

—*No es huérfana. Mira—los zapatos. Habla con ella.*

All the while the small girl had moved up closer to them. She sat glumly looking out to sea, her tiny white face pinched by the wind.

—Are you all right to find your way home from here?

No reply.

—We have a spare jumper here. Would you like one to keep you warm?

The girl looked steadily out to sea as if nothing concerned her.

The woman spoke again softly to the man:

—*Me parece un poco difícil: ella no quiere que nosotros hagamos preguntas.*

—Si, pero quizás su madre está muy preocupada, ha llamado a la policía, busca su hija.

—My mother has to cook dinner and feed my little sister. Afterwards when I get home it will be the right time to give my little sister a bath and read her a story and then I can serve dinner. My mother can manage ok after that.

The words slipped out without disturbing the faraway gaze of the small girl's face.

—Ah, you can talk—and it seems you understand something of Spanish too, he said.

—What's Spanish?

—The language we were speaking.

—No, you were speaking Australian. Everyone speaks Australian because this is Australia—only some people make it sound different.

—Why is that? he asked.

—Because everyone is different, of course. Anyway, she said, looking a little guilty at the confession, it's easy to know when anyone talks about my mother. She's very sensible and she talks very quietly in a special way, and when someone wants to say something about my mother they have to speak like that too.

His curiosity touched, he continued, "If I said, 'Mi hermana y yo hemos venido del otro lado del mundo', would you know what I mean?"

"You shouldn't tell lies", she said. "You can't tell lies and expect me to make sense of it".

Laughing the woman tapped him on the shoulder. "Serves you right," she said. Then turning to the girl she tried again.

—What is your name?

No answer.

—Shouldn't you be going home now the sun is going down?

—What are your names? the girl asked.

—I'm Melu and my friend is Simon.

—My cat's name is Rowena. What day is it today?

—Tuesday, the woman replied.

—Tuesday, and we're the only people on the beach. And you come from far away and are married but have to pretend to be brother and sister. Someone bad must be chasing you.

He was not quite sure if he heard this or if his own thoughts were speaking through the girl's lips. Feigning normality, he resumed the conversation.

—Do you always come to the beach?

—Most of the time. My cats like the beach.

—You have lots of cats?

—Rowena and Sally and Sarah and Susan and Sophie and Susu and Samantha and Sicamore.

—Where are the rest of them?

—They're about.

—I don't see them.

—They don't always want to be seen.

—And you always bring them to the beach with you?

—Only sometimes.

The woman looked anxiously at the girl.

—Shouldn't we take you home.

—Why? My cats might like to stay here all night. They like to chase the waves and there's always plenty of fish. We might live here for a few days or a month.

The man was becoming more and more agitated by the turn of the conversation. The woman, sensing danger, wanted some formula, to keep all in control, to extricate the two of them.

—*Vale, Simón, vámanos. La niña parece loca. Tal vez su madre toma drogas. Quién sabe, hay tanta gente mala en este país que no tiene cuidado con sus niños.*

But the man made no response, sitting there on the darkening beach, vaguely aware of a profound loss of will. And behind his passivity dream fragments rippled, giving the landscape the threatening edge of something recognised.

*

Two days before. Images on waking. I live in a hut in the forest. There is a wolf with me. He has eaten all the chickens in my barn. He and I are doubles, but though he has been beside me a long time I walk in continual fear. His food supply has run out. I am walking away from the hut towards the tall forest. There is a town somewhere out there. I notice that my balls and thighs have scraped against something and there is a smear of blood there. The wolf scents the warmth of nearby blood. He bounds past me and then returns again. He doesn't yet perceive me as food. We have been together so long and have always seemed partners in survival. But there is a side to him which is growing stronger: which will not perceive me as myself but be drawn to that smear, will act mechanically, will find itself ferociously devouring whatever bears that smear of blood. I feel like a woman trapped in shame by nature, seeking to hide the drops of blood at her waist. Suddenly I remember the fridge in the hut: there is meat there I could give him, but would it be enough? Perhaps it would calm him for a while. I could then go to the chemist in town and buy a small white tablet of poison and bury it deep in the meat and kill him. But would the chemist be willing to sell me poison? It would be obvious I was intending to kill someone. Even if the wolf is a monster do I have the right to kill him deliberately?

*

The wind is getting decidedly cold now. Waves lap savagely at the deserted beach.

—*Ay caramba, Simón. Tenemos que hacer algo ahora mismo. Es possible que la gente nos haya visto con la chica; entonces si le pasara algo malo la policía nos buscará.*

—*No puedo hacer nada. Las niñas siempre tienen poder.*

Dropping the Spanish in his anxiety to find a way out, he spoke directly to the girl.

—You should go back to your mother.

—I've already told you that I am not really worried about my mother. She doesn't get bored much.

—But is your mother worried about you?

—Why should she be?

—Why do you like to come here?

—Because I like to look at the sea which is wide and empty.

*

The mind as a basement below street level piled high with rotting suitcases. There are children wearing monster masks, cavorting like demons, trailing their arms on the floor, snarling, yelping, but I feel quite safe. They run off again intent on their own games. Their desire is to impress rather than hurt.

*

—You should come home with us.

—*Simón, no, no toques la niña. Es muy peligroso.*

—*Cállate, Melu. No es possible abandonar la niña aquí en la playa. Hay gente mala que puede asaltarla. Entonces la policía va a seguirnos. No hay otro remedio.*

The girl sits upright on her heels, motionless, taking it all in, watching the ocean. Her hair curls against the wind like thin minted gold and she carries herself with the dignity of one who is the keeper of invisible cats.

At that moment the police car drew closer, slowly, almost brushing the thin man and the woman who could talk with God.

As the waves crashed shoreward a car slowly drew past. The window slid down. Eyes from darkness observed two figures huddling on a beach in the cold wind of nightfall. Two figures only. There were no cats. There was no girl.

PREFACE TO SOME POEMS BY WILLIAM O'SHAUNESSY

A Note by the Editor

When William O'Shaunessy died in March 2002 his flat in St Leonards was littered with drafts of translations, photocopies of Greek and Latin texts, books with lines of poetry scrawled in the margins, and numerous dated notebooks where ideas were sketched and abandoned. O'Shaunessy always found it difficult to complete a piece and, when it came to his own stories and poems, was all too easily put off by rejection.

Of all the poems he wrote in the 1970s and 1980s only two are published here—"At the Northside Clinic" and "St Leonards sunset". Both reflect O'Shaunessy's life-long battle with depression, the illness that overwhelmed him in his second year of a PhD at Cambridge. Returned to Australia, he spent considerable time in the late seventies, early eighties and less frequently during the nineties, as a patient at the Northside Clinic, an institution specialising in anorexia nervosa but also treating patients with a range of psychological/psychiatric issues.

A visit to the Philippines in June 1985 produced the poem "Evening Central Luzon". Travelling alone and trying to face down the paranoid breakdowns that ended both his trip to Spain in the winter of 1975 and his ill-fated bike ride across America in 1979, O'Shaunessy found inspiration in the rugged and often dangerous Sierra Madre cordillera of central Luzon. Counterbalancing personal fears, Luzon was to O'Shaunessy a place attuned to protective presences. The simple tiki, a kind of chameleon gekko to be found everywhere in the Philippines, is the guardian spirit evoked in the poem. The word itself is almost certainly the same as the Maori tiki, the protective amulet. Typically the chameleon that changes colour and masters invisibility to protect itself becomes, in turn, the protector of others. O'Shaunessy was to return to Luzon in late 1997, tracking down indigenous accounts of a pre-Spanish encounter with Europeans—O'Shaunessy was fascinated by the possibility that they were in fact members of the Emperor Antoninus' delegation to China on their return journey.

The year 1993 was unusually productive for O'Shaunessy as writer of his own poems. During a spell when he took a break from work on the Apocrypha a string of rather surreal but still very personal poems came out. The three dated poems—17/4/93, 18/4/93 and 20/5/93—had been accepted for publication by O'Shaunessy's long-term friend and sometime mentor John Forbes in *Scripsi*. (Unfortunately Forbes as poetry editor often accepted more poems than there was room for, creating a backlog in the publication schedule.) O'Shaunessy had become a friend of Forbes during his time at Sydney University in the years 1969 to 1973 and remained on good terms though seeing him much less often in later years. There is a striking photo taken by Vicki Skarrat of Forbes, O'Shaunessy and the real Mark O'Connor at the Harold Park Hotel in 1989, Forbes taking the camera on with full confidence, O'Shaunessy glancing away.

The bleakness of "Clinic" might reflect any of several visits in the late 1990s to specialists for a range of heart problems and cancer scares. "Reading Borges late at night and imagining Buenos Aires" is based loosely around an incident at Ezeiza airport in 1976 when O'Shaunessy was refused entry to Argentina, detained as an IRA suspect and sent back to be interrogated by MI5. For three days O'Shaunessy was held and interrogated without charges being laid. I have searched newspapers of the time for some mention of this incident but nothing appears. Buenos Aires became for O'Shaunessy a magic city, a place he was condemned never to enter, a peculiar Latin American double of Sydney—somewhere he could only inhabit imaginatively through the works of his favourite Borges. With characteristic exactitude of detail O'Shaunessy uses the fact that midnight in Sydney corresponds to 8.30 in the morning of the previous day in Buenos Aires, as if the city of the Harbour Bridge and the Opera House had only to travel some fifteen hours to the East and it would be the imaginative landscape of Borges' fiction.

"Reading Borges late at night and imagining Buenos Aires" also gives a sense of O'Shaunessy's personality. It reveals something of his deep affection for his nephew and niece, his pride in his grandfather,[1] and the various connections that held him to life. (His grandfather, the late Colonel Henry O'Shaunessy, was wounded at Gallipoli but went on to rise through the ranks to the position of Colonel.) It strikes me as especially poignant that the fourth last line of the poem, almost the last line O'Shaunessy wrote, should read "but living would be beautiful". It might serve as an apt tribute to the life of William O'Shaunessy.

—*Peter Boyle, March 2009*

---

[1] The obsessive and complex grandfather in "Death in another's landscape" bears no resemblance to O'Shaunessy's grandfathers. Written in the late 1970s the story is more a reflection of his difficult relationship with his father. The stories, all from the 70s and early 80s, are quite different from the poems written in the 90s after O'Shaunessy had spent over a decade working on the Apocrypha. A first draft of "Reading Borges" was written in April 2001 but O'Shaunessy last revised it only a few weeks before his death.

Nine Poems
by William O'shaunessy

At the Northside Clinic

She is (more than me)
battered by the world
battered by the difficulty of reading the world

Dumb before the letters that go on whispering
she hears with her uncertain hand

This night
riveted eyes downcast
by the lightning that jaggedly splices the room
where she sits alone, timidly restless

How much of the world
pours into each hand

I who am all walls
watch over her tenderness
Darkly she escapes me
I carry nothing
and each raindrop
        goes on falling infinitely
                    within her.

(April, 1979)

St Leonards' Sunset

A man on a cherrypicker cleaning a traffic light
Sunset as wide as the soul and as nameless
The red hospital has beached itself
Above the football field almost crushing
The cluttered cosmopolis of the cemetery
In a surgical cut between the houses
A train speeds the exhausted to life and to sleep
I head back to my purple room my cubicle my silence
I have no wounds in my hands or my side
Tomorrow I turn thirty

Evening, Central Luzon

Above the interminable noise of the TV
the tiki poises on the ceiling,
invisible except for a faint line.
When silence comes
we will see him—
if you place him by water
he is water,
beside the wind
he is wind,
and in the world of men
he is the tongue-click of the clock on the wall,
a tiny hammer
tapping on the tin roof,
brotherhood.

Make it new

The ancient cities have all gone away. Rome left and travelled a thousand kilometres to the west. Athens, Pompey—the same, relocating to camping grounds or broken-down marinas in rusted bayous. The true ancient world has wandered off in search of a more appreciative audience.

We are left to ourselves then—alone and nervous in the ubiquitous modernity of death.

17/4/93

The strange sisters speak to us,
that they are lonely as we are—
all invisible
and breathing in the same quiet,
numbering the same stars.
We wanted to dwell in the future—a water-stained substitute
for the hard earth, the three a.m. chill
of damp grass under elms.

Insignificant things have travelled best.
You gave me a miniature rainforest as a present.
In its small brown pot
I watered it and clipped its canopy.
When the sky disappears beyond its
gnomic and intricately referenced leaves,
I will remember your face
and all its tenderness.
Everything you gave is alive somewhere.
In a world of strident crows
it whispers its litany.
Though I can enumerate nothing
it says, "I am what sustains you.
I am the everlasting catalogue."

18/4/93

Sometimes you have to follow strangeness back to its lair.
The furniture provides limited clues
as do the children
growing into altered versions of yourself but with
a withering refusal to endorse your chosen dead-ends.
If not the bric-à-brac what is it you've accumulated?
And what is this debt you've clocked up
pauperizing you for 25 years after your death?
At least you robbed your own inheritance.
At least you didn't have to blow anyone up
to put water into your bathtub.
Of the future's future less than five minutes is visible,
a haze where loss and guilt merge into green rolling vistas.
Dozo, the Japanese version keeps saying,
dozo, kono hon wa otonyo no skyblaetter desu.
An immense light glows where the words vanish.
Writing in effortless abandon
as befits the last days
of a warrior hermit gone to seed,
this at last could be the true life.

20/5/93

The television sets of my nephews
dispute space with each other.
Caught in the crossfire
I shelter like an artificial plant.
Whatever I plan slips away
beyond the edges of yesterday.
Buffeted by the winds of a great noise
I travel across black evening corridors
like the migration of some great thought from India
over enormous deserts to Alexandria
then by accidental telepathy to New York and Dublin.

Why was I sitting there reading a strange
interminable French novel on a train?
Why was it I never married you?
Between mismanagement and a culpable
fear of life I struggle on
to let yesterday bloom into the white fleeting dazzle
of railway-station pickets passed at great speed.
With my pathological fear of the unknown
I stay behind dragging myself from washbasin to bed,
rocking myself into painlessness
on the shining floor
as vast and incomprehensible as the world.

Clinic

You could have sat in an office
and greeted people one by one
and given them bad news
Or driven a bus
blistering in the heat and all the fumes
Or have lived
as you did neither high nor low
sampling a little of everything

This room waits in the same way
the glow of its lamps
casts downward
an even light

In all the magazines
no one finds anything interesting

5 pm
waiting for results

Reading Borges late at night and imagining Buenos Aires

1.

No one dreams the river as it is.
If I transpose sides
and make new islands,
if I annex one shore
and tie it to another continent,
it is only to remind myself that here is all places.

Nightfall, the concrete slit where snow-melt
and drains from dull backyards
all merge as mud,
the blue lines of maps
like the sky was sketching its own arteries.
No one dreams the river as it is.

2.

I never left the airport.
All I could see
were the lines of light marking the edges
of the harbour.
The metal detectors
went wild as I passed through and two soldiers
trained their machine guns at me
as my arms shot up
in gesture of surrender.
Imagining Buenos Aires from the air.

Lines of light at 2 am
giving the vague curve of river and bay.
I spent hours trying to find change
small enough for the drink machine.
City of Borges and of tangos,
of Palermo, the Recoleta
and the Plaza de Mayo …

Imagining Buenos Aires from the airport lounge:
its décor of posters
(more snowfields of the Andes, more seals),
the internationally flavoured
minidrinks of its bar.
Imagining Buenos Aires from a book of poems
written from the unimaginable year of my father's birth
to the time I turned sixteen—
City of Borges and of tangos,
of Palermo, the Recoleta and the Southside,
of Serrano and the Plaza de Mayo,
Paris of the South,
where are you?

Almost not a sound in all that space.
Cold after the tropics. I imagine a plain of darkness
stretching endlessly beyond the terminal's walls.

City that will never quite make dawn,
I image you as night
and night you stay.

3.

There are days when watches stop,
years when time runs backwards.
My sister's voice, my brother's voice
reach me,
a faint whispering sliding across
the thousand thousand miles of ocean.

I wake and sleep
entrusting all my body
to a room whose name
is Departure.

4.

What was beauty, what was pride
lost in our multiple hands.

In the grainy substance of the documentary
a shadow walks beside Maria Kodama
stroked by the city's tremulous sun
or a voice intones "Sólo del otro lado del ocaso"
on the faded tape playing in a car radio
as my nephew zigzags his way across a soccer field,
the rain sluicing down.

My ancestors roamed the world
leaving Ireland for California, for Dunedin, Melbourne,
the always elsewhere gold
that became treachery and war,

names that echo like Junín or Anzac Cove,
so many young men's bodies
under a limpid sky.

5.

To spin
like the globe gone wild
To drift across continents
like reluctant rainclouds
To arrive
a voice pale as last year's ashes

To claim membership
in the illustrious confraternity of ghosts
To cross in a loop
the Southern Pole
To dream our lives have passed
in an endless prolongation of night

6.

A maid's hands
straighten the blinds in a hotel room
I never stayed in.
Taxi doors open and close
on a trip I never took.
Imagining Borges imagining Buenos Aires—
the labyrinth of streets and names,
the infinite library of first moments.

Shuffling days out of an itinerary
and waking late one afternoon
on a city's outskirts—
the cantinas, the dirt, the sky—

to stumble
face-forward
into a heart attack or a stranger's knife

to claim this destiny
where all depends on never
stepping through a doorway.

7.

Night comes
and poets will climb out of their coffins
and the music will flow:
John Forbes Nazim Hikmet Federico García Lorca
César Vallejo and Yeats and Supervielle
and Wallace Stevens a little aloof
and Whitman at the centre of numerous groups, and Rilke
fuming with the bluster of cigarettes and the silent vibration of angels

and the blind will wonder what skin they are in
and the tormented will find a great quiet
(gently picking the unravelling stitches,
bone that speaks, the pure sun
brought back from its dream of ice:
Elizabeth Bishop, Sylvia Plath and Alejandra Pizarnik;
Señor Borges rolling the patience of syllables

between an absent finger, an absent thumb)

and many will sit quite still
knowing the sea has moved endlessly through them
and a few will turn over stones
that break up into words in their hands.

It will go on
the way it would if there were no walls
as if this life was made
from only our breath.

8.

love and the rain that falls in an unspoken miracle

windows opening on a harbour where the lights continue burning
    long after dawn

the last day in a city you will never return to, saying goodbye to its
    trees, how the drink in a bar goes on trembling lonely in its glass

midday in the drowned city, the facades of buildings scooped up in
    a handful of water

a painting in which everything has been included: a painting from
    which everything has been left out: the same painting

9.

When a breeze comes
and a spider travels upside down

across the ending of the hottest day in Autumn,
I drop into a cool quiet zone
which is the possibility of writing.
East of here
all of South America is making breakfast—
measuring bottled water for the coffee
that will be yesterday.
Shadows of ancestors, possibilities of being
move round me as I write,
cut off by the universal script of night.

10.

So many years adding on,
marking the slow
encroachment of perfection
but living would be beautiful
drinking the still-standing water
in the tall glass
that mirrors the world.